Praise for A Reader's Companion to J.D. Salinger's The Catcher in the Rye

"For those of us who have not read or taught *The Catcher in the Rye* for at least a decade or two, Peter G. Beidler's *A Reader's Companion to J. D. Salinger's* The Catcher in the Rye *(second edition), offers the breadth and detail of a gripping, if not nostalgic, documentary about *The Catcher* and its maker. For those American students in the second millennium who are assigned this book in their high school or college English courses – or who will read it for the first time out of their own literary curiosity – Beidler's book will prove to be a time capsule that will illuminate the world of their grandfathers."

– Joel Salzberg, Emeritus Professor of English, University of Colorado at Denver

"Holden Caulfield is a literary icon of a character, the youth disaffected with the world. *A Reader's Companion to J. D. Salinger's* The Catcher in the Rye is a guide to fully understanding this classic novel and why it has gained fame today. On top of exploring the book, many theories and ideas about the work are explored, such as the fate of Holden after the events of the book and a greater eye on his familial relations. *A Reader's Companion to J. D. Salinger's* The Catcher in the Rye is for fans and those opening the book for the first time. Highly recommended."

—The Midwest Book Review/Small Press Bookwatch

"With a clear presentation of copious facts and insights, accompanied by a wide array of photographs, Professor Beidler's indispensable book enhances the reader's understanding and appreciation of Salinger's landmark novel."

—Bruce F. Mueller, co-author, *Critical Companion to J. D. Salinger: A Literary Reference to His Life and Work* (Facts on File, 2011)

" 'That is so last century!' today's readers and teachers may exclaim as they begin *The Catcher in the Rye*, the 1951 classic by J. D. Salinger. Fortunately, Peter G. Beidler has decoded the cultural information that packs the novel.... A valuable tool for twenty-first century readers. Although now retired from Lehigh University's Department of English, Peter G. Beidler continues to serve the reading community."

– Geraldine A. Richards, ForeWord Digital Reviews

A Reader's Companion
to
J. D. Salinger's
The Catcher in the Rye

Second Edition

For A., P., K., C., N., P., W., L., M., M., E., H., and A.

A Reader's Companion
to
J. D. Salinger's
The Catcher in the Rye

Second Edition

by Peter G. Beidler

A Reader's Companion
to
J. D. Salinger's
The Catcher in the Rye

Second Edition

by Peter G. Beidler

coffeetownpress
Seattle, Washington

Published by Coffeetown Press.

Beidler, Peter G., 1940–
A Reader's Companion to J. D. Salinger's The Catcher in the Rye / Second Edition
by Peter G. Beidler

Includes bibliographical references, map, glossary, photographs, study questions, and indexes.

ISBN 978-1-60381-013-5 (pbk. : alk. paper)
1. Salinger, J. D. (Jerome David), 1919–2010.—The Catcher in the Rye.
2. Characters—Holden Caulfield. 3. Caulfield, Holden (Fictitious character)—Film and video adaptations. 4. Criticism. 5. Explanatory notes. 6. Glossary for ESL and EFL readers. 7. Discussion and essay questions.

Designed in Adobe Jenson Pro font by Publishing Plus, Yardley, PA.

Cover image by Calloway M'Cloud

Cover design by Sabrina Sun

The paper used in this publication meets the minimum requirements of the American National Standard for Information Sciences—Permanence of Paper for Printed Library Materials, ANSI Z39.48-1992.

Coffeetown Press

Contact: info@coffeetownpress.com

Contents

Preface   viii

Note on the Second Edition   x

Acknowledgments   x

Catching *The Catcher in the Rye*   1

   1. Time line of *The Catcher in the Rye*   1
   2. Biographical references   4
   3. Salinger's life in *The Catcher in the Rye*   10
   4. From the stories to *The Catcher in the Rye* 18
   5. Holden Caulfield's appearance   27
   6. *The Catcher in the Rye* in other fiction   32
   7. *The Catcher in the Rye* in movie and song   46
   8. The enduring appeal of *The Catcher in the Rye* 56
   9. The aftermath of J. D. Salinger's death   66

Explanatory Notes to *The Catcher in the Rye*   73

   Holden says good-by to Pencey (chapters 1–7)   74
   Holden goes to Manhattan (chapters 8–14)   112
   Holden wanders Manhattan (chapters 15–20)   145
   Holden goes home (chapters 21–26)   183

Glossary for ESL and EFL Readers   213

Questions for Readers of *The Catcher in the Rye*   241

Index to *The Catcher in the Rye*   257

Index to this Reader's Companion   269

Preface

In 1961 George R. Creeger predicted that "perhaps in fifty years we shall need a scholarly edition of *The Catcher in the Rye*" ("Treacherous Desertion," reprinted in *J. D. Salinger and the Critics*, ed. William F. Belcher and James W. Lee [Belmont, CA: Wadsworth, 1962], p. 99). Creeger was thinking mostly about the prep-school jargon, which he thought would be far outdated by the twenty-first century. In fact, however, the language has remained remarkably fresh and readable, but other features of the novel now require explanations. This reader's companion is by no means a scholarly edition of the novel. Rather, it is designed in part to give twenty-first-century readers and teachers annotations with cultural information about J. D. Salinger's *The Catcher in the Rye*, information that would have been common knowledge to most first readers of the novel, but which is now lost in last-century mists. After all, it has been six decades since the now-classic narrative of the three-day fictional adventures of Holden Caulfield took place. Indeed, the novel now reads almost like a work of historical fiction. In addition to providing as much as I could find about the historical and cultural backdrop to the novel, I include many features not previously available in this detail and between one set of covers:

—some 250 detailed page-by-page explanations of the many references that Holden makes to his contemporary mid-twentieth-century people, places, and events.

—information and speculation on the extent to which Holden's adventures mirror events in Salinger's own life.

—discussion of some of the changes Salinger made when reworking material from two earlier short stories about Holden into a much expanded role for him in the novel.

—a detailed chronology of Holden's adventures.

—information about the relevance of the books and authors Holden mentions.

—information about the movies and the movie actors Holden mentions.

—discussion of several post-*Catcher* novels and movies that show the influence of *The Catcher in the Rye*.

—stills from movies Holden mentions, and lines from several songs referred to in the novel.

—a map of Manhattan showing the places Holden visits.

—photographs of many of the New York City scenes that Holden mentions, particularly in Central Park, the Museum of Natural History, and the Metropolitan Museum of Art.

—brief quotations from literary critics about such issues as why the novel has been so popular, what kind of California institution Holden is in, the significance of Holden Caulfield's name and red hunting hat, Mr. Antolini's motives in patting Holden's head, and Holden's intense relationship with his sister.

—a glossary of more than 150 terms and phrases that ESL amd EFL readers may not understand.

—indexes to the more than 200 characters and people mentioned in *The Catcher in the Rye* and nearly 75 places.

—information about Salinger's January 27, 2010, death at age 91, and a medley of reactions to it.

—study, discussion, and essay questions.

Note on the Second Edition

This second edition of *A Companion to J. D. Salinger's The Catcher in the Rye* is required by the need to acknowledge Salinger's death on January 27, 2010, to report on some of the many reactions to his death, and to incorporate information on two important books that have been published since the first edition: J. D. California's novel *60 Years Later: Coming through the Rye*, and Kenneth Slawenski's biography *J. D. Salinger: A Life Raised High*. Bruce F. Mueller and Will Hochman's *Critical Companion to J. D. Salinger: A Literary Reference to His Life and Work* (New York: Facts on File, 2011) appeared too late for detailed inclusion in this book. Readers of *The Catcher in the Rye* will be interested in pages 55–112 of this 500-page book. The authors kindly acknowledge incorporating material from the first edition of my book. I have also made a number of smaller changes, reported my discovery of the source of the Stekel quotation in chapter 24 of the novel, added a list of questions to guide readers of *The Catcher in the Rye*, and added an index.

Acknowledgments

I owe thanks to several people who have helped me with this project: Kathe Morrow and Pat Ward of the Lehigh University libraries, Molly K. Riley of the University of Washington libraries, and Ellen Fitzgerald of the Seattle Public Library for helping me to find many arcane dates and facts and printed materials; Steven Lichak of the digital media studios at Lehigh University for help in producing usable photographs; Emily Barth for her help in securing from the archives of the American Museum of Natural History photographs of the museum and some of its exhibits and dioramas; Dorothea Arnold for her help in locating information on the Egyptian tombs and mummies at the Metropolitan Museum of Art; Ron Mandelbaum of Photofest in Manhattan for making available stills of a number of movies; Jo B. Lysholdt for help in designing the map of Manhattan; Calloway M'Cloud for the cover design; Marcela B. Gamallo for proofreading and helping with the glossary for ESL and EFL readers; Michele Horwitz for help with the index; and especially Marion Egge for information about the musical references in the novel and for her many helpful editorial and technicsl suggestions on various drafts of this book. I must also gratefully acknowledge the help of the World Wide Web in researching and checking certain facts.

I wish to thank Paul Acker, editor of *ANQ: A Quarterly Journal of Short Articles, Notes, and Reviews*, for permission to use some materials from my article on *Captains Courageous*. I am grateful to the American Museum of Natural History, the Metropolitan Museum of Art, *TIME* magazine, and Photofest for permission to publish photos and stills. I took the photos in and around Central Park.

My quotations from J. D. Salinger's *The Catcher in the Rye* are taken from the widely accessible Little, Brown paperback edition (Boston, 1951). Page reference to quotations from the novel are placed parenthetically (usually without "p." or "pp.") in the text.

Catching *The Catcher in the Rye*

1. Time line of *The Catcher in the Rye*

The Catcher in the Rye apparently takes place in mid-December, 1949, on a Saturday, Sunday, and Monday a week or more before Christmas. There is repeated evidence for such specificity in dating, though not all of the movie and play references jibe perfectly. The key evidence for the year 1949 is that Holden tells us (38) that his ten-year-old brother Allie died on July 18, 1946, when Holden was thirteen. We know that Holden is sixteen (9) during the present action of the novel, which then must take place around three years later. We know from several references that the action takes place in December—"it was December and all" (4)—and in the pre-Christmas season. Given the reference to Holden's going over to Sally Hayes's place to help trim the tree, mid-December seems right. Other references corroborate that dating: "She and old Marty were drinking Tom Collinses—in the middle of December, for God's sake" (74); "Christmas was coming soon" (118); "It was [. . .] pretty near Christmas" (197); and so on. Critics like Robert Miltner are wrong to say that Holden comes of age "in the 1950s" and that his father is a "Fifties male" ("Mentor Mori; or, Sibling Society and the *Catcher* in the Bly" in J. P. Steed, ed., *The Catcher in the Rye: New Essays* [New York: Peter Lang, 2002], pp. 33, 36). By 1950, the main action of the novel has ended.

1

If we assume any sort of temporal accuracy on Salinger's part—that is, if we assume that he was really thinking of 1949 and that he consulted a calendar—we might accurately enough suppose that, since Christmas fell on a Saturday in 1949, the Saturday action of the novel may start on either Saturday, December 10, or Saturday, December 17. The 10th may be a better guess. The 17th seems late, since Phoebe tells Holden that their father will miss her play, which is on Friday, because he is flying to California (162). If the Saturday of the novel were the 17th, that would put her play the following Friday on Christmas Eve—not a probable time for a school pageant—and it would also mean that their father would probably not be home for Christmas Day, either. His missing Christmas is unlikely, in view of Phoebe's reporting that D.B. may be coming home for Christmas (164). Surely Mr. Caulfield would not miss the family holiday reunion. The events of the novel seem to come well before Christmas because Phoebe tells Holden that she hasn't started her Christmas shopping yet (178), and because the workmen are just unloading a big Christmas tree (196). I am, then, skeptical of Robert M. Slabey's complex religious reading, since it is based on the assumption that the novel starts on December 17, during Advent (see "*The Catcher in the Rye*: Christian Theme and Symbol," *CLA Journal* 6 [1963]: 170–83). If the 10th is the right starting date, then the events of the novel take place from Saturday, December 10, to Monday, December 12, 1949. (See **December 2nd** in my explanatory notes to chapter 2, below). Since D.B. is coming home for Christmas, we are perhaps to assume that he takes Holden back with him to California in early 1950, where the change of scene and the sunny California weather will help him to recuperate. Holden would then be writing the novel in a California sanitarium in 1950—probable enough in view of the 1951 publication date of *The Catcher in the Rye*.

Saturday (chapters 1–8). Saturday starts badly for Holden. As manager of the Pencey Prep fencing team, he takes the team to New York City, where he loses the fencing gear on the subway. Unable to compete, he and the rest of the team return to Pencey Prep early, in time for the big football game with Saxon Hall. Then, while most other students are at the game, Holden pays a visit to Mr. Spencer, his history teacher. He returns to his dormitory and talks with his roommates Ackley and Stradlater. While Stradlater is on a date with Jane Gallagher, Holden goes out for burgers with Ackley and Brossard, then returns to write a composition for Stradlater about Allie's baseball glove. When Stradlater returns, Holden picks a fight with him and gets his face bloodied. Around midnight Holden leaves Pencey Prep on the train, where he chats with Ernie Morrow's mother. He finally arrives in New York City.

Sunday (chapters 9–20). Early Sunday morning, at the start of Holden's longest day, he arrives at Penn Station. Following a circuitous cab ride to the Edmont Hotel, he checks in before going down to its Lavender Room, where he dances with three visitors from Seattle until the place closes. He then takes another cab to Ernie's in Greenwich Village, engages in a conversation with Lillian Simmons and her date, and walks back to the Edmont, where he enlists the services of a prostitute named Sunny. Without having had sex with her, he pays and dismisses her, then goes to bed alone. After being beaten up by the pimp Maurice, he leaves the hotel with his bags, checks them at Grand Central Station, and then has breakfast with two nuns before going to—but not into—the Museum of Natural History. Later, he meets Sally Hayes at the Biltmore and takes her to the Sunday matinee of *I Know My Love*. They go skating at Rockefeller Center and part acrimoniously when he insults her. Holden takes in a movie alone at Radio City Music Hall, then meets Carl Luce at the Wicker Bar in the Seton Hotel. He wanders around a bit more, walks to Central Park to see if he can find the ducks, sits mournfully alone on a park bench, and finally walks home for a chat with Phoebe. It is by now very late indeed.

Monday (chapters 21–26). Monday starts early with Holden's arrival home. He wakes Phoebe to talk with her, manages to avoid his parents, and then goes to the apartment of Mr. Antolini, his former English teacher. After talking with Mr. Antolini, Holden sleeps on the living room couch. Waking up to Mr. Antolini's patting his head, Holden rushes away. It is already starting to get light. He goes to Grand Central Station and sleeps on a bench there for a couple of uncomfortable hours, then tries to eat a doughnut before heading north on Fifth Avenue. On the way he decides that he will hitchhike out West, where he plans to work in a gas station and build a cabin near the woods. He leaves a message with Phoebe at her school, instructing her to meet him on the steps of the Metropolitan Museum of Art so he can return her money. He changes his mind about running away when she comes with her suitcase to join him. They go to the zoo in Central Park and then to the carrousel. Abandoning his plan to hitchhike West, Holden goes home.

2. Biographical references

Because I refer to the following works about Salinger's life with some frequency in the pages below, I give the full citations, with brief annotations, here. I list them chronologically by date of appearance:

Henry Anatole Grunwald, "The Invisible Man: A Biographical Collage" in Grunwald, ed., *Salinger: A Critical and Personal Portrait* (New York: Harper, 1962; reissued as a Pocket Books Giant Cardinal edition in 1963), pp. 3–19. This chapter reprints "Sonny: An Introduction," the September 15, 1961, *TIME* magazine cover story on J. D. Salinger (see Figure 1). The *TIME* article says little about Salinger's first novel but speculates on why he had become so reclusive. Its cover is one of the few portraits of Salinger's face. Artist Robert Vickrey painted it based on an earlier photograph of the author, since Salinger of course refused to sit for the portrait.

Warren French, "That David Copperfield Kind of Crap" in *J. D. Salinger* (New York: Twayne, 1963), pp. 21–35. This early sketch of the little that was known about Salinger's life is somewhat helpful, but also snippy and judgmental. French has this to say, for example, about Salinger's insistence on reclusive isolation: "His seclusion may actually result from an inability to make the social adjustments expected of mature members of society" (pp. 32–33).

Ian Hamilton, *In Search of J. D. Salinger* (New York: Vintage, 1988). Abbreviated as *In Search* below. This book, the first attempt at a full-length biography of Salinger, is as interesting for Hamilton's narrative of his methods of uncovering information as it is for what it reveals of Salinger. Hamilton talked with Salinger's friends and publishers, looked at old school records and talked with Salinger's classmates, uncovered files of Salinger's correspondence in university archives, and so on. The narrative ends with Hamilton's somewhat embittered account of the legal issues between him and Salinger. Salinger's lawyers filed an injunction against Hamilton and Random House, mostly on the basis of Hamilton's plan to publish quotations from unpublished letters. By then Random House already had the book in bound galley proofs, a copy of which Salinger read and objected to. The case finally went to the U.S. Supreme Court, which

Figure 1: This September 15, 1961, cover of *TIME* magazine came out ten years after the publication of *The Catcher in tne Rye*. Robert Vickrey's portrait is one of the very few we have of Salinger. Courtesy *TIME*.

refused to review a lower court's ruling that the book not be published. *In Search of J. D. Salinger* is a revision of that book, paraphrasing portions of the letters, and making certain other changes, as well. Hamilton did, however, donate a copy of the bound galley of the original biography to the Princeton University Library.

Joyce Maynard, *At Home in the World: A Memoir* (New York: Picador, 1999). Abbreviated as *At Home* below. When Joyce Maynard published in the *New York Times Magazine*, at age eighteen, a personal essay in which she "looked back" on her life and her generation, J. D. Salinger wrote a letter to her at Yale. That letter started a several-month correspondence that led to her dropping out of Yale and moving into his home in Cornish, New Hampshire. Salinger was 35 years older than she and had a daughter, Margaret (see her book, below), not much more than a year younger than she, and a son considerably younger. At that time, both children spent most of their time living a short distance away with their mother, whom Salinger had long since divorced. Joyce Maynard stayed in Cornish with him for almost a year before he asked her to leave. In *At Home in the World* Maynard tells about her own troubled youth, her correspondence with "Jerry," her stormy year with him, and her grief at their separation. She was by law not permitted to quote from his letters to her, but she paraphrases generously, revealing many details about her infatuation, his medical and dietary proclivities, and their sexual difficulties.

Paul Alexander, *Salinger: A Biography* (Los Angeles: Renaissance Books, 1999). Abbreviated as *Salinger* in the explanatory notes below. This biography has relatively few new insights to offer the reader about its elusive subject. It draws on some new sources, it picks up some materials from the bound galleys of Ian Hamilton's unpublished biography, which Alexander consulted at Princeton, and it brings in information from journalists, most of them women, who managed to interview Salinger. Part of Alexander's book consists of chronologically-organized plot summaries of Salinger's early fiction, interwoven with the few known facts and Alexander's conjectures about Salinger's life. Alexander's approach to Salinger's biography is influenced by his inference that "Much, if not all, of Salinger's writing—at least after his return from the war—was, to a significant degree, autobiographical" (p. 115). Given his approach to a man whom we know mostly through his fiction, Alexander perhaps was compelled to make such an inference, the validity of which is, of course, questionable. Alexander sees a dark pattern in Salinger's attraction to young girls, both as his personal companions and as subjects for his fiction. He even speculates that one reason Salinger has insisted on a life of seclusion is that "he sought and protected his privacy because he had a penchant for young women that he did not want to reveal to the public" (pp. 312–13).

Margaret A. Salinger, *Dream Catcher: A Memoir* (New York: Washington Square Press, 2000). Abbreviated as *Dream Catcher* below. In her book, Margaret ("Peggy") has consulted her mother Claire and her aunt Doris (J. D. Salinger's older sister), as well as recounting her own memories, to write a detailed and personal account of her father's life. She makes much of her father's Jewish roots and possible experiences with anti-Semitism and, later, with various forms of Buddhism. She makes frequent references to Salinger's fiction, which she clearly considers to be strongly connected to her father's own life

experiences. Her father did not cooperate in the book. At
the end of the book a short essay, "The Salingers: A Family
Album," written by her father's first cousin, Jay Goldberg,
gives useful information about her paternal mother's and
her paternal grandfather's origins. Included in the book are
a number of family photos of Doris, Claire, Margaret, and
Salinger himself.

Kenneth Slawenski, *J. D. Salinger: A Life Raised High* (Hebden
Bridge, West Yorkshire, UK: Pomona, 2010). Abbreviated
J. D. Salinger below, this biography came out just a
couple of months after Salinger's death. It builds on
earlier biographies and adds new materials. Slawenski
is especially good on the composition and publication
histories of Salinger's short stories and on Salinger's often
strained relationships with his publishers. He presents
a fair assessment of Salinger's frustration, bordering at
times on paranoia, with people who tried to invade his
copyrights and his privacy. Slawenski's biography also
provides useful plot summaries of Salinger's various
literary works. Readers should, however, be careful
about accepting without skepticism Slawenski's apparent
assumption that virtually all of Salinger's fictional works
are autobiographical. Slawenski thinks, for example, that
the story "Slight Rebellion off Madison" was "a confession,
an explanation of the frustration Salinger was experiencing
in his own life at at the time" (p. 41); that in "This
Sandwich Has No Mayonnaise" the author "casts himself
as Vincent Caulfield who, mirroring his creator, remained
torn between repressing his feelings and admitting the
reality in which he was embroiled" (p. 119); that it is
"likely that the circumstances of his story, 'A Girl I Knew,'
mirrors actual events. [. . .] Salinger's intense feeling for this
family make it inconceivable that he imposed such a fate

upon them through fabrication" (p. 135). Slawenski also reads *The Catcher in the Rye* as heavily autobiographical: "Salinger expresses his depression through his characters, pain that can be felt through the despair of Seymour Glass, the frustration of Holden Caulfield, and the misery of Sergeant X" (p. 226); "Salinger's ability to connect with the remnants of his own childhood is what had allowed him the insight to create the voice of Holden Caulfield" (p. 236–37). There is no doubt some truth behind these kinds of speculations, but we should not try to fill the many gaps in the list of known facts of Salinger's life by assuming that his fiction is little more than his thinly-veiled autobiography.

A forthcoming biography by Shane Salerno and David Shields, reportedly to be entitled *The Private War of J. D. Salinger*, may give a more balanced account of Salinger's life.

3. Salinger's life in *The Catcher in the Rye*

One question that has intrigued many readers of *The Catcher in the Rye* is whether it is based to some extent on J. D. Salinger's own life. One of the curious features of *Catcher* scholarship is that readers seem to want to believe that the novel is largely autobiographical. And of course in some ways it is. Salinger and Holden both grew up on New York's posh Upper East Side, knew Manhattan and some of its museums well, had wealthy parents, attended expensive private schools (one of them in Pennsylvania), were managers of their school fencing team and lost the team equipment on a New York subway, enjoyed movies by Alfred Hitchcock, suffered some sort of physical or nervous breakdown, and so on. Some readers believe they have seen general similarities in Salinger's and Holden's relationships with children and women, reclusiveness, annoyance with certain kinds of movies, leanings toward atheism, cynical views of modern life and culture, and so on.

Overshadowing these surface similarities, however, is a long list of differences. Salinger, born in 1919, would have been thirty in 1949; Holden, just sixteen in 1949, would have been born around 1933. Salinger landed in Normandy on D-Day (June 6, 1944); Holden would have been only around ten or eleven then. After two years at Valley Forge Military Academy, Salinger graduated, creditably enough, in 1936. After only a semester at Pencey Prep, which is not a military academy, Holden fails out and goes home. Salinger's father, a meat-importer, was a Jew, his mother a Catholic-turned-Jew. Holden's father, a corporation lawyer, is a Catholic, and we never find out what his mother's religion is or was. Salinger had a bar mitzvah, but Holden makes no mention of one. Salinger had an older sister; Holden has an older brother as well as younger brother who died at ten of leukemia and a younger sister who is ten in the present time of the novel.

Despite these differences in age and family situation, some of those who have been closest to Salinger personally have heard in Holden Caulfield's voice the voice of his maker. Joyce Maynard, who as a college student began a correspondence with Salinger and eventually moved in with him, read *The Catcher in the Rye* only after she had received many of his letters, but before they had met personally. In *At Home in the World* she writes of reading Salinger's novel for the first time:

> Although this is my first exposure to Salinger's published work, the voice in the novel is instantly recognizable. It could be Jerry talking. It's not just that Jerry has inserted so many of his opinions—about movies, or books, or actors, or music—into *Catcher in the Rye*. What's familiar is the point of view and the eye of the young Holden Caulfield, which is very nearly the same as that of the man with whom I have been corresponding these last few weeks. (*At Home* 88)

Maynard also gives her opinion about what actor might perform the role of Holden in a movie and concludes that only Salinger himself could do it justice:

> "Jerry Lewis tried for years to get his hands on the part of Holden," he tells me. "Wouldn't let up." This is never going to happen, we both understand. The only person who might ever have played Holden Caulfield would have been Jerry Salinger. (*At Home* 93)

Jerry Lewis was not the only person to want to make a movie of *The Catcher in the Rye*. In a *New York Times* article published on January 29, 2010, shortly after Salinger's death, Dave Itzkoff, in "Why J. D. Salinger Never Wanted a *Catcher in the Rye* Movie," reports that such big names as Steven Spielberg, Billy Wilder, Elia Kazan, and Harvey Weinstein approached Salinger about rights to do a stage or film adaptation. Others have reported that Marlon Brando, Jack Nicholson, and Leonardo DiCaprio approached Salinger or his agents about making movies of *The Catcher in the Rye*. Salinger turned them all down. He is reported to have replied to one would-be adapter, "I cannot give my permission. I fear Holden wouldn't like it" (Mel Elfin, *Newsweek*, May 30, 1960).

In 1957 a "Mr. Howard" wrote a letter, not now extant, asking Salinger why he would not let *The Catcher in the Rye* be made into a movie. On July 19, 1957, Salinger wrote a two-page reply to this letter. It is not clear who this "Mr. Howard" was, but Salinger in his reply refers to "your friendly and highly readable letter." Salinger gives several reasons for refusing to sell the rights to his novel. For one thing, he wanted to let his family, after his death, make the decision about—and reap the financial rewards of—the movie rights. It woujld be a kind of legacy or insurance policy for them if he died poor. More importantly, he goes on:

> The *Catcher in the Rye* is a very novelistic novel. There are readymade "scenes"—only a fool would deny that—but, for me, the weight of the book is the narrator's voice, the non-stop peculiarities of it, his personal, extremely

discriminating attitude to his reader-listener, his asides
about gasoline rainbows in street puddles, his philosophy
or way of looking at cowhide suitcases and empty
toothpaste cartons—in a word, his thoughts. He can't
legitimately be separated from his own first-person
technique. True, if the separation is forcibly made,
there is enough material left over for something called
an Exciting (or maybe just Interesting) Evening in the
Theater. But I find that idea if not odious, at least odious
enough to keep me from selling the rights [. . .] And
Holden Caulfield himself, in my undoubtedly super-
biased opinion, is essentially unactable.

"Essentially unactable," perhaps, but Hillel Italie wrote in
an Associated Press release just after Salinger's death that at one
point Salinger had contemplated permitting a stage adaptation of
the novel—"with the author himself playing Holden" ("*Catcher in
the Rye* Author J. D. Salinger Dies," January 28, 2010). If Salinger
considered Holden unactable by anyone except himself, then it
may well be that at some fundamental level, in some fundamental
ways, *The Catcher in the Rye* is what might be termed emotionally
autobiographical.

In a letter that Salinger much later (on March 25, 1972)
wrote to a young woman named Liz Rosenberg, he said,
apparently in response to a question she had written to him about
whether he is like any of the Glass characters who had appeared
in his later fiction, that the simple fact was that he was more like
Holden than like any of the Glass men or women. At the time
Salinger was in his early fifties, while Liz Rosenberg was just
seventeen. (The letter is in the Berg collection in the New York
Public Library.)

In *Dream Catcher*, Salinger's daughter Margaret recalls the
advice her father once gave to "a young lady, an English student"
who had asked for his help in sorting out the autobiographical
origins of his fiction. "He was very polite," Margaret writes, "and
said he appreciated her good will; nevertheless, he told her, the

biographical facts you want are in my stories, in one form or another, including the traumatic experiences you asked about" (*Dream Catcher* xiii–xiv).

Holden tells us that W. Somerset Maugham's *Of Human Bondage*, first published in 1915, is "a pretty good book and all" (18). Salinger would no doubt have agreed with Maugham's statement in the preface that "it is easier to write of what you know than of what you don't," and perhaps he would have nodded in sympathy with Maugham's statement that *Of Human Bondage* "is not an autobiography, but an autobiographical novel; fact and fiction are inextricably mingled; the emotions are my own, but not all the incidents are related as they happened, and some of them are transferred to my hero not from my own life but from that of persons with whom I was intimate" (New York: Modern Library, 1999, pp. xxxviii–xxxix).

There can be no question that in writing his novel about Holden Caulfield, Salinger drew in some general and also some quite specific ways on what he knew personally and on his own life. Beginning writers are routinely advised to write about what they know, and no doubt Salinger did draw from his own life experiences as he worked on his first novel. Salinger attended Ursinus College for a short time—less than a semester. Ian Hamilton reports that a classmate named Frances Thierolf said that she recognized autobiographical elements in Holden: "'When we knew Jerry, he was Holden Caulfield, although when *The Catcher in the Rye* burst upon the literary world, he expressed surprise when I recognized him as Holden. I guess he never knew his adolescence was showing'" (*In Search* 45). To call the novel autobiography, however, is surely to misrepresent the slippery relationship between the cloudy facts of Salinger's early life and the sharply-etched fiction of Holden's. Perhaps we can do no better than the editors of *TIME* who wrote, in 1961, "Salinger, like a lonely child inventing brothers and sisters, has drawn most of his characters out of his own rare imagination" (quoted from the reprint in Henry Anatole Grunwald, ed., *Salinger: A Critical and Personal Portrait* [New York: Harper, 1962], p. 11).

We should keep in mind that if we did want to seek an autobiographical figure in the novel, D.B. would be a strong candidate. Like Salinger, D.B. is a writer of short stories, and, like Salinger, he goes by his initials, not his given name. D.B. is roughly the same age as Salinger, and, like Salinger, landed in Normandy on D-Day and returned after the war to take up the writer's craft. He apparently shares some literary tastes with Salinger. As for D.B.'s going out to Hollywood to be a "prostitute," it is possible to see in Salinger's own life a rough parallel to that migration. Salinger sold the movie rights to his story "Uncle Wiggily in Connecticut" and in 1950, just a year before he published *The Catcher in the Rye*, saw the resulting Samuel Goldwyn film, *My Foolish Heart*, starring Susan Hayward and Dana Andrews (see Figure 2). Salinger was reportedly horrified by what Hollywood had done to his story and resolved never again to allow a movie to be made of his fiction. He broke that resolve only once, in 1956, when he offered to sell the movie rights to his story "The Laughing Man" to Hollywood. Hollywood writers, however, found the story too slight for a movie, and nothing came of the offer. After that, Salinger's days of prostituting himself to Hollywood were over; D.B.'s, apparently, are not.

We must also keep in mind that, while there are certainly elements of Holden's life that sound autobiographical, the hero of *The Catcher in the Rye* bears a remarkable similarity to earlier fictional characters. Certain young innocents on a journey leap immediately to mind as literary antecedents for Holden. Melville's handsome young Billy Budd is too good for the world that victimizes him. Twain's Huck Finn bears several clear parallels with Holden (discussed in more detail in my notes below). Hemingway's Nick Adams, like Holden, is puzzled by

Figure 2: From *My Foolish Heart* (Samuel Goldwyn, 1950), starring Dana Andrews and Susan Hayward, which was based on Salinger's story "Uncle Wiggily in Connecticut." Salinger hated the movie. Courtesy Photofest.

the human cruelty he sees around him as he comes of age. For even more specific parallels, we can look to Willa Cather's Paul, a troubled youth who runs away from home for a fling in the big city. Salinger could easily have known "Paul's Case," first published in 1905 and widely anthologized. It concerns the brief odyssey of young Paul, a tall, skinny teenager whose propensity for lying puts him in repeated trouble in his Pennsylvania high school. He is often at odds with his father, who finally takes him out of school and apprentices him to a business firm. Paul steals money from the firm and takes a train to New York for a week-long fling.

He buys fancy clothes, stays at the ritzy Waldorf-Astoria, and indulges his dreams by enjoying plays and concerts. In the end, faced with a return home to Pittsburgh, he commits suicide by flinging himself in front of a train. Holden is far different from Paul, of course, but the similarities are obvious enough that this story almost surely contributed to the characterization, setting, and themes of Salinger's story.

In 1953 Salinger moved to Cornish, New Hampshire. That fall a high school student named Shirlie Blaney interviewed him over lunch in Windsor, Vermont (across the Connecticut River from Cornish). When she asked Salinger directly whether *The Catcher in the Rye* was autobiographical, he said it "sort of" was: "My boyhood was very much the same as that of the boy in the book, and it was a great relief telling people about it" (quoted in Alexander, *Salinger* 177–78). Much later, in 1980, when Salinger was in his early sixties, another young woman interviewed him. Betty Eppes asked the same question about whether the novel was autobiographical. Salinger replied, "I don't know. I don't know. I've just let it all go. I don't know about Holden anymore" (quoted in Alexander, *Salinger* 266). Whether we like it or not, most readers who know anything about Salinger think they hear his voice behind Holden's. As Joseph S. Walker puts it, "it is the rare reader who can meditate on Holden's voice as an autonomous object distinct from the celebrated silence of his creator" ("The Catcher Takes the Field: Holden, Hollywood, and the Making of a Mann," in J. P. Steed, ed., *The Catcher in the Rye: New Essays* [New York: Peter Lang, 2002], p. 80). We can probably safely assume that though Holden Caulfield is very much a literary creation, he is in some ways somewhat like the young Salinger. *The Catcher in the Rye* can perhaps best be described as a brilliantly original work of fiction that combines elements of the biographical facts and the traumatic experiences of Salinger's own life with those of the lives of others he knew and of other cinematic and literary lives he was familiar with—all combined with the artistic creativity that is the mark of the greatest literature.

Still, any consideration of the possible autobiographical basis of *The Catcher in the Rye* must acknowledge that Salinger's conception of the narrative changed over the years. Since the basic facts of Holden's familial, educational, military, and romantic experiences developed in the course of the decade in which he worked on what eventually emerged as the novel, there can be no question that autobiography yielded to artistry as the story line grew from divergent short stories into a unified novel.

4. From the stories to *The Catcher in the Rye*

On the facts-of-publication page immediately following the title page of *The Catcher in the Rye*, Salinger reports that two of the "incidents" in the novel had appeared "in a different form" as stories in magazines. The two stories are not named, but the names of the magazines and the years of publication are given, so it is easy enough to find them. Reading the two stories helps us to make an assessment of the ways Salinger developed the story line over time and enlarged his conception of Holden in the five years between the publication of the stories and the publication of *The Catcher in the Rye*.

Salinger wrote the story "I'm Crazy" while he was still in Europe following World War II, apparently not many weeks from the time that he suffered a nervous breakdown as a result of battle fatigue (now called post-traumatic stress disorder or PTSD). Whether or not Salinger was feeling that he was in some sense "crazy," he checked himself into an Army hospital in Nuremberg. "I'm Crazy" appeared in the December 22, 1945, issue of *Collier's* (see Figure 3), a popular American weekly that competed with *The Saturday Evening Post* for readers and circulation. At its height during World War II, *Collier's* had a weekly readership of well over two million.

"I'm Crazy" begins with a comparison of the weather to
that in a grade B movie: "It was about eight o'clock at night, and
dark, and raining, and freezing, and the wind was noisy the way
it is in spooky movies on the night the old slob with the will
gets murdered" (p. 36). In addition to its narrator's interest in
movies, that early story, which took up parts of three pages of the
magazine (pp. 36, 48, 51), will sound familiar indeed to readers
of Salinger's novel, though some differences are apparent. Its
first-person narrator Holden Caulfield is going home a day early
(not five days, as in the novel) because he is failing out at his prep

Figure 3: From the first page of "I'm Crazy" in *Collier's,* December
22, 1945. Note that Holden here carries his suitcases with him to the
Spencers, having already decided to go home early, and that he has not
yet in this story acquired a peaked hunting hat.

school Pentey (not Pencey Prep as in the novel). Trying to feel a good-by to the place, he stands beside the cannon on a bitterly cold night on top of Thomsen Hill listening to the sounds of a game of basketball (not football), where his team is playing the Saxon Charter (not Saxon Hall) team. He thinks of the good time he had tossing a football around with Buhler and Jackson (not Tichener and Campbell) one fall day at dusk. Then he runs down the hill and crosses Route 202 (not 204) with his suitcases (rather than packing them later) to say good-by to his history teacher, Mr. Spencer. Mrs. Spencer lets him in and sends him into the bedroom where grippe-ridden old Spencer reads to him from his final exam on the Egyptians and their mummies. During part of Spencer's castigation of him, Holden thinks about the lagoon in Central Park and what happens to the ducks when the lagoon freezes over. Spencer asks what his plans are and whether he will miss Pentey. Holden says he'll miss the Pentey stickers on his suitcases and tells Spencer about the time he had lied to Andy Warbach's mother (not Ernie Morrow's) about what a great guy her son is. Holden then says he has to catch a train, declines the offer of hot chocolate, and leaves the Spencer's home with his suitcases.

At his parents' apartment in New York, Holden has a brief conversation with Jeannette, the "colored maid" (not Charlene, who is not identified by race in the novel), and then goes to see his two sisters, named Phoebe, age ten, and Viola, who seems to be around three. When his parents come home, Holden talks with them. We are not shown the conversation, but Holden goes to bed in his own room afterward. The story ends with this paragraph:

> I lay awake for a pretty long time, feeling lousy. I knew everybody was right and I was wrong. I knew that I wasn't going to be one of those successful guys, that I was never going to be like Edward Gonzales or Theodore Fisher or Lawrence Meyer. I knew that this time when Father said I was going to work in that man's office that he meant it, that I wasn't going

back to school again ever, that I wouldn't like working in an office. I started wondering again where the ducks in Central Park went when the lagoon was frozen over, and finally I went to sleep. ("I'm Crazy" 51)

Salinger made many small changes when he expanded "I'm Crazy" to *The Catcher in the Rye*: Holden's passing one course at Pencey Prep, rather than failing every single one; his losing the fencing team equipment, his red hunting hat, his wanting to be a catcher in the rye, his remembering the death of James Castle, and so on. Each of these was an important change and worth considering, but I want to discuss here only two of the larger changes.

First, Salinger increased the length and scope of Holden's journey. The material from "I'm Crazy" finds its way into only four chapters of the novel, chapters 1–2 (mostly the visit to the Spencers) and chapters 21–22 (his return to his family's apartment in Manhattan). Virtually all of chapters 3–30 is new in the novel: the Ackley-Stradlater material; the near obsession with Jane Gallagher; the actual train trip, including his talk with Mrs. Morrow; the taxi ride to the Edmont Hotel, where he meets the three women from Seattle; the taxi to Greenwich Village and Ernie's, where he meets Lillian Simmons; his walk back to the hotel, where he encounters Maurice and Sunny; his cab ride to Grand Central Station and his encounter with the two nuns; his disastrous date with Sally Hayes; his going to a show at Radio City Music Hall; his visit to the Wicker Bar, where he meets Carl Luce; and his nocturnal visit to Central Park. On his return home in chapters 21 and 22, he talks with Phoebe, but then after a short while his parents come home and, to avoid a confrontation with them, he sneaks out. The rest of *The Catcher in the Rye* is all new: the visit to Mr. Antolini; the subway ride to Grand Central; the visit to the pharaoh's tomb at the Metropolitan Museum of Art; the visit with Phoebe to the carrousel in Central Park; and the decision to go home again after a half-year in California. In

"I'm Crazy," Salinger gave us two scenes—at the boarding school and at home—with no travel time in between. In *The Catcher in the Rye*, he gives us those two scenes, more or less, but with the journey-plot inserted—the travel by train, taxi, subway, and foot, with reference also to a journey west, not to cowboy country but to a California sanitarium. I speak here, of course, not just of a physical journey from one place on the map to another, but also of the emotional journey in which the young rebel grows into maturity. In "I'm Crazy," Holden ends the story as he began it—a brash and "crazy" kid who has given up on school—"I wasn't going back to school ever again"—and is resigned to start an office job he knows he will hate. In the novel Holden has matured enough to end his journey ready to give school another chance. When asked whether he is going to "apply himself" at school in the fall, he replies with realistic uncertainty, "I *think* I am, but how do I know?" (213).

The second large change that Salinger made in transforming his story into a novel was the addition of Holden's two brothers. In "I'm Crazy," Holden has two younger sisters and no brothers. In *The Catcher in the Rye*, he has one younger sister and two brothers, one older and one younger. His older brother D.B. is a writer of short stories who Holden thinks has sold out to Hollywood. His younger brother Allie had died at age ten of leukemia. The addition of these brothers is a brilliant move on Salinger's part. Whether or not Allie can be said to represent to Holden his own lost innocence, while D.B. represents to Holden his own grim future as a successful writer with his own fast sports car and his own beautiful "English babe" (213), there is no denying their importance to him. Allie was smart, friendly, and likable—but just as dead as Holden at times wishes he himself were. D.B. is smart, friendly, likeable, and successful—but with the kind of success that Holden does not respect. Surely one aspect of Holden's growth is that he comes to envision for himself some sort of realistic alternative to Allie's death-in-innocence and D.B.'s life-in-success, some alternative to being an idealistic savior catching innocent children before they fall off a crazy cliff or riding off into the western sunset to live in deaf-and-dumb isolation in a remote cabin.

The other early-published "incident" of *The Catcher in the Rye* appeared in the *New Yorker* a year later, on December 21, 1946, entitled "Slight Rebellion Off Madison." Salinger had written the story and had it accepted by the *New Yorker* back in 1941, but the attack on Pearl Harbor on December 7 of that year delayed actual publication until four years later, when Salinger was still in the Army. "Slight Rebellion Off Madison" gives us the origins of the telephone call to Sally Hayes in chapter 15 of the novel, of his date with her in chapter 17, and later of his drunken call to her in chapter 20. Home for Christmas vacation from the "Pencey Preparatory School for Boys," Holden Morrisey Caulfield in the story drops his suitcase in the foyer, kisses his mother, and calls his girlfriend Sally Hayes. He takes Sally dancing to the Wedgwood Room. They neck in the taxi on the way home. The next afternoon they see the matinee of a play starring the Lunts. During the intermission they talk about the play with a snobbish man named George Hamilton. Afterwards they go to Radio City to ice skate. They sit down and have a heated conversation during which Holden tells Sally all the things he hates and says he wants to quit school and run off with her to New England. When she refuses, he insults her and goes out drinking with a Pencey Prep classmate named Carl Luce (quite a different Carl Luce than in the novel) at the Wadsworth Bar. At 2:00 a.m., dead drunk, he calls Sally to say he'll help her trim the Christmas tree. He makes his way to the men's room, soaks his head in the washbowl, talks with a wavy-haired piano player, and goes out to wait for the Madison Avenue bus.

Salinger made several small changes that need not concern us here—for example, Holden wears not a red hunting hat, but a conventional hat with a sharp "V" in the crown. Several of the larger changes, however, deserve mention.

First, "Slight Rebellion Off Madison" has a third-person narrator, which Salinger shifts, for the sake of consistency with the point of view in the rest of *The Catcher in the Rye*, to first-person. This change makes our identification with Holden more immediate and lets us hear his famously judgmental voice more consistently. In the story we read this:

> As soon as Holden got into New York, he took a cab home, dropped his Gladstone in the foyer, kissed his mother, lumped his hat and coat into a convenient chair, and dialed Sally's number.
> "Hey!" he said into the mouthpiece. "Sally?"
> "Yes. Who's that?"
> "Holden Caulfield. How are ya?" ("Slight Rebellion" 82)

In the novel we read this:

> Anyway, I gave her a buzz. First the maid answered. Then her father. Then she got on. "Sally?" I said.
> "Yes—who is this?" she said. She was quite a little phony. I'd already told her father who it was.
> "Holden Caulfield. How are ya?" (105–06)

Second, in "Slight Rebellion Off Madison," Holden is home just for vacation and is not failing out of school. He seems like a regular teenaged kid who dutifully kisses his mother but whose first priority is to call his girlfriend, also just home on vacation from her school. He is apparently in a long-term and serious relationship with Sally Hayes, who comes across as less shallow and flirtatious than in the novel. Holden's diatribe to her about the hatefulness of the world around him is less sweeping and bitter in the story than in the novel.

Third, there is no mention in "Slight Rebellion Off Madison" of any of Holden's siblings. So far as we can tell from the story, he is an only child. In the novel he is one of four siblings, one of them dead. Still, all in all, Salinger made fewer changes in Holden's character and situation in adapting this second story to its place in the novel than he made in adapting "I'm Crazy." The biggest changes, once again, were expanding Holden's family and his inserting new events into Holden Caulfield's journey. Although the novel tracks the story fairly closely, Salinger breaks it up with other pieces of Holden's odyssey: his talk with the two nuns, his trip to the Museum of Natural History, his seeing the show at Radio City, and his long talk with an older Carl Luce at the Wicker Bar.

A fourth change that Salinger made in adapting the two stories to the expanded novel format was to transfer the "I'm crazy" refrain from the boarding school chapters to the Sally Hayes chapters. In "I'm Crazy," Holden identifies his craziness with his decision to stand on Thomsen Hill trying to feel a good-by, with his inability to express to old Spencer his real feelings, and, in his talk with Phoebe, with his inability to cope at school:

> Boy, I was cold. Only a crazy guy would have stood there. That's me. Crazy. No kidding. I have a screw loose. ("I'm Crazy" 36)

> Anyway, I wasn't saying much that I wanted to say. I never do. I'm crazy. No kidding. [. . .] I told him I'd write him a letter sometime, that he shouldn't worry about me, that he oughtn't to let me get him down. I told him that I knew I was crazy. ("I'm Crazy" 48)

> "I couldn't help it, Phoeb," I said. "They kept shoving stuff at me, exams and all, and study periods, and everything was compulsory all the time. I was going crazy." ("I'm Crazy" 48–51)

Title line of the short story "I'm Crazy" does carry over into the novel, but in quite different situations. Holden refers to his craziness not in connection with the school or Spencer or Phoebe, but in the episodes with Sally Hayes and the nature of his emotional connection with her. There had been no mention of anything "crazy" in that connection in "Slight Rebellion Off Madison," but there are several in the novel:

> I'm crazy. I didn't even *like* her much, and yet all of a sudden I felt like I was in love with her and wanted to marry her. I swear to God I'm crazy. I admit it. (124)

> Then, just to show you how crazy I am, when we were coming out of this big clinch, I told her I loved her and all. It was a lie, of course, but the thing is, I *meant* it when I said it. I'm crazy. I swear to God I am. (125)

> She wouldn't have been anybody to go with. The terrible part, though, is that I *meant* it when I asked her. That's the terrible part. I swear to God I'm a madman. (134)

> I wished to God I hadn't even phoned her. When I'm drunk, I'm a madman. (151)

Biographer Paul Alexander reports that Salinger himself apparently did not think that Holden Caulfield was really crazy. The first publisher he had lined up for *The Catcher in the Rye* was Harcourt Brace. When Salinger heard that one of its senior editors, Eugene Reynal, read the manuscript and asked whether Holden was supposed to be crazy, an annoyed Salinger withdrew the book and published it with Little, Brown (*Salinger* 146–47).

Salinger wrote short stories about the Caulfield family, but they were never published. Two are now archived in the Princeton University library. "The Ocean Full of Bowling Balls" was sold in 1947 to *Woman's Home Companion*, but it was never published. The story is narrated by Vincent Caulfield, an early study of the character to be named D.B. in *The Catcher in the Rye*. Vincent has a girlfriend named Helen who, like Jane Gallagher in the novel, keeps her kings in the back row. Vincent's younger brother Kenneth suffers from a heart condition and dies while swimming in the ocean. Like Allie in *The Catcher in the Rye*, Kenneth has bright red hair and leaves behind a baseball mitt covered with poetry. Another brother named Holden is away at summer camp but writes a letter from Camp Wigwam complaining about some of the people he encounters there. "The Last and Best of the Peter Pans" also centers on Vincent Caulfield. It is mostly a dialogue between Vincent and his mother about Vincent's joining the army. Holden and Phoebe are mentioned, as is the deceased brother Kenneth.

Other stories centering on Vincent Caulfield's World War II experiences were published. In "This Sandwich Has No Mayonnaise," which appeared in *Esquire* in 1945, Vincent is in basic training in the army in Georgia. He is worried because his younger brother Holden, also a soldier, has been reported missing on the Pacific front. His concern causes him to remember certain scenes involving Holden. In "The Last Day of the Last Furlough," which appeared in the *Saturday Evening Post* in 1944, Vincent visits his friend Babe Gladwaller, who is about to ship out to his military assignment. Vincent reports that his brother Holden is missing in action. In "The Stranger," which appeared in *Collier's* in 1945, Babe Gladwaller visits Vincent's former girl friend Helen to tell her how Vincent had been killed in action. Holden is not mentioned.

The obvious conclusion is that Salinger initially conceived *The Catcher in the Rye* as a series of short stories. Only later did he refashion portions of some of them into a novel that focused on a few days in the life of Holden Caulfield, who was far too young to have served in the war. In doing so, Salinger was guided more by the need for consistency of characterization and artistic integrity than by the need to be faithful to his own experiences or his early expression of Holden Caulfield's experiences.

5. Holden Caulfield's appearance

One of the built-in problems with first-person narration is that we usually know little about what the narrator looks like. First-person narrators are, after all, more interested in describing those around them than describing themselves. Unless the narrator resorts to the mirror trick ("I looked into the mirror and saw the face of a slender young man whose two-day growth of black beard was not enough to conceal the mole below his right ear . . ."), we know little enough about his own appearance. Holden gives us a good bit of information about what he looks like, but the information he gives us is scattered and selective, with much of it having to do with his efforts to appear older than his sixteen years so that he can order alcoholic drinks and impress women.

We know something of Holden's physical stature—"I'm six foot two and a half" (9)—and that he can sometimes get away with ordering alcohol "on account of my heighth" (57). At the Wicker Bar he orders "a couple of Scotch and sodas. [. . .] I stood up when I ordered them so they could see how tall I was and not think I was a goddam minor" (142). We know that he is thin and narrow-shouldered because he is concerned about letting Stradlater borrow his jacket: "We were practically the same heighth, but he weighed about twice as much as I did. He had these very broad shoulders" (25–26). Holden tells us later that his sister Phoebe is "quite skinny, like me" (67) and "I'm a very light eater. I really am. That's why I'm so damn skinny" (107).

Holden seems especially focused on his hair. He tells us right off that "I wear a crew cut" (6) and, later, just before Sunny the prostitute comes in, "I went to my room and put some water on my hair, but you can't really comb a crew cut or anything" (91). It may be that Holden is eager to let us know that he does not have long hair, since this kind of hair he associates with "flits" when he describes the men at the Wicker Bar: "They weren't too flitty-looking—I mean, they didn't have their hair too long or anything—but you could tell they were flits anyway" (142). Interestingly, Sally Hayes seems not to make such associations with long hair. Just after she tells Holden she loves him, she says "Promise me you'll let your hair grow. Crew cuts are getting corny. And your hair's so lovely" (125). Holden himself is particularly proud of the gray hair he has: "I have gray hair. I really do. The one side of my head—the right side—is full of millions of gray hairs. I've had them ever since I was a kid" (9). He tells Mrs. Morrow about it: "'And I have quite a bit of gray hair.' I turned sideways and showed her my gray hair" (57). He is pleased to show off his gray hair especially because it makes him look older, as when, drunk, he talks to the hat-check girl: "I showed her my goddam gray hair and told her I was forty-two—I was only horsing around, naturally" (153).

As for what his face looks like, we have Lillian Simmons's general judgment when, accompanied by her date at Ernie's, she bumps into Holden: "'Isn't he handsome?' she said to the Navy guy.'Holden, you're getting handsomer by the minute'" (87). We cannot necessarily trust Lillian Simmons's judgment though, since she may have motives of her own. She may want to make the "Navy guy" jealous, or she may want to flatter Holden so he will want to give his brother D.B. her flirtatious message. Besides, what does she mean by "handsome"? Does her epithet mean anything more specific than Mr. Antolini's when he tells Holden, "Good night, handsome" (191)? These "handsomes" are about as vague as Sunny the prostitute's declaration to Holden that "You're cute" (97). How fully can we trust the judgment of a hooker who stands to gain from flattering one of her johns? If she thought him ugly, would she have told him so?

There is no reason to think that Holden is ugly. He is probably what most people would call a "nice-looking kid," but it is impossible to translate such terms into a drawing or mental picture of what his face looks like. The only real clue we get as to what Holden's face looks like comes indirectly from Sunny as she sits, uninvited, on Holden's lap:

> "You look like a guy in the movies. You know. Whosis. You know who I mean. What the heck's his name?"
> "I don't know," I said. She wouldn't get off my goddam lap.

"Sure you know. He was in that pitcher with Mel-vine
Douglas? The one that was Mel-vine Douglas's kid brother?
That falls off this boat? *You* know who I mean."
"No, I don't. I go to the movies as seldom as I can." (97)

In fact, Holden seems to go to movies as often as he can. Bernard
S. Oldsey, who wrote an early article on movies in *The Catcher
in the Rye*, reminds us that Holden's imagination "battens on
the movies: his reveries revolve around them; and his narrative
depends heavily upon them. [...] As a child of his times he is
automatically a child of the movies" ("The Movies in the Rye,"
College English 23 [1961]: 210).

Although Holden denies recognizing the movie she refers
to, he would probably not feel flattered by the comparison she
draws. The reference is to *Captains Courageous*, the 1937 movie
based on Rudyard Kipling's novel of fishing on the Grand Banks
east of New England (see Figure 4). The movie starred Spencer
Tracy, who won the best actor Academy Award for his portrayal
of Manuel, the Portuguese fisherman who rescues the ten-year-
old Harvey Cheyne when he falls off a passenger liner on its
way to Europe. Harvey is a spoiled little brat who is sailing with
his father—not his older brother—played by Melvyn Douglas.
Harvey, played by the twelve-year-old child actor Freddie
Bartholomew, is a small and round-faced preadolescent boy with
curly locks, scarcely the sort of person the insecure Holden would
have wanted to resemble. In *Captains Courageous*, thanks to the
tough-loving guidance given him by Manuel, the childish Harvey
eventually matures and, months later, drives west with his father.
Perhaps we are to understand that Holden, despite his height and
gray hair, has something of a baby face. Perhaps the point is that
Holden, like Harvey, is a spoiled brat who needs a strong friend to
make him into a man. I have more to say about
Captains Courageous in my notes to chapter 13 below.

Figure 4: From the film version of *Captains Courageous*. Note the boyish face of Harvey Cheyne, played by child-actor Freddie Bartholomew. It is interesting that Sunny thinks Holden looks like him. The fisherman Manuel is played by Spencer Tracy. Courtesy Photofest.

6. *The Catcher in the Rye* in other fiction

Salinger's novel has been widely read in English and in translation in other countries. Stephen J. Whitfield tells us that it has been translated into thirty languages ("Cherished and Cursed: Toward a Social History of *The Catcher in the Rye*," *New England Quarterly* 70 [1997]: 568). Although translators of *The Catcher in the Rye* into other languages have come up with a variety of substitutions for the title, the novel is still—well, substantially—the same. According to Donald M. Fiene, some of the foreign titles, back-translated into English, are "Life of a Man," "The Young Holden," "Cursed Youth," "Heart-Catcher," "Savior in Time of Need," "The Man in the Rye," "Lonely Journey," "I, New York, and All the Rest," "Above the Precipice in the Ryefield," "Wanderer in the Rye," and "The Hidden Hunter" ("J. D. Salinger: A Bibliography," *Wisconsin Studies in Contemporary Literature* 4 [1963]: 109–11). By whatever title, Salinger's novel has undoubtedly reached many readers around the globe, and without doubt it has influenced later novelists. Biographer Paul Alexander gives a list of books in English influenced by *The Catcher in the Rye*:

> [Salinger's] importance can best be measured in the way *Catcher* has influenced books that have been written after it. *Last Summer* by Evan Hunter, *The Bell Jar* by Sylvia Plath, *The Last Picture Show* by Larry McMurtry, *The Basketball Diaries* by Jim Carroll, *A Separate Peace* by John Knowles, *Birdy* by William Wharton, *Less than Zero* by Bret Easton Ellis, *Bright Lights, Big City* by Jay McInereny, *Girl, Interrupted* by Susanna Kaysen—these are just a few books written in the tradition of *The Catcher in the Rye*. (*Salinger* xiv)

Others would add to the list. Louis Menand, for example, would add *Fear and Loathing in Las Vegas* by Hunter S. Thompson ("Holden at Fifty: *The Catcher in the Rye* and What It Spawned," *New Yorker*, October 1, 2001, p. 86). And Matt Evertson makes a long argument about Salinger's influence on Cormac McCarthy's 1993 *All the Pretty Horses* ("Love, Loss, and Growing Up in J. D.

Salinger and Cormac McCarthy," in J. P. Steed, ed., *The Catcher in the Rye: New Essays* [New York: Peter Lang, 2002], pp. 101–41).

Sometimes the influence of *The Catcher in the Rye* is made explicit by the author. In John Fowles's *The Collector* (1961), for example, the neurotic narrator stalks and abducts the lovely Miranda Grey, locking her away in his basement. Miranda tries various methods to persuade her captor, whom she calls "Caliban," to set her free. One of her methods of getting through to Caliban is to lend him her copy of *The Catcher in the Rye*, hoping he'll see some connection between himself and Holden. When Caliban eventually—but reluctantly—does read it, they have this conversation:

> M. Well?
> C. I don't like the way he talks.
> M. I don't like the way you talk. But I don't treat you as below any serious notice or sympathy.
> C. I suppose it's very clever. To write like that and all.
> M. I gave you that book to read because I thought you would feel identified with him. You're a Holden Caulfield. He doesn't fit anywhere and you don't.
> C. I don't wonder, the way he goes on. He doesn't try to fit.
> M. He tries to construct some sort of reality in his life, some sort of decency.
> C. It's not realistic. Going to a posh school and his parents having money. He wouldn't behave like that. In my opinion.
> (Little, Brown 1997 edition, pp. 219–20)

Another contemporary work in which the characters make specific and extended reference to *The Catcher in the Rye* is John Guare's play *Six Degrees of Separation* (1990). In this play a young black man named Paul, bleeding from a knife wound, bursts into the home of a middle-aged New York couple and claims to know their children, who, he says, are his classmates at Harvard. He also claims to be the son of actor Sidney Poitier and to have been beaten in Central Park by muggers who had stolen his briefcase with the only copy of his thesis. When asked what the thesis was about, he mentions that he was interested in the fact that several young men who had been reading *The Catcher in the Rye*—an unnamed school teacher, assassin Mark David Chapman, and would-be assassin John Hinckley—had committed violent acts in apparent response to the novel. Paul is somewhat vague about precisely what the point of his thesis was, but he gives a learned-sounding three-page disquisition on the novel. Among other things, he says that in his view *The Catcher in the Rye* is "about paralysis [. . .] emotional and intellectual paralysis" and "the death of the imagination" (New York: Vintage Books, 1990, p. 33). Both Fowles and Guare assumed that their audiences would already know about Salinger's novel and its hero. The 1993 film version of *Six Degrees of Separation*, starring Will Smith as Paul, and Donald Sutherland and Stockard Channing as his hosts (see Figure 5), is somewhat different from the play, but director Fred Schepisi retains the long scene on *The Catcher in the Rye*.

Without question, Stephen Chbosky's *The Perks of Being a Wallflower* (New York: Pocket Books, 1999) builds on *The Catcher in the Rye*. Its first-person fifteen-year-old male narrator tells the story of his troubled first year of high school in the early 1990s in Pittsburgh, Pennsylvania. He describes the books he reads and the movies he sees and the songs he hears, the crush he has on a senior girl, his discovery of masturbation, his fumbling discovery of necking and petting, his brush with friends who are gay, and his close connection with a favorite English teacher whom he visits in his home. Like Holden, Charlie has a brother and sister and is haunted by the tragic death of a favorite relative—so haunted and guilt-ridden that he has a nervous breakdown, thinks of suicide, and has to be taken to a hospital, where he talks with a psychiatrist. Eventually he is released and comes home, ready to start school again. There are other connections to Salinger's

Figure 5: From the film version of *Six Degrees of Separation* (Metro-Goldwyn-Mayer, 1993), starring Will Smith, Donald Sutherland, and Stockard Channing. Young Paul claims to have been mugged in Central Park and to have written a Harvard thesis on *The Catcher in the Rye*. Courtesy Photofest.

book, but they are obvious enough to anyone who has read both of them. Chbosky would surely not deny the connection, since he has Bill, the English teacher, recommend *The Catcher in the Rye* to Charlie, who reads it no fewer than four times and eventually gives it to the girl he loves, Sam (apparently short for "Samantha"), when she graduates. There are plenty of differences in the novels—*The Perks of Being a Wallflower* is epistolary in form, for example, and Charlie not only smokes and drinks but also experiments with drugs—but for all its delightful originality, Chbosky could scarcely have written this novel had Salinger not shown him the way.

Novels that make no explicit mention of *The Catcher in the Rye* also show its influence. A novel that immediately comes to mind is Philip Roth's blockbuster *Portnoy's Complaint* (1967). Like Holden, Alex Portnoy is a smart and confused New York-area resident who gives a retrospective first-person account of his experiences as a young man. Indeed, it is possible to see *Portnoy's Complaint* as a continuation of *The Catcher in the Rye*, with Alex adding his youthful masturbatory excesses and his later exploits with a series of female sexual partners. Although there are many and important differences between the two novels, there are so many similarities that direct influence is unmistakable: both young men use such slang expressions as "it kills me" and "in my entire life" (*Portnoy*, p. 40; all page numbers in this paragraph are to the Vintage International edition first published in 1994); both have conflicted relationships with powerful mothers; both have ineffectual fathers who are consumed by their business dealings; both have sisters to whom at times they are drawn; both refer to relatives who were in the D-Day invasion at Normandy (see Heshie in *Portnoy*, p. 143); although Jewishness lies at the origins of both novels, both protagonists are vague about their own religious orientation; both refer to the possibility of escaping to the countryside (*Portnoy*, p. 196); both refer to baseball players named Allie (*Portnoy*, p. 242) and to special baseball mitts (*Portnoy*, p. 243); both attempt sexual encounters with women but fail (the Jewish lieutenant scene, *Portnoy*, pp. 256–57); both wind up talking to psychiatrists (indeed, the whole *Portnoy* novel is Alex's oral unloading to his psychiatrist, Dr. Spielvogel). It is difficult to believe that *Portnoy's Complaint* could have been written, at least in its present form, had *The Catcher in the Rye* not preceded it.

Indeed, so influential has *The Catcher in the Rye* been that it is difficult to imagine any contemporary American writer of fiction about adolescence who has not been influenced by it in one way or another. Russell Banks's troubling *Rule of the Bone* (New York: Harper Collins, 1995) is an example. Chappie, its fourteen-year-old first-person narrator, talks about how, after being abandoned by his father and sexually abused by his stepfather he leaves home and school for a life of drugs and petty crime in upstate New York. There he comes under the influence of several questionable mentors before he stumbles into the presence of a Jamaican migrant worker named I-man. Chappie eventually flees to Jamaica with I-man, where he chances upon the biological father who had abandoned him a decade earlier. This "real" father, like I-man, turns out to be a pot-headed drug lord. He can do little good for his son, who has renamed himself "Bone." In the end, Bone, now aged fifteen, has first sex with his father's girlfriend and then leaves Jamaica, armed with little more than a rough-and-tumble knowledge of the corrupt world, an instinct for survival in that world, and an innate knowledge of good and evil. Readers can believe, if they want to, that this weed-puffing young man has learned enough about evil that, with a little luck, he may turn out not only to prosper but even to do some good. Although Bone is subjected to a far rougher world than anything Holden experiences—a world of lust, porn purveyors, dangerous drugs, corrupt law-enforcers, and even murder—he shares with

Holden a certain adolescent charm as he encounters loneliness, disappointment, and confusion. Like Holden, he contemplates a suicidal retreat from life. Bone also has Holden's ability to tell creative on-the-spot lies about himself, and he cares enough about a young girl, a surrogate sister, to attempt to protect her from the evils of the adult world.

Once we start looking for them, we find influences all around, even in unlikely quarters such as Native American fiction. In James Welch's *Winter in the Blood* (1974), for example, we hear echoes and see reflections of Salinger's novel. This fine first novel by a Blackfeet/Gros Ventre Montanan has a young first-person narrator who acts much younger than he is. This unnamed Indian is confused, sexually immature, and sometimes suicidal as he goes off on an odyssey around northern Montana. On his Holden-like journey he gets drunk and is beaten up. His father is absent and he has trouble relating to his mother. He talks about movies and movie stars, tells lies, and makes unemotional connections with a series of young women in bars and hotels. He confronts a series of men, and is even grabbed in the crotch by a bullying antagonist (parallel to Maurice who "snaps" Holden). He has a wounded leg (parallel to Holden's wounded hand). He is haunted by the death of a brother, Mose, who died when just a boy. Holden admits near the end of *The Catcher in the Rye* that he best likes people who are dead: "'I know he's dead! Don't you think I know that? I can still like him, though, can't I? Just because somebody's dead, you don't just stop liking them, for God's sake—especially if they were about a thousand times nicer than the people you know that're alive and all'" (171). Similarly, near the end of *Winter in the Blood* the narrator, thinking of his dead brother and father, tells us, "They were the only ones I really loved, I thought, the only ones who were good to be with" (New York: Harper and Row, 1974, p. 172).

A more recent Native American novel also shows the influence of *The Catcher in the Rye*, Spokane/Coeur d'Alene writer

Sherman Alexie's *The Absolutely True Diary of a Part-Time Indian* (New York: Little Brown, 2007). The novel is about a Washington State fourteen-year-old Spokane Indian who decides to leave his reservation school and attend an off-reservation white high school, where he is made to feel very much like a misfit. Young Arnold Spirit sounds a lot like Holden Caulfield: he has a disfunctional family, a dead sibling, a talent in sports, and a propensity to tell lies. Like Holden, he focuses at times on his pubescent sexuality—indeed, one might call him "Holden with a boner." Like Salinger, Alexie tells the heavily autobiographical story in the first-person colloquial voice of a confused teenager. The connection to Salinger's novel is made even more explicit when Arnold lets us know that second on his list of favorite books is *The Catcher in the Rye*. Alexie's novel, of course, is remarkably fresh and original, but the connection with Salinger's novel is obvious enough, and certainly not one he would deny.

Even in the work of a writer as different from Salinger as Stephen King, we find what may be echo-influences of *The Catcher in the Rye*. In King's novella *The Body* (1984, published as part of *Different Seasons*), a successful writer whose career sounds suspiciously close to that of King himself, writes what he calls a "memoir" of an experience he and three other boys, all around twelve or thirteen, had when they went in search of the dead body of an acquaintance. Its first-person narrator, named Gordon Lachance, has a voice that sounds somewhat like Holden's, refers to songs and literary works as Holden does, and lives his life in the haunting shadow of a dead brother.

Dave Eggers's *A Heartbreaking Work of Staggering Genius* (2000), a heavily autobiographical work somewhere between a novel and a memoir, looks back to *The Catcher in the Rye* as well. In language that Salinger might appreciate, Eggers says in the preface that his book "is not, actually, a work of pure nonfiction. Many parts have been fictionalized in varying degrees, for various purposes" (p. ix in the 2001 Random House Vintage edition).

Dave, its young first-person male narrator, is, like Holden, the son of a big-city lawyer. Like Holden, he feels responsible for the welfare of a younger sibling, in this case a brother named Toph (aged seven at the start of the book and gradually growing older). Like Holden, Dave likes to tell outlandish lies, goes to California after a traumatic event, has a stormy love life, spends some lonely nights on the town telephoning and calling on male and female friends, uses profanity and related raunchiness, and writes with self-critical humor. So Holden-like is he that G. William Gray, an early reviewer, has this to say of Eggers's novel:

> For 40 years readers have been waiting around on J. D. Salinger to send down a new manuscript from high atop his reclusive Vermont [sic] mountain. Well, the vigil is over and we can forget hearing from Salinger. He's been replaced by a stunning new writer. His name is Dave Eggers. Eggers is the Holden Caulfield of the 1990s: a bit older, perhaps a bit brighter, and definitely more perceptive. He's hyper on latte and tacos, and already wise to the phoniness of his 20-something generation. (*Tampa [Florida] Tribune*, February 20, 2000, Commentary section, p. 4)

Tobias Wolff's *Old School* (2003) is about a young part-Jewish man who attends, on scholarship, an exclusive private high school for boys. His confused fascination with things Jewish ultimately leads him to plagiarize a story about a Jew. When the plagiarism is discovered, he is expelled without a degree. Although this book is far different from *The Catcher in the Rye*, its first-person narrator bears a number of similarities to Holden: his feeling like an outsider in this all-boys school, his hero-worshiping of certain authors, his confusion about his religion, about truth, and about honor, his encounters with his teachers and his roommates, his going to New York when he is expelled—"I didn't go home. Instead I got off the train in New York" (New York: Random House [Vintage], 2003, p. 155). According to Carmela Ciuraru, "*Old School* [. . .] exposes the kind of class-based phoniness that Holden Caulfield so famously detested" ("Lessons Learned in Old School," *Los Angeles Times*, December 10, 2003, p. E-11).

Frank Portman's *King Dork* (2006) capitalizes on the popularity of *The Catcher in the Rye*. Indeed, its paperback cover reproduces the well-known maroon cover of the paperback edition of Salinger's novel, but with the title and Salinger's name in yellow letters not quite whited out and Portman's name and *King Dork* scribled in over the white paint. The sixteen-year-old first-person narrator, Tom Henderson, reminds us in many ways of Holden Caulfield, but he does not share his teachers' admiration for *The Catcher in the Rye*:

> It is every teacher's favorite book. The main guy is a kind of misfit kid superhero named Holden Caulfield. For teachers, he is the ultimate guy, a real dreamboat. They love him to pieces. They all want to have sex with him, and with the book's author, too, and they'd probably even try to do it with the book itself if they could figure out a way to go about it. [...] I've been forced to read it like three hundred times, and don't tell anyone but I think it sucks. (Delacorte Press edition. p. 12)

Henderson gets more interested in the book, however, when he finds his father's marked-up copy of *The Catcher in the Rye*, which gives him some clues about his father's mysterious death many years earlier. Most of *King Dork* is about the adventures of young Henderson: his getting beaten up by the "normal" students, his starting a band with a friende named Sam Hellerman, his conflicts with his mother and his teachers, his sexual experiences with two high school girls, and so on. Even though Portman was unquestionably influenced as a writer by Salinger's novel, and even though he has Sam Henderson at the end of *King Dork* grudgingly admit that *The Catcher in the Rye* "is not that bad of a book," he still has him refer to it as "a sucky book you read only to suck up to teachers holding a gun to your head" (p. 322).

Although the influence of Salinger and Holden is most often seen in novels by men, women also enter the literary arena created by *The Catcher in the Rye*. A recent entrant is Curtis Sittenfeld—"Curtis" is here a woman's name—with her novel *Prep* (New York: Random House, 2005). *Prep* is a 400-page novel about a young woman from South Bend, Indiana, who gets a scholarship to an exclusive preparatory school named Ault School, not far from Boston. While the novel is apparently based to some extent on Sittenfeld's own experiences at Groton, it shows a more-than-coincidental knowledge of *The Catcher in the Rye*. The novel's first-person narrator, Lee Fiora, doesn't fit in well with most of her classmates, but she manages to negotiate her way successfully in her new world of teachers, friends, roommates, snobbery, jobs, sports, crushes, dating, sexuality, parental disapproval, eating disorders, suicide attempts, cheating, racial prejudice, and so on. Unlike Holden, she is not kicked out of school, though she comes close. The novel takes place almost entirely on or very near the Ault campus and ends with Lee's graduation. Some of the characters seem to leap right off the pages of Salinger's novel. The sexually omnivorous basketball player Cross Sugarman, for example, sounds a lot like Ward Stradlater. So obvious is *Prep*'s similarity to *The Catcher in the Rye* that many of the reviewers of this best-seller mention the connection. A glance at the excerpted reviews of the novel inside its cover reveals the influence: "Holden Caulfield would love this heroine" (*The Washington Post*); "the new *Catcher in the Rye*" (*Westchester Journal*); "Lee Fiora [is] a teenager as complex and nuanced as those of Salinger" (Thisbe Nissen); "Speaking in a voice as authentic as Salinger's Holden Caulfield" (Wally Lamb).

I close this section on *The Catcher in the Rye* in other fiction by discussing two audacious novels in which J. D. Salinger himself is made a character. The first is W. P. Kinsella's *Shoeless Joe* (1982). Kinsella creates a fictional character named J. D. Salinger, a writer

who is without question based on the real J. D. Salinger. In one
passage, for example, we learn that

> Salinger, almost everyone knows, has been holed-up like a
> badger, on an isolated hilltop in New Hampshire, for over
> twenty-five years. He has published nothing since a story in *The
> New Yorker* in 1965. He virtually never gives interviews, guards
> his privacy as if it were a virgin bride, even refuses to let his
> stories be anthologized. (Boston: Houghton Mifflin [Mariner
> Books edition, 1999], pp. 32–33)

This character plays an important role in the novel and speaks
often, as when he says, "Once and for all, *I am not Holden
Caulfield!* I am an illusionist who created Holden Caulfield
from my imagination" (p. 87). The fifth and last section of the
novel is entitled "The Rapture of J. D. Salinger." Kinsella did
not get permission from Salinger to put a character with his
name into a novel, nor did Salinger sue him. For discussion of
the relationships between the two novels and of the legal issues
involved, see Dennis Cutchins, "*Catcher* in the Corn: J. D. Salinger
and *Shoeless Joe*" in J. P. Steed, ed., *The Catcher in the Rye: New
Essays* (New York: Peter Lang, 2002), pp. 53–77. Interestingly,
when the novel *Shoeless Joe* was turned into a movie called *Field of
Dreams*, Salinger had his lawyers threaten a lawsuit if his name or
image was used. The director then renamed the Salinger character
as Terence Mann, and had him played by the African-American
actor James Earl Jones. For discussion of the film and its
connection with *The Catcher in the Rye*, see Joseph S. Walker, "The
Catcher Takes the Field: Holden, Hollywood, and the Making
of a Mann," in J. P. Steed, ed., *The Catcher in the Rye: New Essays*
(New York: Peter Lang, 2002), pp. 79–99.

   A more recent novel in which J. D. Salinger is portrayed
as a character is John David California's controversial *60 Years
Later: Coming through the Rye* (2009). Brought out in England by
Windupbird Publishing, this novel bills itself as "An Unauthorized
Fictional Examination of the Relationship Between J. D. Salinger

and His Most Famous Character.'"John David California" is the
pseudonym of a young American-born Swedish author named
Fredrik Colting, living in Sweden in 2010.

Although the first-person narrator of *60 Years Later* is
never directly called "Holden Caulfield," there is no question that
the seventy-six-year-old "Mr. C." in the retirement home is the
central character of *The Catcher in the Rye*. He is referred to as
the creation of "Mr. Salinger." He has a sister named Phoebe and
brothers named Allie and D.B. We learn only sketchily what Mr.
C. has done for a living between the end of the 1951 novel and the
beginning of the 2009 one. He apparently worked for a time as a
teacher, and at some point he married a woman named Mary—
now dead. They had a son named Daniel who visits Mr. C. at
the very end of California's novel. By then Mr. C. has joined his
demented sister in a mental institution. Mr. C.'s final words in the
novel are spoken to Daniel: "Did I ever tell you about the catcher
in the rye?" (p. 277).

The plot of *60 Years Later* bears several broad similarities
to that of *The Catcher in the Rye*. At the start of the earlier novel,
the sixteen-year-old Holden Caulfield escapes his confining prep
school and sneaks off to New York City. There he wanders around
the lonely streets and has experiences in sleazy hotels and bars,
visits the Museum of Natural History, strolls through Central
Park to its carrousel, connects with his beloved sister Phoebe,
then ends the novel in a sanitarium out West. At the start of the
later one, the seventy-six-year-old Mr. C. escapes his retirement
home and sneaks off to New York City. There he wanders around
the lonely streets and has experiences in sleazy bars, visits the
Museum of Natural History, strolls through Central Park to its
carrousel, connects with his beloved sister Phoebe, then ends the
novel in a sanitarian out West.

Although *60 Years Later* clearly grows out of *The Catcher
in the Rye*, it is very much its own creation. Mr. C. encounters
Stradlater, but finds him in Manhattan, not in Pennsylvania.

There is no Mr. Antolini—he would almost certainly be dead when Mr. C. is seventy-six. Unlike Holden, Mr. C. has several near-death experiences by bizarre accidents—a runaway truck, a mad woman with a knife, debris falling from a construction site—and two suicide attempts. But what is most original is the way California gives Salinger a voice in *60 Years Later*. More than five per cent of the novel is made up of italicized sections in which Salinger writes about the novel he is writing and the character he created but cannot always control. He reveals that, curiously, he does not like his protagonist and wants to kill him off. In each of these excerpts, "I" is Mr. Salinger, "he" and "him" are Mr. C.:

> *I'm bringing him back. After all these years I've finally*
> *decided to bring him back.* (p. 9)
>
> *I have to give him a past for the simple reason that you can't*
> *kill what doesn't exist.* (p. 36)
>
> *I will wipe my slates clean and finish what I've started.*
> *And that's the irony of it all. I worked so hard to*
> *get him to leave me alone, and now I'm the one*
> *bringing him back just so that I can kill him.*
> (p. 48)
>
> *What an arrogant little shit! Who does he think he is? My*
> *creation, a piece of living art, seems to have grown*
> *a will of its own.* (p. 83)
>
> *What a schmuck! Why can't he just lay down and die? . . .*
> *I'm his God. I'm the only God there is for him. . . .*
> *He's merely puppet on a string.* (p. 211)

Such "authorial" commentary has no parallel in *The Catcher in the Rye*. Nor is there a parallel for the chapters, late in the novel, when the puppet on a string decides to take a bus to Cornish to pay a personal visit to the reclusive puppeteer who created him.

Not surprisingly, when the real J. D. Salinger of the real Cornish, New Hampshire, got wind of plans to distribute *60 Years Later* in the United States, he directed his lawyers to try to stop such distribution. They did so on the basis that California's novel was a copyright infringement. Salinger, then ninety and

in fragile health, did not appear at the hearing. After listening
to arguments on both sides, federal judge Deborah Batt ruled
in July, 2009, that the characater Holden Caulfield is protected
by copyright and issued a restraining order blocking sale of
California's novel in the United States. It remains to be seen
whether Salinger's death in January, 2010, will alter that decision.

7. *The Catcher in the Rye* in movie and song

Paul Alexander gives a list of movies he thinks have been
influenced by Salinger's novel:

> A host of films—*Rebel Without a Cause, American Graffiti,*
> *Dead Poets Society, Summer of '42, Stealing Home, Risky Business,*
> *Running on Empty, Dirty Dancing, I Never Promised You a*
> *Rose Garden, The Graduate, Stand By Me,* and *Fast Times at*
> *Ridgemont High* are only a few—could not have been made in
> the way they were if *Catcher* had not existed as a model before
> them. Indeed, one could argue that the entire teen-movie
> subgenre, which has become a staple of the film industry in
> Hollywood, owes a debt to Holden and *Catcher*. (*Salinger* xiv)

Dana Stevens makes a smiliarly extravagant claim that Holden
Caulfield shows up "thinly disguised, in the majority of American
coming-of-age films of the past half-century. Though *Catcher*
was never filmed, Holden Caulfield has had perhaps the longest
cinematic afterlife of any modern fictional hero" ("Goddam
Hollywood Phonies," in *Slate*, January 28, 2010). Stevens adds
a half-score more more movies to Alexander's list, among them
The Wild One, Tadpole, Donnie Darko, Igby Goes Down, Sixteen
Candles, Ghost World, The Slums of Beverly Hills, and *Rushmore.*
He also mentions Nigel Tomm's 2008 "film adaptation" of *The*
Catcher in the Rye, which is nothing more than 75 minutes of
watching a solid blue and unchanging screen.

Scholars like Paul Alexander and Dana Stevens may
exaggerate, but there is no question that Salinger's first and only

novel has gained such iconic status in American culture that
moviemakers can refer to and build on it with confidence that
enough viewers will see the connection and know what is going
on.

The 1997 film *Conspiracy Theory* (see Figure 6), directed
by Richard Donner, builds part of its complex plot on the fact
that musician John Lennon's assassin Mark David Chapman
had on his person when he pulled the trigger a copy of *The
Catcher in the Rye* and that a copy was also found four months
later in John Hinckley's apartment after Hinckley attempted to
assassinate President Ronald Reagan. The protagonist in the
movie, Jerry Fletcher (played by Mel Gibson), mind-controlled
to be an assassin himself, has been programmed to buy every
copy of *The Catcher in the Rye* he can find. When his thirteen
copies are destroyed he feels compelled to buy another one. His
buying of that one in a Barnes and Noble store tips off the bad
guy (played by Patrick Stewart) about how to find him again, and
the chase is on. The novel is not mentioned in the second half of
the film, which focuses more on Jerry Fletcher's adventures with
Alice Sutton (played by Julia Roberts). There is no way to know
whether the protagonist's first name is meant to reflect J[erome].
D. Salinger's, but Jerry Fletcher does mouth some Holdenisms
like, "I was just horsing around."

In the 2000 film *Finding Forrester* (see Figure 7), starring
Sean Connery and Rob Brown (directed by Gus Van Sant),
neither Salinger nor *The Catcher in the Rye* is mentioned, but few
viewers or reviewers have missed the allusions to both. The central
character is an aging reclusive writer named William Forrester
who befriends a young African-American sixteen-year-old named
Jamal Wallace in the Bronx. Forrester has published only one
novel (called *Avalon Landing*), but even now, some fifty years after
its initial publication, it still is assigned in high school classrooms
and still earns its author healthy royalties. A number of other

Figure 6: From *Conspiracy Theory* (Warner, 1997), starring Mel Gibson as Jerry Fletcher and Julia Roberts as Alice Sutton. Jerry's obsession with *The Catcher in the Rye* plays a key role in the plot. Courtesy Photofest.

Figure 7: From *Finding Forrester* (Columbia, 2000) starring Sean Connery as the reclusive novelist William Forrester, whose wall of isolation is slowly broken down by a Bronx high school student named Jamal Wallace, played by Rob Brown. Courtesy Photofest.

parallels help to clinch the film's allusiveness to Salinger and *The Catcher in the Rye*. Forrester, like Holden, lives with the guilt of thinking that he is responsible for the death of a younger brother; Forrester, like Salinger, likes young people, has published in the *New Yorker*, distrusts English teachers who write about his work, types with two fingers, and is a military veteran. And young Jamal, like Holden, at times wears his hat backwards. Because Jamal likes to write but feels out of place in the private prep school where he has been offered a scholarship, it is almost as if *Finding Forrester* is the story of the young Holden meeting his future self in the person of a much older writer, and the story of an older Salinger meeting his former self in the person of a confused street kid.

A more recent film that is even more obviously based on Salinger's life is the 2006 *Winter Passing* (see Figure 8), directed by Adam Rapp. Ed Harris plays a famous but reclusive Michigan Upper-Peninsula novelist and ex-English-professor named Don Holdin ("Holden," get it?) who is struggling to move his writing career back on track after two dry (except for alcohol) decades. He lives and writes in the garage-shack behind the big house, which he allows to be occupied by stacks of books, a washed-up rock singer handyman named Corbit, and a pretty former student from England named Shelly, with whom he may once have had an affair. Corbit protects Don Holdin from invasive strangers who try to take photos, while Shelly prepares his meals and quietly worships him. The plot deals mostly with the return of Holdin's estranged daughter Reese Holdin, played by Zooey Deschanel. Reese is a just-barely-making-it Broadway actress, with a side job as a cocaine-snorting bartender. At the end of her current role, apparently as Miranda in an avant-garde version of Shakespeare's *Winter's Tale*, a book publisher offers her $100,000 for her mother's and father's love letters. Needing money, she hops a bus from New York to Michigan to claim her inheritance. Her encounters there are somewhat reminiscent of encounters that Salinger's one-time girlfriend Joyce Maynard had with his daughter Margaret Salinger, when their paths intersected at the Salinger retreat near Cornish, New Hampshire. The idea of publishing a famous author's letters has been a common theme in Salinger's life, one that Salinger's lawyers pursued all the way to the Supreme Court. The movie has a happy ending when Reese Holdin voluntarily destroys her parents' love letters and returns to New York to take up a more solid acting career, and when Don Holdin completes and publishes a new book.

Another filmic attempt to build on the almost universal knowledge of *The Catcher in the Rye* is the 2000 film *Chasing Holden* (see Figure 9), directed by Malcolm Clarke. The film

Figure 8: From *Winter Passing* (Yari Film Group, 2005), starring Ed Harris as Don Holdin, a reclusive alcoholic writer who has stopped writing, and Zooey Deschanel as his daughter Reese, who visits her father on a mission to publish her parents' love letters. Courtesy Photofest.

Figure 9: From *Chasing Holden* (Lions Gate, 2000), starring D. J. Qualls as Neil Lawrence and Rachel Blanchard as his companion. Neil's obsession with Holden Caulfield takes him to Strawberry Fields in Central Park and to Salinger's home in the hills, where he hopes to kill the uncommunicative author. Courtesy Photofest.

concerns the adventures of a nineteen-year-old boy named Neil, played by D. J. Qualls, recently released from a mental institution after he puts his hand through a window following the death of his brother—a clear parallel to Holden's own history. Neil is the son of the governor of New York—we recall that Holden had pretended to Stradlater to be "the little ole goddam Governor's son" (29)—who on his release is sent off to an exclusive prep school, where one of his teachers gives the class the assignment of writing an essay on what happened to Holden after the end of the novel. Frustrated but resourceful, Neil runs off with a fellow student, the lovely T. J. (played by Rachel Blanchard) to New York. They visit the Strawberry Fields memorial in Central Park (see Figure 10), where the disturbed Mark David Chapman

Figure 10: This photograph of the Strawberry Fields memorial in Central Park shows a spot near where Mark Chapman shot John Lennon in 1980. Chapman had with him at the murder scene a copy of *The Catcher in the Rye.*

had on December 8, 1980, shot John Lennon. At the time of the murder, Chapman had on his person a copy of *The Catcher in the Rye*. (For a cinematic attempt to make sense of the senseless murder, see *Chapter 27* [2008], directed by J. P. Schaefer and starring Jared Leto as Mark David Chapman.) After further adventures in New York—involving, among other things an encounter with a prostitute whose john refuses to pay her—Neil and T. J. set off by bus to New Hampshire to find J. D. Salinger himself. Neil packs a gun with which he plans to murder the author for not responding to a letter he had sent demanding an interview. Although the plot differs greatly from that of *The Catcher in the Rye*, Neil clearly sees himself as a modern-day Holden, and the audience is meant to notice many parallels with the confused hero of Salinger's novel.

I must mention one more movie, *The Good Girl* (2002) (see Figure 11), starring Jennifer Aniston as Justine, a frustrated and lonely housewife, and Jake Gyllenhaal as Tom, a confused and unhappy college dropout, now living with his stony-faced parents. Tom takes a job as a cashier in the same variety store where Justine works as a makeup artist. Tom, who in the opening scene is reading a dog-eared copy of *The Catcher in the Rye*, tells everyone at work that his name is Holden. Directed by Miguel Arteta, the film is about the furtive and ill-considered affair that leads to Holden's unhealthy dependency on Justine. As the story progresses, people learn of their affair and Justine, finding herself pregnant, has to make a decision: to stay with her bland-and-boring house-painter husband or to run off with Holden. The choice is forced upon her when Holden steals $15,000 from the store and begs Justine to run off with him. Her choice has tragic consequences for the distraught Holden. Although the *Catcher*-connections are not as glaringly obvious here as they were in *Chasing Holden*, they are unquestionably apparent in both films. Tom-as-Holden, like Neil-as-Holden, is a young man whose fixated identification with the hero of *The Catcher in the Rye* is evidence of a disturbed, if not neurotic or pathologically dangerous, personality.

That image of Holden as neurotic depressive has found its way also into several recent rock-band songs that showcase the

Figure 11: From *The Good Girl* (Fox Searchlight, 2002), starring Jake Gyllenhaal as a frustrated Holden Caulfield wannabe and Jennifer Aniston as Justine Last, a frustrated housewife who becomes his lover. Their efforts to end their frustration have comic—and tragic—consequences. Courtesy Photofest.

dark, despairing, crazy, negative aspects of the famous Holden Caulfield. The band Green Day in 1992 released a song called "Who Wrote Holden Caulfield?" The refrain of the song is:

> There's a boy who fogs his world and now he's getting lazy.
> There's no motivation and frustration makes him crazy.
> He makes a plan to take a stand but always ends up sitting.
> Someone help him up or he's gonna end up quitting.

That same year (1992) a group named The Offspring did a song entitled "Get It Right" about a boy who hopes things will get better for him, but they don't. Some of the lines are:

> For the thousandth time you turn and find
> That it just makes no difference to try.
> Like Holden Caulfield, I tell myself
> There's got to be a better way.

Then, in 2000, a group called the Bloodhound Gang put out "Magna Cum Nada," a song with grimly nihilistic lyrics that begin:

> Why try? I'm that guy
> Holden Caulfield from *Catcher in the Rye.*

Holden Caulfield was an icon of the troubled youth of the twentieth century. Surely he continues in that iconic role in the twenty-first.

8. The enduring appeal of *The Catcher in the Rye*

The continuing appeal of *The Catcher in the Rye* is nowhere more apparent than in its numbers. Almost immediately after its release in July of 1951, Salinger's first and only novel made the *New York Times* list of bestsellers. Its popularity was due initially to the fact that it was a Book-of-the-Month Club summer selection, but increasingly people felt connected to it. In 2001, Louis Menand reported that *The Catcher in the Rye* had sold more than sixty million copies since its publication fifty years earlier—averaging more than a million copies a year in its first half-century. Menand offered a rather simplistic explanation of the popularity of the novel: "The book keeps acquiring readers [. . .] not because kids keep discovering it but because grownups who read it when they were kids keep getting kids to read it. This seems crucial to making sense of its popularity" ("Holden at Fifty: *The Catcher in the Rye* and What It Spawned," *New Yorker*, October 1, 2001, p. 82). Menand's statement is no doubt true—parents and teachers do like to encourage young people to read the novel—but they encourage them to read other books as well. None of those other books captures so many eager readers.

Salinger's novel continues to sell impressively in the new century. BookScan, a division of Nielsen Media Research, which tracks book sales for the publishing industry, reports that by early 2007, the mass-market edition of *The Catcher in the Rye* had, since January 1, 2001, sold more than a million-and-a-half copies, while the trade paper edition sold nearly another half million, for a total of more than two million copies. For comparison, Fitzgerald's *The Great Gatsby*, in its two paperback editions, sold fewer than one-and-a-half million copies in that same period. It appears that Salinger's novel continues to be America's most-read novel among high school and college students. If any modern novel can claim to be the best-known in America, surely that novel is *The Catcher in the Rye*.

On May 29, 2006, there appeared on pages 42–43 in the *New Yorker* magazine a short article entitled "Caught" purportedly written by a Central Park coyote. It started with this sentence:

> If you're really interested in hearing all this, you probably first want to know where I was whelped, and what my parents' dumb burrow was like, and how they started me out hunting field mice, and all the "Call of the Wild" kind of crap, but I'd really rather not go into it, if that's all right with you.

Ian Frazier, the author, and the editors of the magazine never announce that the piece is written as a parody of Salinger's *The Catcher in the Rye*. They could assume that virtually all readers of

the *New Yorker* would remember the famous opening lines of the
novel and enjoy the parody:

> If you really want to hear about it, the first thing you'll
> probably want to know is where I was born, and what my lousy
> childhood was like, and how my parents were occupied and
> all before they had me, and all that David Copperfield kind of
> crap, but I don't feel like going into it, if you want to know the
> truth.

In the May 17, 2010, issue of *Newsweek*, editor Jon
Meacham wrote this sentence about his magazine: "We are not
the only catcher in the rye standing between democracy and the
abyss of ignorance and despair." Meacham never in his article
directly mentions Salinger or Holden or their novel. He never
explains the comparison he draws between Holden's desire to
protect endangered little children from falling off a cliff and his
own desire to use *Newsweek* to protect endangered American
democratic principles.

Even cartoonists build on the wide name-recognition of
The Catcher in the Rye. On page D4 of the May 25, 2010, issue
of the *Bucks County* [PA] *Courier Times*, there appeared Dana
Summers's syndicated cartoon *Bound & Gagged*. The cartoon is
a single-frame drawing with the caption "Canine Literature." It
shows a large grinning dog in a purple suit and red bow tie sitting
in an armchair in his living room reading a book. The title of the
book is *Dog Catcher in the Rye*.

For what other novel, American or British, could writers,
editors, and cartoonists have assumed that readers would
recognize its opening sentence or the preferred occupation of
its troubled hero? Why has this one novel been so appealing
that most high school and college graduates can be expected to
recognize undocumented phrases from it?

It is surprising that a novel that takes place almost entirely
in the world of money and privilege should have such universal
appeal. The schools Holden and his friends attend are all

expensive private college prep schools: Andover, Choate, Elkton Hills, McBurney School, Mary A. Woodruff, Pencey Prep, Saxon Hall, Shipley, the Whooton School. And the places where the students and the parents of the students who attend these schools speak of going to college are private and expensive: Columbia, Oxford, Princeton, Harvard, Yale. The only public university mentioned in the book is New York University (N.Y.U.), but that is not where Holden and his friends will go. It is where Mr. Antolini, once a lowly school teacher, now teaches. Where do the public school readers who have found the book so endearing locate themselves in this snobbish world of preppy privilege?

The answer is clear enough: they locate themselves in Holden Caulfield, a rich boy who, despite his parents' wealth and his history at an array of expensive private prep schools, rejects or at least questions almost everything that Pencey Prep, his exclusive little school in Agerstown, Pennsylvania, stands for. Despite his narcissism, his prejudice against "flits," "old guys," and "colored" people, his fearfulness, his lack of direction and motivation, his quickness to judge people he barely knows, his sweeping criticisms of society, his eagerness to blame others for his own shortcomings, his self-pitying arrogance, his inconsistency and even hypocrisy, his impractical plans about escaping to life as a deaf-mute in the wilderness, his inveterate resistance to growing up, Holden Caulfield is still a likeable, even admirable, young man. There is no question that several generations of readers have been drawn to *The Catcher in the Rye* because they are drawn, in quite personal ways, to Holden himself. Despite his flaws and weaknesses—indeed, in part because of them—Holden has many enduringly endearing qualities:

—he is, like most boys at sixteen, uncertain, frightened, confused, lonely, unsure of his sexuality.

—he is kind to weak and unpopular underdogs like Robert Ackley and James Castle.

—he boldly strikes out against privileged predators like Ward Stradlater and exploitative thugs like Maurice.

—he has a noble, if unrealistic, goal of protecting innocent children from falling off a cliff or from reading "Fuck you" messages.

—he tries to correct injustices, even attempting to "sort of even up the weight" when he sees a "sort of fat" kid overbalancing a "skinny kid" on the seesaw (122).

—he has a strong sense of fairness, lashing out when Sunny asks for ten dollars for a five dollar deal; it's not the money that upsets him, but the unfairness.

—he tries to protect young women like Jane Gallagher from the groping seductions of men like her stepfather and like Stradlater, and ones like Sunny from the pay-and-run sexuality of men like himself.

—he can have sex only with someone he really likes ("'I can never get really sexy—I mean *really* sexy—with a girl I don't like a lot'" [148]), and in any case he won't force himself on women ("They tell me to stop, so I stop. I always wish I *hadn't*, after I take them home, but I keep doing it anyway" [92]).

—he recognizes and admires skill in almost anything—dancing, whistling, drumming, writing.

—he hates phoniness, snobbery, false intellectualism, and pretentiousness, whether he sees them in the home, in the dorm room, in the school auditorium, in bars, in movies, or on stage.

—he has such loving memories of his dead brother Allie that he writes a composition about him, and he cares so deeply about his living sister Phoebe that he goes out of his way to buy her a record he thinks she'll like and decides on her account to stay home rather than go out West to work on a ranch.

—he feels sorry for false snobs like Ernie ("In a funny way, though, I felt sort of sorry for him when he was finished" [84]), pretentious liars like Lillian Simmons ("You had to feel sort of sorry for her, in a way" [87]), and girls who marry bores like Harris Macklin ("Maybe you shouldn't feel too sorry if you see some swell girl getting married to them" [124]).

—he misses people, forgiving even the ones he has reason to dislike ("I sort of *miss* everybody I told about. Even old Stradlater and Ackley, for instance. I think I even miss that goddam Maurice" [214]).

—he tells a good story. Frank McCourt, who worked much of his adult life teaching high school English in the New York Public School System, spent much of his class time doing not "traditional English" but entertaining and informing his students by telling them stories about his own life. In *Teacher Man: A Memoir* (New York: Scribner, 2005), McCourt tells how he made his stories relevant by comparing them with those of the famous literary characters he was teaching about: "The students never stopped trying to divert me from traditional English, but I was on to their tricks. I still told stories, but I was learning how to connect them with the likes of the Wife of Bath, Tom Sawyer, Holden Caulfield, Romeo and his reincarnation in *West Side Story*. English teachers are always being told, You gotta make it relevant" (pp. 203–04). That statement is interesting for several reasons, but two reasons stand out. First, McCourt (author of *Angela's Ashes*) without apology places Holden Caulfield in the company of the most famous literary characters of Chaucer, Twain, and Shakespeare. Second, he recognizes the appeal of a good story. Readers are drawn to Holden in part because he tells a compelling story in a compelling way.

A number of scholars have tried to account for the appeal of the novel:

—Ernest Jones: "Why has this unpretentious, mildly affecting chronicle of a few days in the life of a disturbed adolescent been read with enthusiasm? [. . .] Entirely, I think, because [. . .] it reflects something not at all rich and strange but what every sensitive sixteen-year-old since Rousseau has felt" ("Case History of All of Us," *Nation* 173 [Sept. 1, 1951]: 176).

—Warren French: "I think that young people read Salinger because he writes in their language about the world they know or would like to know" ("Preface" to *J. D. Salinger* [New York: Twayne, 1963], p. 7).

—Clinton W. Trowbridge: "[I]n this age of atrophy, in this thought-tormented, thought-tormenting time in which we live, perhaps it is not going too far to say that, for many of us, at least, our Hamlet is Holden" ("Hamlet and Holden," *English Journal* 57 [1968]: 29).

—Nancy C. Ralston: "Holden Caulfield is not likely to go away. The echo of his voice hovers over the ubiquitous examples of phoniness whenever and wherever they dare to appear. His shadow haunts every display of obscene graffiti scrawled in millions of public places. Holden knows no generation gap. He is the super-adolescent of yesterday, today, and tomorrow" ("Holden Caulfield: Super-Adolescent," *Adolescence*, No. 24 [1971]: 432).

—David J. Burrows: "Certainly every reader, no matter how young, has at least begun to make his own compromise with the adult society he is entering, and still may identify his own plight very strongly with Holden's, feel compassion for him, and have brought to the surface while reading the book great reservoirs of wistfulness and nostalgia for an innocence perhaps quite recently lost" ("Allie and Phoebe: Death and Love in J. D. Salinger's *The Catcher in the Rye*," in *Private Dealings: Modern American Writers in Search of Integrity*, ed. David J. Burrows, et al. [Rockville, MD: New Perspectives, 1974], p. 107).

—Philip Roth: "The response of college students to the work of J. D. Salinger indicates that he, more than anyone else, has not turned his back on the times, but, instead, has managed to put his finger on whatever struggle of significance is going on today between self and culture" (written in 1974, as quoted by Charles McGrath in his obituary "J. D. Salinger, Literary Recluse, Dies at 91" in the *New York Times*, January 28, 2010).

—Carol and Richard Ohmann: "For us, as for almost all readers, Holden's sensitivity is the heart of the book, that which animates the story and makes it compelling" ("Reviewers, Critics, and *The Catcher in the Rye*," *Critical Enquiry* 3 [1976]: 27).

—June Edwards: "Holden Caulfield emerges as a confused but moral person. He befriends the friendless. He respects those who are humble, loyal, and kind. He demonstrates a strong love for his family. He abhors hypocrisy. He values sex that comes from caring for another person and rejects its sordidness" ("Censorship in the Schools: What's Moral about *The Catcher in the Rye*," *English Journal* 72 [1983]: 42).

—Ian Hamilton: "*The Catcher in the Rye* exercises a unique seductive power—not just for new young readers who discover it, but also for the million or so original admirers like me who still view Holden Caulfield with a fondness that is weirdly personal, almost possessive" (*In Search of J. D. Salinger* [New York: Random House (Vintage), 1988], pp. 4–5).

—Harold Bloom: "All readers receive him into their affection, which may be the largest clue to his book's enduring charm. As a representation of a sixteen-year-old youth, the portrait of Holden achieves a timeless quality" ("Introduction" to *Holden Caulfield* [New York: Chelsea House, 1990], p. 1).

—Sanford Pinsker: "Salinger's novel is the best account of prep school despair we are likely to get. It is perhaps the most rounded, most affecting portrait of a sixteen-year-old American boy we shall ever have. Holden Caulfield has joined the gallery of great American characters" (*The Catcher in the Rye: Innocence Under Pressure* [New York: Twayne, 1993], p. 16).

—Tom Wolfe: "*The Catcher in the Rye* captures the mood of the adolescent who wants desperately to fit in but doesn't want to seem as if he does, who wants to act flippantly but who, underneath that flippancy, has great sorrow" (from an interview with biographer Paul Alexander, quoted in his *Salinger: A Biography* [Los Angeles: Renaissance Books, 1999], p. 25).

—Carl Freedman: "There are more than a few of us for whom *The Catcher in the Rye* still feels less like a canonical book than like a personal experience, and one of the most powerful of our lives. [. . .] [T]here is not a novel in American literature, perhaps not a novel in the world, that more convincingly invents and sustains a young colloquial voice, page after page after page, with virtually not a single false note" ("Memories of Holden Caulfield—and of Miss Greenwood," *Southern Review* 39 [2003]: 401, 404–05).

—Michael Chabon: "*Catcher in the Rye* made a very powerful and surprising impression on me. Part of it was the fact that our seventh grade teacher was actually letting us read such a book. But mostly it was because *Catcher* had such a recognizable authenticity in the voice that even in 1977

or so, when I read it, felt surprising and rare in literature"
(quoted in Hillel Italie's Associated Press obituary, "*Catcher
in the Rye* Author J. D. Salinger Dies," January 28, 2010).

Of course, not all readers sing in the chorus of critics who
connect in such personal or positive ways with *The Catcher in the
Rye* or with Holden Caulfield:

—Maxwell Geismar: "This is surely the differential revolt of the
   lonesome rich child, the conspicuous display of leisure-class
   emotions, the wounded affections, never quite faced, of the
   upper-class orphan. [. . .] He is still, and forever, the innocent
   child in the evil and hostile universe, the child who can never
   grow up" (*American Moderns: From Rebellion to Conformity*
   [New York: Hill and Wang, 1958], pp. 198–99).

—Robert G. Jacobs: "The reader cannot, finally, identify
   himself with Holden Caulfield, for Holden is hilariously,
   ridiculously sick, and the reader lives in a world where
   adulthood is health" ("J. D. Salinger's *The Catcher in the Rye*:
   Holden Caulfield's 'Goddam Autobiography,'" *Iowa English
   Yearbook* [Fall 1959]: 14).

—Mary Suzanne Schriber: "How have critics managed to
   magnify to such proportions a protagonist who is, after all,
   but a sixteen-year-old urban, male, WASP preppie? How
   has it happened that critics have persuaded themselves that
   this carefully delimited young male is the whole of youth,
   male and female, and the whole of America as well? [. . .]
   The essential ingredient in the phenomenal success and the
   critical reception of *The Catcher in the Rye* is the propensity
   of critics to identify with Salinger's protagonist. Holden
   Caulfield, c'est moi. Falling in love with him as with their
   very selves, they fall in love with the novel as well" ("Holden
   Caulfield, C'est Moi" in Joel Salzberg, ed., *Critical Essays on
   Salinger's* The Catcher in the Rye [Boston: G. K. Hall, 1990],
   pp. 226–27).

—Mark Silverberg: "What Schriber does not ask is with whom
these critics fall in love. In other words, whom do they
imagine Holden (and by extension, themselves) to be? I
have suggested two main identifying stories: Holden the
sensitive outsider and Holden the perennial adolescent,
which account for critical acts which simultaneously valorize
Holden and validate their authors" ("'You Must Change
Your Life': Formative Responses to *The Catcher in the Rye*"
in J. P. Steed, ed., *The Catcher in the Rye: New Essays* [New
York: Peter Lang, 2002], p. 28).

—Michael Kimmel: "[W]hat makes him so endearing and *The
Catcher in the Rye* so enduring, is that he actually believes his
own hype. Holden believes that he and he alone is morally
superior to all the phonies he sees around him" ("Guy
Lit—Whatever," *Chronicle of Higher Education*, May 26,
2006, p. B13).

—Barbara Feinberg: "Holden is somewhat a victim of the current
trend in applying evermore mechanistic approaches to
understanding behavior. Compared to the early 1950s, there
is not as much room for the adolescent search, for intuition,
for empathy, for the mystery of the unconscious and the
deliverance made possible through talking to another
person. [One fifteen-year-old boy from Long Island told
me:] 'Oh, we all hated Holden in my class. We just wanted to
tell him, Shut up and take your Prozac'" (quoted in Jennifer
Schuessler's "Get a Life, Holden Caulfield," *New York Times*,
June 21, 2009).

9. The aftermath of J. D. Salinger's death

J. D. Salinger was born in Manhattan on January 1, 1919. He died
of natural causes after more than fifty years of quiet seclusion in
his home near Cornish, New Hampshire, on January 27, 2010.
The previous May he had suffered a broken hip, but except for

that, he was in generally good health. Among his survivors were
Colleen O'Neill, his wife since the late 1980s, his two children,
Matt and Margaret, and three grandsons. Shortly after Salinger's
death, his literary agents issued a statement that "in keeping with
his lifelong, uncompromising desire to protect and defend his
privacy, there will be no service, and the family asks that people's
respect for him, his work, and his privacy be extended to them,
individually and collectively, during this time" (quoted by Charles
McGrath in his obituary "J. D. Salinger, Literary Recluse, Dies at
91" in the *New York Times*, January 28, 2010).

The wall of privacy that Salinger erected began to
disintegrate soon after his death. For example, an artist named
Michael Mitchell, who had become Salinger's friend when
he designed the cover illustration for *The Catcher in the Rye*,
received some eleven letters from Salinger. He eventually sold
them to a man named Carter Burden. Burden donated them to
the Morgan Library in Manhattan. The curators kept them in a
vault, but prepared a public exhibit of them within weeks after
Salinger's death. Some of the letters give revealing glimpses into
Salinger's work and work habits. In a 1966 letter, for example,
Salinger wrote that he had been working on "two particular
scripts—books, really—that I've been [. . .] picking at for years"
(quoted by Alison Leigh Cowan, "Unsealed Letters Offer Glimpse
of Salinger," *New York Times*, February 11, 2010). Letters like
that, coupled with one written in the 1980s in which Salinger
says that he started writing every morning at 6:00—or 7:00 at
the latest—suggest that there may be quite a lot of material ready
to be published posthumously. If that material does exist, and
if Salinger's literary executors permit it to be published, then
Salinger's four slender books may soon be joined by others.

Not surprisingly, Salinger's death inspired an outpouring of
statements in the public press and on blog and other computer
venues about how important *The Catcher in the Rye* had been to
its readers. Here are a few of them:

—David Remnick: "Everyone who works here and writes here at
the *New Yorker* even now, decades after his silence began,
does so with keen awareness of J. D. Salinger's voice. He
is so widely read in America, and read with such intensity,
that it's hard to think of any reader, young or old, who does
not carry around the voice of Holden Caulfield" (quoted in
Hillel Italie's Associated Press obituary, "*Catcher in the Rye*
Author J. D. Salinger Dies," January 28, 2010).

—Adam Gopnik: "Salinger's voice [. . .] remade American writing
in the fifties and sixties in a way that no one had since
Hemingway. [. . .] In American writing, there are three
perfect books, which seem to speak to every reader and
condition: *Huckleberry Finn*, *The Great Gatsby*, and *The
Catcher in the Rye*. Of the three, only *Catcher* defines
an entire region of human experience: it is—in French
and Dutch as much as in English—the handbook of the
adolescent heart" ("J. D. Salinger," *New Yorker*, February 8,
2010, pp. 20–21).

—Michiko Kakutani: "What really knocked readers out about
The Catcher in the Rye was the wonderfully immediate voice
that J. D. Salinger fashioned for Holden Caulfield. [. . .] Mr.
Salinger had such unerring radar for the feelings of teenage
angst and vulnerability and anger that *Catcher*, published in
1951, remains one of the books that adolescents first fall in
love with—a book that intimately articulates what it is to
be young and sensitive and precociously existential, a book
that first awakens them to the possibilities of literature.
[. . .] It is a novel that still knocks people out, a novel, if you
really want to hear about it, that is still cherished, nearly six
decades after its publication, for its pitch-perfect portrait of
adolescence and its indispensable hero" (*New York Times*,
January 28, 2010).

—Lillian Ross: "Salinger was one of a kind. His writing was his and his alone, and his way of life was only what he chose to follow. He never gave an inch to anything that came to him with what he called a 'smell.' [. . .] Getting back to work, he said, was 'the only way I've ever been able to take the awful conventional world. I think I despise every school and college in the world, but the ones with the best reputation first'" ("Bearable," *New Yorker*, February 8, 2010, p. 22).

—Charles McGrath: "I first read J. D. Salinger's *Catcher in the Rye* in the summer of 1960, when I was twelve. I heard about it from an older boy who was an unerring guide to books that were racy. So I went to my local library, in Brighton, Mass., asked for *Catcher*, and was told that I would need a note of permission from my parents. The librarian glared at me as she said this. My mother, who was not a big reader herself, wrote a note saying I should be allowed to read whatever I wanted, which now seems one of her greatest gifts to me. That little piece of paper got me into the other, grownup side of the library, where I found a lot of books that opened my eyes and, I suppose, led me eventually to become a writer myself. I have since read better books than *Catcher* but few that made a more lasting impression. I still recall reading the first papagraph and thinking to myself, 'You can really do that?'" (*The Catcher in the Rye* in 1960: Permission Slip Required," *New York Times*, January 28, 2010).

—Henry Allen: "When I was twelve or thirteen [. . .] I was looking at my parents' bookshelves and asked about that odd title. 'It's too old for you,' my mother said with a tone bearing not a little ulterior motive. That night, after my parents had gone to bed, I turned on my light and started reading. *Catcher* got me with the first line, and I became a devotee, newly coined from the dross of adolescence into the gold of irony and self-consciousness. I wasn't just agonized with my despairs. I was a member of some order of righteous adolescence, a kid standing in the corner and watching the phonies at the party" (*Washington Post*, January 29, 2010).

—Bart Barnes: "Caulfield became a teenage Everyman whose wry and caustic observations seemed outrageous, clever, and on the mark" (*Washington Post*, January 29, 2010).

—Richard Lacayo: "Salinger's only novel, *The Catcher in the Rye* [...] was a universal rite of passage for adolescents, the manifesto of disenchanted youth. [...] Holden Caulfield, Salinger's petulant, yearning young hero, was the original angry young man, created at the very moment that American teenage culture was being born. A whole generation of rebellious youths discharged themselves into him" (*TIME*, February 15, 2010, p. 66).

—John Seabrook: "So when my college friend Matt invited us to his dad's house in Cornish, New Hampshire [...] I got to see what a sweet, swell guy he was" ("A Night at the Movies," *New Yorker*, February 8, 2010, p. 23).

—Marie in North Stratford, NH: "I am sad because somehow he has been part of my life as a teacher for the past fifty years, and his book, *Catcher in the Rye*, is as relvant today as it was way back when I first began teaching it. My students just finished reading it, and some of the best classroom discussions we have had all year centered around Holden. Teenagers still comment that Salinger was able to get to them and understand just how they feel" (quoted in Blake Wilson, "Readers Respond to J. D. Salinger's Death," *New York Times*, January 28, 2010).

—Jane in Fairfax, VA: "In 1975, when I was eighteen and a freshman in college, I along with two friends trudged up

to J. D. Salinger's house in Cornish and knocked on his
door. We wanted to meet him. (I know now it was a gross
invasion of his privacy. At the time I didn't know better.)
One of my friends had a dog-eared copy of *Catcher in the
Rye* that he asked Salinger to sign. Salinger refused, saying
it would mean nothing to him to sign my friend's book.
He added, 'That was a silly book when I wrote it twenty-
five years ago and it's a silly book today'" (quoted in Blake
Wilson, "Readers Respond to J. D. Salinger's Death," *New
York Times*, January 28, 2010).

—Leslie in England: "*Catcher in the Rye* was about a self-absorbed,
privileged, ungrateful little snot and the two-dimensional
female stand-in of a character. The only thing more
depressing than that book is the fact that it apparently
resonates with most of America" (quoted in Blake Wilson,
"Readers Respond to J. D. Salinger's Death," *New York
Times*, January 28, 2010).

—Kenneth Slawenski: "Salinger the man may be gone—and for
that the world is an emptier place—but he will always live
within the pages he created, and through his art remain
as vital today and tomorrow as when he walked the
boulevards of New York and strolled the woods of New
Hampshire" (*J. D. Salinger: A Life Raised High* [Hebden
Bridge, West Yorkshire, UK: Pomona, 2010], p. x).

Admiration for *The Catcher in the Rye*, and for its
adolescent hero, then, has not been universal, and we all know
that many readers, troubled by the attitudes, the language, and
the scatological and sexual explicitness of the novel, have with
varying degrees of success sought to have *The Catcher in the
Rye* banned from certain school systems and libraries. For an
extended discussion of the issues involved in censoring Salinger's
novel, see Pamela Hunt Steinle, *In Cold Fear: The Catcher in the*

Rye Censorship Controversies and Postwar American Character (Columbus: Ohio State University Press, 2000). The censorship controversies, of course, would not have arisen at all if Salinger's novel had not been so popular, had not spoken what sounded like the truth to so many generations of readers.

It is impossible to predict what will happen to Salinger's reputation and influence after his death. Much will depend on whether he did indeed continue to write during his half-century of seclusion in Cornish, New Hampshire, and, more important, what he wrote. Even a year after his death, there was still no public release of information about Salinger's literary remains or whether his family had plans to publish any of them. In its January 3, 2001, issue (p. 147), *TIME* reported that "It's said he went on writing. If that work ever comes to light, you can bet we'll go on reading." In its January 3, 2011, issue (p. 72). *Newsweek* put it this way: "Was he writing? If so, did he preserve it? Considering how Salinger's published work shaped the postwar zeitgeist, the shape of America's 21st-century literary life might hinge on the answers."

If you really want to hear about it, my own guess is that Salinger did preserve a great deal of what he wrote, that it will gradually be published in the coming years, but that none of it will change the fact that his first book was his most influential. *The Catcher in the Rye* will continue to be Salinger's most-read book, and Holden Caulfield's is the voice most people will hear when they listen to J. D. Salinger.

Explanatory Notes to
The Catcher in the Rye

In what follows, I provide information designed to help twenty-first-century readers understand some of the terms Salinger uses in *The Catcher in the Rye*, and to identify the books, movies, songs, biblical passages, people, and places referred to in a novel written in the middle of the previous century. I also include a taste of some of the scholarship on some of the issues, particularly the meaning of Holden's name and his red hunting hat, what kind of California institution Holden is in, what to make of Holden's encounter with Mr. Antolini, and Holden's relationship with his sister. To help readers of the novel follow its larger movements, I divide the novel into its four large sections: Holden's time at Pencey Prep, Holden's journey to Manhattan, Holden's wanderings in Manhattan, and Holden's return to his home. Salinger did not physically divide the novel into sections, but these four are natural chronological and spacial divisions. Salinger gave no chapter titles to the twenty-six chapters, but to guide readers I have provided a brief descriptive title for each chapter, along with short italicized summaries of the main action in that chapter. Capital letters in those summaries are keyed to a map (see p. 116) showing the main locations that Holden visits in his Manhattan odyssey. I also give some hints about ways some parts of *The Catcher in the Rye* may reflect aspects of Salinger's biography.

Holden says good-by to Pencey (chapters 1-7)

Chapter 1: Standing on Thomsen Hill

Holden Caulfield announces that he is going to start his story not with his birth or childhood, but with what happened on the Saturday of the big annual football rivalry with Saxon Hall. Instead of going to the game, he walks off campus to say good-by to his history teacher, Mr. Spencer. Holden gives some background information about Pencey Prep, the school he has just "got the ax" from, about his having lost the fencing equipment earlier in the day, and about his brother, D.B. Mrs. Spencer welcomes him into the house.

David Copperfield "If you really want to hear about it, the first
thing you'll probably want to know is where I was born, and
what my lousy childhood was like, [. . .] and all that David
Copperfield kind of crap" (1). David Copperfield is the
central character in Charles Dickens's 800-page *The Personal
History of David Copperfield*, first published in 1850. Holden
almost certainly refers here to the first-person narrator's
opening of the novel with information that Holden Caulfield
considers self-indulgent and irrelevant. The first chapter,
entitled, "I Am Born," starts off with these three sentences:

> Whether I shall turn out to be the hero of my own
> life, or whether that station will be held by anybody
> else, these pages must show. To begin my life with the
> beginning of my life, I record that I was born (as I have
> been informed and believe) on a Friday, at twelve o'clock
> at night. It was remarked that the clock began to strike,
> and I began to cry, simultaneously. (Penguin Classics
> edition [New York, 1996], p. 11)

Holden, of course, refuses to talk about such matters: "I'm not
going to tell you my whole goddam autobiography or anything"
(1). There are other differences between the two works. Dickens's
narrator, for example, writes in the sophisticated language and
with the perspective of a much older man looking back on a long
life. Holden, on the other hand, writes in the teenage vernacular
of a seventeen-year-old looking back only one year on events
that covered only three days. The names of the two protagonist
narrators have interesting possible connections. For example,
"Copperfield" and "Caulfield" both start with the letter C- and end
in -field. Also, David Copperfield is born with a "caul" (p. 11) or
fetal membrane covering his head. Such a caul was supposed to
protect its owner from drowning, which explains why his mother
attempts to sell it. Might Holden *Caul*field be named so because
he has a similar "caul," perhaps suggested in part by the red
hunting hat that figures so prominently in the novel? For other
speculation on the name, see **Holden** below.

Several scholars have speculated about Holden's use of the
word "crap" in the first sentence of the novel. A linguist named
Donald P. Costello, for example, finds that Holden uses the word
"in seven different ways" in the novel and proceeds to list them:
"It can mean foolishness, as in 'all that David Copperfield kind of
crap'" ("The Language of *The Catcher in the Rye*," *American Speech*
34 [1959]: 176). Another scholar, Edwin Haviland Miller, thinks
that while "crap" is Holden's "ultimate term of reductionism for
describing the world, like 'crap' it serves to identify another of his
projections. He feels dirty and worthless, and so makes the world

a reflection of his self-image" ("In Memoriam: Allie Caulfield in *The Catcher in the Rye*," *Mosaic* 15 [1982]: 130).

Hollywood "He's in Hollywood" (1). Hollywood, of course, is in Los Angeles, California. We learn on the next page that Holden considers his brother D.B. to have sold out to the big money in the film industry. Holden's view that only "prostitute" writers would write for Hollywood may stem from the views of his teacher, Mr. Antolini, who had urged D.B. not to go (see p. 181 of the novel). We may also see in the reference to selling out to Hollywood a veiled reference to the life of F. Scott Fitzgerald, whose writing Salinger admired and whose signature novel draws praise from Holden: "I was crazy about *The Great Gatsby*" (141). Three times in his stormy life Fitzgerald went to Hollywood to write screenplays, the last time in 1937. Although he was a serious alcoholic by then and able to work only sporadically, his work in Hollywood met with some success. He died there in 1940. Several readers of *The Catcher in the Rye* have speculated about what the letters "D.B." might suggest. Dexter Martin, for example, believes "D.B. is supposed to remind us of V.D. and t.b. And maybe Dead Body" (in a 1962 letter excerpted in *College English*, reprinted in full in Malcolm M. Marsden, ed., *If You Really Want to Know: A Catcher Casebook* (Chicago: Scott, Foresman [1963], p. 83). Another reader, Yasuhiro Takeuchi, thinks "it seems likely that the initials D.B. are an abbreviation of Death and Birth." Takeuchi suggests, further, that by the end of the novel "D.B. experiences a rebirth like that of Mary Magdalene, the penitent prostitute who first bore witness to the resurrected Savior" ("The Burning Carousel and the Carnivalesque: Subversion and Transcendence at the Close of *The Catcher in the Rye*," *Studies in the Novel* 34 [2002]: 330–31).

"The Secret Goldfish" "The best one in it was 'The Secret
Goldfish'" (1). We learn nothing about this story except
what Holden tells us in the next sentence. Holden's liking
of the story in some ways anticipates his own desire for
privacy—his reluctance, for example, to show his own
secrets to others, even to the reader, by making up so many
lies to those he encounters about who he is and why he is
where he is and does what he does. He tells Mrs. Morrow,
for example, that his name is Rudolf Schmidt and that he is
going to New York for an operation to remove a small brain
tumor (54, 58). Ian Hamilton says that one of Salinger's
interests at the McBurney School was "tropical fish" (*In
Search* 21).

Jaguar "He just got a Jaguar" (1). A Jaguar is a low-slung
ostentatious British sports car, almost always purchased
in part to show the owner's affluence. The company was
founded as the Swallow Sidecar Company in 1922 to
make motorcycle sidecars, but soon became better known
for its line of prestige sports cars. After World War II, the
company was renamed Jaguar Cars Ltd. to avoid unfavorable
connotations of the initials, "SS" (the German Secret
Service). The company was acquired by the Ford Motor
Company in 1990. The particular model that D.B. has is
probably the Jaguar XK120, a sports model manufactured
between 1948 and 1954. Available as a coupe, convertible,
or roadster, it could do around 120 miles per hour. In 1949,
of course, $4,000 would have been a great deal of money, at
least $35,000 in 2010 dollars, depending on what inflation
adjuster we apply. That, of course, would be a bargain for a
new Jaguar, so D.B.'s Jaguar might have been a used model.
The point is that D.B. apparently is doing very well indeed in
Hollywood, and is spending his money ostentatiously.

this crumby place "That isn't too far from this crumby place"
(1). Apparently Holden has been sent to a sanitarium or
hospital not far from Los Angeles to recuperate from a
physical or emotional breakdown. He refers later in this
chapter to how "I practically got t.b. and came out here for
all these goddam checkups and stuff" (5). Ignoring that line,
many readers assume that Holden is in a mental institution.
Arthur Heiserman and James E. Miller, Jr., confidently
report that Holden "has no place to go—save of course, a
California psychiatrist's couch" ("J. D. Salinger: Some Crazy
Cliff," *Western Humanities Review* 10 [1956]: 131). Frederic
I. Carpenter says that Holden "thinks of fleeing West, but
is dissuaded by his attachment to his family, and is sent to a
psychiatrist instead" ("The Adolescent in American Fiction,"
English Journal 46 [1957]: 315). Peter J. Seng thinks Holden
has had "a mental breakdown" and that his story "reads like
an edited psychoanalysis" ("The Fallen Idol: The Immature
World of Holden Caulfield," *College English* 23 [1961]: 205).
James Lundquist puts Holden "out in California in the
psychiatric ward" (*J. D. Salinger* [New York: Ungar, 1979],
p. 51), and A. Robert Lee puts him in "a West Coast
psychiatric ward in the wake of his nervous breakdown"
("'Flunking Everything Else Except English Anyway':
Holden Caulfield, Author" in Joel Salzberg, ed., *Critical
Essays on Salinger's* The Catcher in the Rye [Boston: G. K.
Hall, 1990], p. 185). James M. Mellard thinks that Holden
is telling his story "from a psychoanalytic ward somewhere
out West" ("The Disappearing Subject: A Lacanian Reading
of *The Catcher in the Rye*" in Joel Salzberg, ed., *Critical Essays
on Salinger's* The Catcher in the Rye [Boston: G. K. Hall,
1990], p. 198). The persistence of this view is apparent in
Lisa Privitera's statement that *The Catcher in the Rye* is "the
story of a young man's sad spiral into a nervous breakdown"
("Holden's Irony in Salinger's *The Catcher in The Rye*,"

Explicator 66 [2008]: 205), in Sean McDaniel's that Holden
is a "nut case" (*A Catcher's Companion* [Santa Monica: Lit.
Happens Publishing, 2009], p. 25), and in John Timpane's
that he narrates the book from a "mental facility" ("Reclusive
Author Spoke for Alienated Youth," *Philadelphia Inquirer*,
January 29, 2010, p. A16). An alternate view is that Holden
is in a medical sanitarium in southern California because
the dry, sunny climate had been prescribed for his incipient
tuberculosis. If all Holden needed was a psychiatrist or a
mental ward, he could have found plenty of them in New
York.

prostitute "Now he's out in Hollywood, D.B., being a prostitute"
(2). It may be that Holden's harsh words about writers
who do Hollywood scripts reflect Salinger's own recent
experience with Hollywood, which had turned his story
"Uncle Wiggily in Connecticut" into a Samuel Goldwyn film
called *My Foolish Heart*, staring Dana Andrews and Susan
Hayward. Directed by Mark Robson, the film bears but
slender resemblance to Salinger's spare narrative about two
former college roommates who get together for an afternoon
of talk and inebriation. With a screenplay by Julius J. and
Philip G. Epstein, the film has an elaborate plot of romance,
betrayal, marital misery, concealed paternity, and divorce
that both surprised and angered Salinger. It gives major
roles to Lew and Walt, who are mentioned only in passing
in the story and never actually appear, and it invents entire
characters, like Eloise's parents, who are never mentioned
in the story. *My Foolish Heart* follows parts of Salinger's
story in a general way—the credits indicate that it is "Based
on a story in the *New Yorker* by J. D. Salinger"—but it is
essentially a whole new plot. For a detailed comparison of
Salinger's story with the Epsteins's film, see Warren French,
"The Phony World and the Nice World" in *Wisconsin
Studies in Contemporary Literature* 4 (1963): 21–30. *My*

Foolish Heart tells not a bad story, but it is surely not Salinger's story. The film came out in 1950, just as Salinger was finishing *The Catcher in the Rye*, which appeared in 1951. It is interesting that *My Foolish Heart* was featured starting January 19, 1950, in Radio City Music Hall, which may be where Salinger first saw it. If so, that fact may have influenced the snide remarks he has Holden make later about Radio City. In any case, the film that botched his story would have been fresh in his mind as he completed his novel, so his castigation of a brother who was a literary "prostitute" in Hollywood may have been in part a castigation of himself for selling the rights to his work for money.

the movies "If there's one thing I hate, it's the movies" (2). This is one of Holden's many references to movies. It is a curious statement because there is ample evidence that he both enjoys and admires many movies.

Pencey Prep "Where I want to start telling is the day I left Pencey Prep" (2). Pencey Prep is modeled in some ways on Valley Forge Military Academy, in Wayne, Pennsylvania, not far west of Philadelphia. Later in the chapter (p. 5) Holden refers to crossing Route 204. There is no such route near Wayne, though there is a Route 202. In "I'm Crazy," an early story about Holden Caulfield published in *Collier's* for December 22, 1945, Holden is said to cross Route 202 on his way from "Pentey Prep" to Spencer's off-campus house (p. 36). Salinger attended Valley Forge for two years and appears to have enjoyed most aspects of the experience. He did not fail, but in fact graduated in 1936. The fictional Pencey Prep is not a military academy, though it is an all-boys' school.

Agerstown, Pennsylvania "Pencey Prep is this school that's in Agerstown, Pennsylvania" (2). There is no town named Agerstown in Pennsylvania. In northern Maryland, just over

the Pennsylvania border from the town of Waynesboro,
is the city of Hagerstown—perhaps just a coincidental
similarity in names.

Saxon Hall "Anyway, it was the Saturday of the football game
with Saxon Hall" (2). There is no prep school named
Saxon Hall, though it may be that Salinger selected this
name in reminiscence of an actual private school in nearby
Essex County, New Jersey. Seton Hall Preparatory School,
founded in 1856, is a private all-male high school in West
Orange. It is the oldest Catholic college preparatory school
in New Jersey.

Revolutionary War "I was standing way the hell up on top of
Thomsen Hill, right next to this crazy cannon that was in
the Revolutionary War and all" (2). The end of this war in
the late-eighteenth century, of course, marked the end of
the colonial period of American history, the beginning of
American independence from England. Salinger wrote *The
Catcher in the Rye* not long after the end of another war,
World War II. Like Holden's brother D.B., Salinger had
fought in this war and had, like D.B., landed in Normandy
on D-Day (June 6, 1944). Salinger's novel is not a war
novel, though some passages seem to reflect or parallel the
psychological damage done to returned soldiers.

fencing team "I was the goddam manager of the fencing team"
(3). Margaret Salinger remembers her father talking about
"the time he, like Holden, lost the fencing team's gear on the
subway" (*Dream Catcher* 33). See next item.

McBurney School "We'd gone into New York that morning for
this fencing meet with McBurney School" (3). Salinger
himself actually attended the McBurney School in New
York before leaving and going to Valley Forge Military
Academy. According to his daughter Margaret, it was
"a private Young Men's Christian Association movement

school" where school records show that he was "hard hit
by adolescence" (*Dream Catcher* 30). Salinger, as usual,
shifts the facts somewhat. He was actually the manager
of the fencing team at McBurney when he lost the fencing
equipment on the subway en route to a match. According to
Kenneth Slawenski, Salinger was expelled from McBurney
for bad grades, despite his I.Q. of 111 (*J. D. Salinger* 9–11).
If we assume that *The Catcher in the Rye* is somewhat
autobiographical, then Salinger shifted Holden's expulsion
from the McBurney of his own experience to the Pencey
Prep of Holden's fictional life.

ostracized "The whole team ostracized me the whole way back on
the train" (3). By this fancy term Holden apparently means
simply means "kidded" or "made fun of." The term has a
Greek origin and refers to a group's banishment or exclusion
of an individual, decided on by popular vote. Here it serves
to indicate Holden's desire to flaunt his knowledge of a fancy
term he may have learned in one of his classes.

grippe "He had the grippe" (3). The "grippe" was actually an earlier
term for flu or influenza, but sometimes it was used for what
we would now call a very bad cold.

reversible "I only had on my reversible" (4). A reversible is a light
jacket or windbreaker that could be worn with either side
out, one side usually being rainproof.

camel's-hair coat "The week before that, somebody'd stolen my
camel's-hair coat right out of my room, with the fur-lined
gloves right in the pocket" (4). A camel's-hair coat would
have been both warm and expensive. There is probably no
intended reference to John the Baptist in Mark 1:6: "And
John was clothed with camel's hair, and with a girdle of a
skin about his loins; and he did eat locusts and wild honey."
The points, rather, seem to be that Holden's wealth was
indicated by his good clothing, that there are thieves among

his fellow students at Pencey Prep, and that during Holden's odyssey on this and the next two days, he is not warmly dressed for cold winter weather, a fact that may contribute to his breakdown and his possible tuberculosis (see **t.b.** below).

Anthony Wayne Avenue "He lived on Anthony Wayne Avenue" (5). Although there is no Anthony Wayne Avenue in Wayne, Pennsylvania, home of Valley Forge Military Academy, there are an Anthony Wayne Drive, an Anthony Wayne movie theater, and several Wayne avenues (North Wayne Avenue, West Wayne Avenue, and so on) not far from the campus. It is perhaps appropriate that history teacher Spencer lives on an avenue named for an important military figure in American history. General Anthony Wayne (1745–1796) served with some distinction in various battles in the Revolutionary War and, later, against Indian tribes in the Northwest. Fort Wayne, Indiana, was named for him, as was the town of Wayne (Delaware County, Pennsylvania), not far from Anthony Wayne's Pennsylvania birthplace. Wayne fought with George Washington at Valley Forge. It is probably idle to speculate on Salinger's possible interest in Anthony Wayne, but they shared a January 1 birthday (though 174 years apart). Wayne was nicknamed "Mad Anthony Wayne" for the bravado of some of his military exploits.

heavy smoker "I'm quite a heavy smoker, for one thing—that is, I used to be. They made me cut it out" (5). In the late 1940s, smoking was not yet known to be a serious health risk. Indeed, more than half of the men in the United States smoked, and many people, encouraged by the advertising of tobacco companies, believed not only that it was "manly" to smoke, but that it was actually healthy to smoke, if only because it relaxed the smoker. Movies tended to reinforce that image. In the 1949 movie *The Sands of Iwo Jima*, after the mighty warrior played by John Wayne slaughters an unrealistic number of Japanese enemy soldiers, he says, "I never felt so good in my life. How about a cigarette." In a scene in the movie *My Foolish Heart*, based in a general way on Salinger's story "Uncle Wiggily in Connecticut," Eloise, alone with Walt in his tiny apartment, asks for a couple of puffs of his cigarette. It was not until 1964 that the Surgeon General's report on the negative effects of smoking to the smoker's health was released, and even then it had little immediate effect on the prevalence of smoking. For an informative history of tobacco and smoking, see Iain Gately's *Tobacco: A Cultural History of How an Exotic Plant Seduced Civilization* (New York: Grove Press, 2001).

t.b. "That's also how I practically got t.b. and came out here for all these goddam checkups and stuff" (5). The abbreviation "t.b.," usually written "TB," stands for tuberculosis, an infectious disease, usually of the lungs. If not treated, it can be fatal. There are now medicines effective in treating the disease, but one of the standard treatments in earlier decades was to move, at least for a time, to a sunny, dry climate like that found in southern California. Virtually all doctors, of course, would have told tuberculosis patients to quit smoking.

a maid "They didn't have a maid or anything" (5). Holden's noticing that the Spencers have no maid is one of several indications in this first chapter that Holden is used to wealth. We find out later that the Caulfields have a live-in maid in their New York apartment.

Holden "'Holden!' Mrs. Spencer said" (5). This is the first use of the protagonist's name in the novel. Several scholars have speculated on Holden's name. According to Robert G. Jacobs, "'Holden,' the first name, suggests the action which the Catcher means to perform. He intends to hold

children back from the cliff on the edge of the rye field"
("J. D. Salinger's *The Catcher in the Rye*: Holden Caulfield's
'Goddam Autobiography,'" *Iowa English Yearbook* [Fall
1959], p. 11). In another attempt to find a pun in the name,
Stanley Bank, who thinks Holden tells his story from a
mental hospital and that he gives us the means to "follow
his behavior as he crosses the line into psychosis," sees his
name as suggesting that he is "'holdin' on as hard as he can
to a comfortable, secure world-view which he must lose"
("A Literary Hero for Adolescents: The Adolescent," *English
Journal* 58 [1969]: 1015–16). Bernard S. Oldsey speculates
that Holden Caulfield's name is "an ironic amalgam of
the last names of movie stars William Holden and Joan
Caulfield" ("The Movies in the Rye," *College English* 23
[1961]: 210). This last speculation seems to gain support
in Joyce Maynard's report that Salinger had told her "how
he came up with the name of Holden Caulfield (names on
a movie marquee: William Holden and Joan Caulfield)" (*At
Home* 88). The reference here is presumably to two films,
Dear Ruth (1947, see Figure 12) and *Dear Wife* (1949),
comedies starring the two actors. The dates don't work,
though, since Salinger had already used the name "Holden
Caulfield" in several stories already published by then, "I'm
Crazy" (1945), and "Slight Rebellion Off Madison" (1946).
In this last story, written and accepted by the *New Yorker* in
1941, Holden Caulfield's middle name is given as "Morrisey."
Salinger's use of the name Holden Caulfield predates the
time when he could have seen a marquee with the two movie
stars' names on it.

Dexter Martin suggests that "Salinger's primary
reason for selecting Caulfield is obviously the fact that it
means 'cold field'; and therefore, within the book, it signifies
'cemetery'—specifically the one in which Allie is buried.
Since Holden means 'deep valley,' it may also imply 'grave' or

Figure 12: This advertisement for the film *Dear Ruth* (Paramount, 1947) shows William Holden and Joan Caulfield as co-stars. Some have thought their names on a movie marquee suggested to Salinger the name "Holden Caulfield," but in fact Salinger had used the name at least as early as 1941. Courtesy Photofest.

'abyss'; but certainly its primary significance is 'trying to find somebody or something to hold on to'" (in a 1962 letter excerpted in *College English*, reprinted in full in Malcolm M. Marsden, ed., *If you Really Want to Know: A Catcher Casebook* [Chicago: Scott, Foresman, 1963], p. 83). William Glasser also speculates on the name: "Holden is an archaic past participle of 'hold,' and Caul, traced back to Old French cale, a kind of cap, is a membrane sometimes enveloping the head of a child at birth. Within the limits of Holden's narrative, that which is 'held' by him as a 'caul,' a kind of cap, is obviously his red hunting hat" ("*The Catcher in the Rye,*" *Michigan Quarterly Review* 15 [1976]: 443).

Chapter 2. Playing by the rules

Holden has a long talk with Mr. Spencer, though his teacher does most of the talking. Spencer asks Holden how many subjects he is failing, why he doesn't play the game of life by the rules, how he feels about leaving Pencey, whether he worries about the future, and so on. Holden does not enjoy the conversation and zones out by thinking about the ducks in Central Park. He leaves as soon as he can, annoyed that Spencer wishes him "Good luck."

Navajo blanket "[H]e showed us this old beat-up Navajo blanket that he and Mrs. Spencer'd bought off some Indian in Yellowstone Park" (7). The Navajos are a large tribe whose home reservation is in northeastern Arizona and northwestern New Mexico. They raise sheep whose wool they weave into lovely saddle blankets, larger blankets, and rugs. Yellowstone National Park, the oldest of the U.S. national parks, is further north in northwestern Wyoming.

Atlantic Monthly "He was reading the *Atlantic Monthly*" (7). The *Atlantic* was an established, serious, almost highbrow, magazine read mostly by intellectuals, with articles about current events, politics, travel, literature, and the like.

Vicks Nose Drops "[E]verything smelled like Vicks Nose Drops" (7). These nose drops came in a small bottle with a squeeze-dropper as a lid. The users tilted their heads back and put a drop or two in each nostril to loosen nasal blockage. The liquid had a pungent odor.

Whooton School "'I had all that Beowulf and Lord Randal My Son stuff when I was at the Whooton School'" (10). There is no actual school by that name. The literary works Holden mentions are standard British literature anthology pieces. Holden talks about them later, in a little more detail, with the two nuns (110).

December 2nd "'We studied the Egyptians from November 4th to December 2nd'" (11). The mention of these specific dates lets us know that the events of the novel took place at least a week after December 2, since that would have given Mr. Spencer time to grade the test Holden and his classmates

Figure 13: This street sign for Central Park South is situated on the southern border of the park, not far from the little lake or lagoon where Holden remembers having seen ducks.

took and then report the results to Dr. Thurmer. In 1949, both November 4 and December 2 fell on Fridays. That would have made for a four-week unit on ancient Egypt. Ending a pedagogical unit on a Friday would have permitted a test the following Monday. In "I'm Crazy," the short-story version of this scene, Mr. Spencer had given the dates for the unit on the Egyptians as November 3 to December 4. That Salinger meant for us to think of December 10–12, 1949, as the dates for Holden's Saturday-Sunday-Monday odyssey is corroborated by his changing the end-date for the Egyptian unit in the story from December 4, a Sunday in 1949, to December 2, a Friday.

chiffonier "'Your, ah, *exam* paper is over there on top of my chiffonier'" (11). A chiffonier is a bureau or chest of drawers, sometimes with a mirror on the top.

Central Park South "I was thinking about the lagoon in Central Park, down near Central Park South" (13). Central Park South is the east-west street at the south border of Central Park (see Figures 13 and 14), the large park in the center of New York City. The park is bounded on the south by 59th Street and on the north by 110th Street.

Elkton Hills "'I believe you also had some difficulty at the Whooton School and Elkton Hills'" (13). There is no actual school called Elkton Hills.

shoulder "I sort of put my hand on his shoulder" (15). It is easy to imagine that by touching Mr. Spencer's shoulder here and shaking his hand a few lines below, Holden could be contracting "grippe" germs that, combined with his failure to dress warmly, eat sensibly, and get enough sleep, and his then wandering around in wintry New York for three days, could have made him sick enough to need hospitalization in California.

Figure 14: This shot, looking south, is one of many vistas of the little lagoon in the southeast corner of Central Park. Note the city buildings visible just over the trees.

Chapter 3: Robert Ackley

Holden returns to his room and starts reading a book, but Robert Ackley comes in from the other side of the shared shower and bothers him. They talk for a while—mostly Ackley complaining about Holden's roommate Stradlater—and Ackley borrows Holden's scissors to cut his fingernails. Then Stradlater comes in and prepares to go out on a date. He goes down to the "can" (toilet) to shave.

first gear "I can just see the big phony bastard shifting into first gear and asking Jesus to send him a few more stiffs" (17). The reference, of course, is to shifting gears on a car. At the time of this novel, while automatic transmissions were available in some models, most cars had standard clutch shift.

fart "[T]hen all of a sudden this guy sitting in the row in front of me, Edgar Marsalla, laid this terrific fart" (17). The mention of farting in literary works goes back at least six centuries, to Chaucer's *Miller's Tale*: "This Nicholas anon leet fle a fart / As greet as it had been a thonder-dent" (lines I 3806–07).

red hunting hat "It was this red hunting hat, with one of those very, very long peaks" (17). This hat, and the ways Holden wears it, reappears many times in the novel (see especially pages 18, 21, 22, 29, 37, 45, 52, 53, 61, 88, 122, 153, 157, 180, 205, 207, and 212). Not surprisingly, several scholars have seen significance in the hat. Robert M. Slabey says that the hat's "redness and Holden's wearing it backwards (like a 'catcher') symbolizes his rebellion against society. [...] The hat also represents his 'looking backward' towards childhood; he puts it on whenever he feels depressed, lonely, or insecure but does not wear it when he wants to look grownup" (*"The Catcher in the Rye*: Christian Theme and Symbol," *CLA Journal* 6 [1963]: 174). Robert P. Moore sees it as Holden's security blanket: It is "to Holden what the blanket is to Linus [a character in the *Peanuts* comic strip]. The hat is something that he wears when others aren't around, when he is walking to the train, sitting in Central Park, standing in the rain watching Phoebe, and writing, alone in his room, a composition for Stradlater" ("The World of Holden," *English Journal* 54 [1965]: 163). Clinton W. Trowbridge sees the hat as symbolizing Holden's "desire to break through the phony conventions of his world; not wearing the cap dramatizes his failure to destroy what is phony" ("Salinger's Symbolic Use of Character and Detail in *The Catcher in the Rye*," *Cimaron Review* 4 [1968]: 9). James Bryan finds the suggestion of "a masculine symbol" in "Holden's long-peaked hunting cap," but also something more broadly symbolic: "At its deepest level, the hat symbolizes something like Holden's basic human resources—his birthright, that lucky caul of protective courage, humor, compassion, honesty, and love—all of which are the real subject matter of the novel" ("The Psychological Structure of *The Catcher in the Rye*," *PMLA* 89 [1974]: 1074). Edwin Haviland Miller believes that Holden, who is obsessed with his younger brother's death, "assumes Allie's red hair when he puts on the red cap" ("In Memoriam: Allie Caulfield in *The Catcher in the Rye*," *Mosaic* 15 [1982]: 130). Similarly, James M. Mellard emphasizes the color of the hat "that dominates Holden's consciousness and exposes his unconscious. The reference is to Allie's bright red hair" ("The Disappearing Subject: A Lacanian Reading of *The Catcher in the Rye*" in Joel Salzberg, ed., *Critical Essays on Salinger's* The Catcher in the Rye [Boston: G. K. Hall, 1990], p. 206). Alan Nadel sees Holden's red hat as evidence that he is an anticommunist in the Cold War: "Donning his red hunting hat, he attempts to become the good Red-hunter, ferreting out the phonies and the subversives"

(*Containment Culture: American Narratives, Postmodernism, and the Atomic Age* [Durham, NC: Duke University Press, 1995], p. 71). Yasuhiro Takeuchi, connecting the novel with Mikhail Bakhtin's ideas of the carnivalesque, suggests that the shifts of the hat between Holden and his sister "signal not merely exchanges of fixed hunter/catcher-prey/caught roles, but also rebirth through these role changes" ("The Burning Carousel and the Carnivalesque: Subversion and Transcendence at the Close of *The Catcher in the Rye*," *Studies in the Novel* 34 [2002]: 329). Interestingly, virtually no one has commented on the traditional reason for wearing a red hunting hat—so as not to be shot by other hunters. It seems obvious enough that Holden wears the hat in paranoid self-protectiveness.

Out of Africa "They gave me *Out of Africa*, by Isak Dinesen" (18). Isak Dinesen is the pen name of the Danish writer Karen von Blixen-Finecke (1885–1962). *Out of Africa*, which Holden gets by mistake from the library, is the 1937 memoir of Dinesen's years in Kenya, where she tries to help her husband make a success of coffee farming. *Out of Africa* was known to be one of Salinger's favorite books. Its interest to Holden may have been its precise descriptions of the landscape, climate, and people of Africa, all of whom would have offered stark contrasts with the privileged phonies of Pennsylvania and New York. Holden would perhaps have found a particular fascination in two free-spirited European men who refuse to come back from Africa and eventually die there, having refused there to play life by the rules. The Englishman Denys Finch-Hatton, who loves books and runs safaris, refuses to be tied down to much of anything and dies in the crash-wreckage of the small airplane he pilots. The blind Danish former sailor referred to as Old Knudsen, who dies of a heart attack on the farm, has a philosophy that the rebellious Holden might have approved:

One strong feeling ran through his Odyssey: the abomination of the law, and all its works, and all its doings. He was a born rebel, he saw a comrade in every outlaw. A heroic deed meant to him in itself an act of defiance against the law. He liked to talk of kings and royal families, jugglers, dwarfs and lunatics, for them he took to be outside the law,—and also of any crime, revolution, trick, and prank, that flew in the face of the law. But for the good citizen he had a deep contempt, and law-abidingness in any man was to him the sign of a slavish mind. (Modern Library edition, New York, 1992, p. 198)

We recall that Holden's father, whom he does not much like, was a lawyer.

a book by Ring Lardner "My brother gave me a book by Ring Lardner for my birthday, just before I went to Pencey" (18). Lardner was an American humorist (1885–1933). The book Holden received may have been *The Portable Ring Lardner* (Viking Press, 1946). That selection of Lardner's work has a section of "Parodies and 'Plays.'" It also contains Lardner's short novel *The Big Town*, about an Indiana woman who comes to New York in 1920 (shortly after the end of World War I) to catch a husband. That novel might have suggested some ideas that Salinger worked into *The Catcher in the Rye*—such as the three naive young women from Seattle with whom Holden dances in the Lavender Room of the Edmont. *The Portable Ring Lardner* contains another story that would have interested Salinger, "A Caddy's Diary," on pp. 467–87. For a comment on the possible influence on Salinger of Lardner's use of a semi-literate first-person narrator to tell "A Caddy's Diary," see **caddy'd** in my notes to chapter 4 below.

traffic cop "[I]t had this one story about a traffic cop that falls in love with this very cute girl that's always speeding" (18).

Holden refers here to Ring Lardner's story, "There Are
Smiles," originally published in *Cosmopolitan* in late April,
1928. "There Are Smiles" is not in *The Portable Ring Lardner*
(see previous note) but is available in other collections,
like *Round Up: The Stories of Ring W. Lardner* (Charles
Scribner's Sons, 1941), pp. 271–81. "There Are Smiles"
fits pretty well the summary Holden gives here, except that
there are hints that the pretty young woman, who is named
Edith Dole, commits suicide to avoid having to marry a man
she does not love rather than Ben Collins, the policeman
she has fallen for. The theme of innocent love thwarted by
external circumstances would have appealed to Holden, and
he would perhaps have felt a fellowship with Edith, who is
being coerced by a wealthy and powerful father to live her
life in a way not congenial to her own inclinations. The title
of Lardner's story apparently comes from the first four lines
of the refrain of "Smiles," a 1917 popular love song by
J. Will Callahan:

> There are smiles that make us happy,
> There are smiles that make us blue,
> There are smiles that steal away the tear drops,
> As the sunbeams steal away the dew.

The Return of the Native "I read a lot of classical books, like
The Return of the Native and all, and I like them" (18). The
reference is to Thomas Hardy's 1878 novel about lives and
loves on Egdon Heath. See **Eustacia Vye**, below.

Of Human Bondage "You take that book *Of Human Bondage*,
by Somerset Maugham" (18). W. Somerset Maugham
(1874–1965) based his novel largely on his own life, though
with some large and small changes. The main character,
Philip Carey, is much like himself, though he is hampered
by a deformed foot that Maugham himself did not have.
Like Philip, Maugham had lived with his aunt and uncle in

the nearby seaside town of Whitstable (thinly disguised as Blackstable in *Of Human Bondage*) and had gone to school in the cathedral town of Canterbury (thinly disguised as Tercanbury in the novel). Maugham had withdrawn from that school, as Philip does at the end of the twenty-first chapter (of more than a hundred chapters in the novel), and for some of the same reasons: because he had friendships that went sour there, because he felt lonely and isolated, because he did not respect most of his teachers, because he did not want to be a cleric like his caretaker uncle, because he saw no reason to go to Oxford, as almost everyone around him expected him to do, because he wanted to see more of the world than he saw opening before him if he stayed and succeeded in school, and so on. Holden in *The Catcher in the Rye* would have had many reasons to identify with young Philip Carey: a dead younger brother, a love of reading, an unhappy boys' boarding school experience, parental pressure to go to a prestigious university, a feeling of isolation among other boys, a teacher whom he both respects and despises, and so on.

Eustacia Vye "I like that Eustacia Vye" (19). Eustacia is a central character in Thomas Hardy's *The Return of the Native*, a woman whose bewitching loveliness draws many men to her. There are several reasons why Holden might like her, besides of course her loveliness. He might well have identified with her loneliness, her feeling of isolation and superiority among the people around her, her need for love, her vigorous independence and insistence that she matters, her restless desire to leave what has become her home, her flirtation with suicide. Holden might have felt a particular affinity with this description of her:

> Thus we see her in a strange state of isolation. To have
> lost the godlike conceit that we may do what we will,

and not to have acquired a homely zest for doing what
we can, shows a grandeur of temper which cannot be
objected to in the abstract, for it connotes a mind that,
though disappointed, forswears retreat. (Penguin edition
[London, 1999], p. 73)

One possible view of Holden is that, like Eustacia, he no
longer quite believes that he can do whatever he wants to
do, but has not yet developed an excitement about doing
what he can do. He is, then, in a frustrating limbo between
knowing what he cannot do and working with what he can
do. Holden mentions *The Return of the Native*, its author,
and Eustacia Vye again on pp. 110–11 of the novel.

Ackley "It was Robert Ackley, this guy that roomed right next
to me" (19). The name may derive from Salinger's having
read William Saroyan's 1943 novel *The Human Comedy*.
A minor character in that novel is named Hubert Ackley.
Because Hubert is a rich kid from an aristocratic family, the
high school track coach favors him over the main character,
Homer Macaulay, who comes from a poor and lower-class
farm family. The distant similarity in the names of *Homer
Macaulay* and *Holden Caulfield* is probably coincidental,
but there are some interesting similarities between the
two novels. Homer Macaulay, like Holden, studies ancient
history with an ancient teacher in high school and, like
Holden, has two brothers and a sister. One of the brothers,
like Holden's brother D.B., goes off to fight in World War II.
Unlike D.B., that brother is killed in action, leaving Homer
distraught about how to deal with the death of a brother:
"What's a man supposed to do? I don't know who to hate. I
don't know what to do. How does a man go on living? Who
does he love?" (Dell Laurel edition, 1966, pp. 186–87).
Holden feels similar frustration at Allie's death in *The
Catcher in the Rye*.

Mother darling "'I think I'm going blind,' I said in this very hoarse voice. 'Mother darling, everything's getting so *dark* in here'" (21). Holden is probably making an oblique reference to the ancient Greek story of Oedipus, a man who inadvertently falls in love with and marries his mother. When he realizes what he has done he gouges his own eyes out. While no lines in the fifth-century B.C.E. *Oedipus the King* by Sophocles match these lines precisely, after he destroys his eyes, the blind Oedipus does say, "Darkness! Horror of darkness enfolding, resistless, unspeakable visitant" (from the David Grene translation in the *Norton Introduction to Literature* [6th edition, New York: Norton, 1995], lines 1389–90).

a goddam prince "'He told me he thinks you're a goddam prince,' I said. I call people a 'prince' quite often when I'm horsing around" (24). Biographer Paul Alexander said that Richard Gonder, Salinger's senior-year roommate, reports that "Jerry" used the term "prince" in a pejorative sense: "His favorite expression for someone he did not care for was, 'John, you really are a prince of a guy.' What he meant by this, of course, was 'John, you really are an SOB'" (*Salinger* 43–44). Holden uses the term in speaking of Ackley again on pages 47 and 50 of the novel.

hound's-tooth jacket "'If you're not going out anyplace special, how 'bout lending me your hound's-tooth jacket?'" (25). The reference is to a jacket made of cloth with a repeated jagged pattern that looks like a series of sharp teeth (referred to again on pp. 33 and 40).

Chapter 4: Ward Stradlater and Jane Gallagher

Holden goes down to the can with Stradlater to chat while Stradlater shaves. Stradlater asks him to write a descriptive composition for him. Holden horses around a bit, pretending, for example, to be a governor's son who wants to be a tap dancer and is about to play an important part in the Ziegfeld Follies. When Holden finds out that Stradlater is going on a date with Jane Gallagher, he becomes very much interested but then, knowing what a "sexy bastard" Stradlater is, he becomes nervous. He asks Stradlater to ask Jane if she still keeps her kings in the back row. Then Holden goes back to his dorm room and kills time until dinner, trying not to think of Stradlater's date with Jane.

"Song of India" "Stradlater kept whistling 'Song of India' while he shaved" (26–27). This 1937 song was made famous by Tommy Dorsey's orchestra. There are no lyrics, but the tune is both catchy and complex.

"Slaughter on Tenth Avenue" "[H]e always picked out some song that's hard to whistle even if you're a good whistler, like 'Song of India' or 'Slaughter on Tenth Avenue'" (27). This ballet, originally choreographed by George Balanchine, is from Rogers and Hammerstein's 1936 *On Your Toes*.

Oxford "'He wants me to go to Oxford'" (29). Oxford University is one of the oldest and most prestigious universities in England. Holden's claiming to be the "Governor's son" refers, of course, to his father's desire for him to attend Yale or Princeton. Philip Carey's father in Maugham's *Of Human Bondage* had wanted his son to go to Oxford (see **Of Human Bondage** in my explanatory notes to chapter 3, above).

Ziegfeld Follies "'It's the opening night of the *Ziegfeld Follies*'" (29). Holden's humorous fantasy may have been inspired by his having seen the movie *Ziegfeld Follies* (see Figure

15), directed by Vincente Minnelli, that came out in 1946. It featured Fred Astaire, Lucille Ball, Gene Kelly, Lena Horne, Judy Garland, Red Skelton, Esther Williams, and many others. In *Ziegfeld Follies* Mr. Ziegfeld, now dead and in heaven, imagines that he will have one more great show, featuring songs, dances, and vaudeville-type skits by a few older artists, but mostly by newer artists. There may also be a side allusion to the earlier (1936) movie, *The Great Ziegfeld*. Holden's fantasy of being the "Governor's son" (29) who wants to be a tap dancer rather than go to Oxford is not precisely paralleled in either movie, but Holden may have been remembering a sequence in which Fred Astaire and Gene Kelly do an extended tap-dance routine. Of course, Holden's fantasy more precisely reflects his own situation as the son of a corporate lawyer who wants him to go to an Ivy League university. It may also reflect Salinger's relationship with his father, Sol Salinger, a successful importer of Polish meats and cheeses, who had hoped that his son would take over the business. Interestingly, in the modern (2000) movie *Chasing Holden*, the lead character is a governor's son, a confused young man obsessed with *The Catcher in the Rye*, who takes a bus trip to the woods of New Hampshire to find J. D. Salinger.

half nelson "I felt like jumping off the washbowl and getting old Stradlater in a half nelson" (30). When an attacker grabs someone's arm from behind and locks it, keeping his opponent's head in a downward grip, that is called a half nelson. The more the victim struggles to escape, the tighter the grip becomes.

B.M. " 'Does she go to B.M. now?' " (31). The reference may be to the Bryn Mawr School, a private preparatory school for girls in Baltimore, Maryland. On their 2006 web site we read: "The Bryn Mawr School continues to provide one of

Figure 15: From the movie *Ziegfeld Follies* (Metro-Goldwyn-Mayer, 1946). The film contains many short dance and comedy routines. This photo shows Lucille Ball with a whip taming some young lioness-dancers. Courtesy Photofest.

the best educational curricula in the country supported by
highly qualified faculty and exceptional teaching, innovative
college-preparatory courses, robust offerings in athletics
and the arts, and a diverse community that welcomes
and provides opportunities for every girl." The school is
mentioned again in chapter 9 when Holden thinks of
"giving old Jane a buzz—I mean calling her long distance at
B.M., where she went" (63). The fact that for her date with
Stradlater she had "signed out for nine-thirty" (34) does not
jibe well with her attending a school in Baltimore (around
a hundred miles away), especially since Stradlater thinks
of driving her to New York City, the opposite direction, for
their date. Jane would not have been old enough yet to go
to Bryn Mawr College, in Bryn Mawr, Pennsylvania. For a
possible explanation of the confusion, see next item.

Shipley "'She said she might go to Shipley, too'" (31). Shipley
School is a private preparatory school in Bryn Mawr,
Pennsylvania, thus reasonably close to Pencey Prep, another
southeastern Pennsylvania school. From their 2006 web
site: "The Shipley School, a prekindergarten through grade
12 coeducational day school, is committed to educational
excellence and dedicated to developing in each student a love
of learning and a compassionate participation in the world."
Salinger's daughter Margaret writes that her mother Claire
was a student at Shipley in the 1950–1951 school year
when she and her father began corresponding: "She knew
from his letters that he was hard at work finishing a novel.
She thinks he changed the school that Holden's friend Jane
Gallagher attended to Shipley for her. 'It was the sort of
thing he'd do, but I was too in awe and on my best behavior
to ask'" (*Dream Catcher* 11). Later we learn that Jane
Gallagher apparently went to "B.M." instead, though there is
a contradiction. In chapter 4 Holden tells Stradlater, "'I

thought she went to Shipley'" (31) and "'I thought she went
to Shipley. I could've sworn she went to Shipley'" (33),
whereas in chapter 9 he refers with more certainty to "B.M.,
where she went" (63). The confusion lends support to the
idea that Salinger originally had Jane be a student at B.M.,
but when he changed it to Shipley to honor Claire, he forgot
to change the second reference.

Vitalis "Old Stradlater was putting Vitalis on his hair" (31).
Vitalis was a mousse or cream that men put on their hair to
give it shine and to keep it from blowing around.

checkers "'I used to play checkers with her all the time'" (31).
Checkers is a simple board game in which the red pieces
and the black ones compete. If a player jumps his opponent's
piece, the jumped piece is removed from the board. All
pieces can move only forward, not backward, unless the piece
has been moved all the way to her opponent's back row. At
that point it is "kinged" with a second checker on top and
can be moved in any direction, thus making it capable of
attacking from the rear. For Jane to keep her kings in the
back row would have been strategically foolish since her
most valuable pieces would then be useless. See **kings in the
back row**, below.

caddy'd "'I caddy'd for her mother a couple of times. She went
around in about a hundred and seventy, for nine holes'" (32).
That, of course, is an exceedingly high—and therefore bad—
score for a nine-hole course. We find here almost certainly
the influence of Ring Lardner, one of Salinger's and Holden's
favorite writers. One of the stories in *The Portable Ring
Lardner* (1946), the book that D.B. may have given Holden
for his birthday, is "A Caddy's Diary," about a sixteen-year-
old golf caddy named Dick who is a far better player than
the wealthy men and women who play at the Pleasant View
Golf Club. He is even better than its golf pro: "I use to play

around with our pro Jack Andrews till I got so as I could
beat him pretty near every time we played and now he won't
play with me no more" (p. 469). Lardner's colloquial style
would have interested, and perhaps influenced, Salinger.
Other features of the story might have interested Salinger,
as well. Dick, for example, has a crush on one of the pretty
women who plays at the club, makes comments on what
bad golfers women players are, and learns firsthand about
the sleazy morality of the country club set—the men, the
women, and the caddies—who lie and cheat regularly. We
find out later in *The Catcher in the Rye* that Holden, like
Dick, is an excellent golfer. Of course, there are many telling
differences between the two narratives, the most obvious
one being the class origins of the two caddies. Dick has poor
lower-class parents who will not allow him to finish high
school because they want him to earn a living. Holden, by
contrast, is from a family that has money to burn and wants
to pay for him to graduate from an exclusive prep school and
attend an Ivy League college.

kings in the back row "'Ask her if she still keeps all her kings in
the back row'" (34). Carl F. Strauch comments on what he
sees in "the symbolism of this imagery, portraying defense
against sexual attack" as Holden's "secret warning against
the slob who would himself be the bearer of the message"
("Kings in the Back Row: Meaning through Structure: A
Reading of Salinger's *The Catcher in the Rye*," *Wisconsin
Studies in Contemporary Literature* 2 [1961]: 13). On the
other hand, the kings in the back row may indicate no more
than Jane's own conservative desire—foolish in a game of
checkers—not to make strategic use of her most powerful
and versatile checker pieces. She cannot hope to win a game
in which she refuses to use her kings, and her kings kept
there cannot protect her other checkers. The kings in the

back row are mentioned elsewhere in the novel, as well (see pp. 31–32, 42, 44, 78). Bernard S. Oldsey thinks that Jane Gallagher's character and situation derive from *Kings Row*, a 1940 novel by Henry Bellaman and later a 1942 movie: "*King's Row* shares with *The Catcher in the Rye* three notable elements: youthful innocence in a world of adult cruelty, possible confinement in a mental institution, and a muted theme of incest" ("The Movies in the Rye," *College English* 23 [1961]: 213).

Chapter 5: Allie's baseball mitt

After a disappointing meal that Saturday night, Holden, Ackley, and Mal Brossard take a bus into Agerstown for a hamburger and a movie, but they skip the movie. They return to the dorm, where Ackley goes to bed and Holden writes the composition for Stradlater. The composition is about his brother Allie's left-handed baseball mitt. We learn in the process about Allie's death from leukemia three years earlier and about Holden's distressed reaction: damaging his hand by smashing the windows in the garage.

Brown Betty "You always got these very lumpy mashed potatoes on steak night, and for dessert you got Brown Betty, which nobody ate" (35). Brown Betty is spiced baked pudding, usually made with apples and raisins, with bread crumbs on top.

Cary Grant "It was supposed to be a comedy, with Cary Grant in it" (37). A versatile and prolific film actor, Cary Grant (1904–1986) was born to working-class parents in England. When he was nine, his mother was placed in a mental institution. To support himself he joined an acting and acrobatic troupe. He did well enough that he parlayed that modest start into one of the most successful Hollywood careers ever. He had his pick of parts and leading ladies. He turned down many roles, including the role of Agent 007 in the first James Bond series. The comedy movie that Holden and his friends do not see that Saturday might have been *Night and Day* (1946) or *Arsenic and Old Lace* (1944, see Figure 16)—or any of several other 1940s comedies Cary Grant starred in.

laughed liked hyenas "They both laughed like hyenas at stuff that wasn't even funny. I didn't even enjoy sitting next to them

Figure 16: From the film version of *Arsenic and Old Lace* (1944), starring Cary Grant. This is possibly the movie that Holden, Brossard, and Ackley decide not to see in Agerstown. Cary Grant is at the left. Peter Lorre is the short man to the right. The scar-faced actor in the center is Raymond Massey. Courtesy Photofest.

in the movies" (37). Holden uses a similar expression later
to describe people on the streets late at night—"hoodlumy-
looking guys and their dates, all of them laughing like hyenas
at something you could bet wasn't funny" (81) and "morons
that laugh like hyenas in the movies at stuff that isn't funny"
(84). Margaret Salinger remembers the advice her father
gave her about finding a mate: "'Make sure you marry
someone who laughs at the same things you do.' Sometimes
he'd add a cautionary tale such as the one about a date who,
in the middle of a movie theater, actually laughed at a bit of
slapstick, the pain it caused him and so on" (*Dream Catcher*
226).

bridge "Old Brossard was a bridge fiend, and he started looking
around the dorm for a game" (37). Bridge is a popular card
game that requires four players, with two of them playing
partners against the other two.

describing rooms "I'm not too crazy about describing rooms and
houses anyway" (38). Holden may here be making another
side allusion to "all that David Copperfield kind of crap" (1).
The opening chapters of Dickens's novel are full of detailed
descriptions of the kind that Holden refuses to write.

leukemia "He got leukemia and died when we were up in Maine,
on July 18, 1946" (38). Leukemia is a cancerous disease
of the blood that causes anemia and excessive production
of white blood cells. In the time we are speaking of, the
disease was almost always fatal. It is interesting that the
only specific date that Holden refers to in the book is the
day Allie died, some three-and-a-half years before the
December, 1949, time when most of the events of the novel
take place. Holden seems to be aware that he may have
stopped maturing on that date: "I was sixteen then, and I'm
seventeen now, and sometimes I act like I'm about thirteen"
(9). Some critics, thinking Holden is mad, date his madness

from Allie's death. In her introduction to *Depression in J. D. Salinger's* The Catcher in the Rye (Detroit: Greenhaven Press, 2009, pp. 14–15), Dedria Bryfonski says:

> Depression and madness are certainly major themes of *The Catcher in the Rye*, and part of the power of the narrative emerges from the way Salinger captures the angst of a sensitive teenager driven into mental illness. What causes Holden Caulfield's depression and descent into madness is the subject of debate [...]. What is clear, however, is that many of the symptoms Holden displays in the course of the novel mirror the classic symptoms of post-traumatic stress disorder. The death of his younger brother, Allie, was a traumatic event in Holden Caulfield's life and is perhaps at the root of the depression he battles in the novel.

my hand "My hand still hurts me once in a while, when it rains and all, and I can't make a real fist any more—not a tight one" (39). Holden's wounded hand connects him with other wounds in modern literature, such as Jake Barnes's genital wound in Hemingway's *The Sun Also Rises* (1926) and Philip Carey's club foot in Maugham's *Of Human Bondage* (1915).

Chapter 6: Fighting Stradlater

Holden worries about Jane Gallagher until Stradlater comes home. When Stradlater does return and complains about the composition Holden wrote about Allie's baseball glove, Holden tears the essay up. Holden asks him about Jane and what they did together, but Stradlater won't tell, saying it is a "professional secret." The two roommates get into a fight in which Holden's nose is badly bloodied. Stradlater goes down to the can and Holden goes into Ackley's room.

my right hand "It probably would've hurt him a lot, but I did it
with my right hand, and I can't make a good fist with that
hand" (43). Holden is referring, of course, to the time he
hurt his hand smashing the garage windows after Allie's
death. His bad hand would explain why he manages the
fencing team rather than fences on it, but it does not jibe
well with his later statements that he plays tennis (see pages
76 and 180 in the novel) and is an excellent golfer (77).

pacifist "I'm a pacifist, if you want to know the truth" (46). To
profess to be a pacifist shortly after World War II would
have had political and social implications. That war, fought
against the tyrannical Hitler whose ambition was to
dominate the world, was widely thought to be necessary if
American freedom, democracy generally, and civilization
itself were to survive. Salinger himself was scarcely a pacifist.
He joined the U.S. Army on April 27, 1942, reported to
Fort Dix, and eventually scaled the cliffs at Normandy on
D-Day. Holden's professed pacifism comes, ironically, just a
couple of pages after he attacks Stradlater: "I tried to sock
him [. . .] so it would split his goddam throat open. [. . .]
I'd've killed him" (43).

Chapter 7: Packing up

*Ackley is asleep, but Holden is so lonely that he wants to talk with
almost anyone, so wakes him up and asks if he wants to play cards.
Ackley doesn't, so Holden lies down on the bed of Ackley's roommate
Ely. All he can think about is what Stradlater did to or with Jane
in Ed Banky's car. Holden wakes Ackley again to ask whether only
Catholics can join monasteries. Then Holden decides to get out of
Pencey that very night and spend the time until Wednesday, when he
is expected home, in New York City. He has no definite plan except to*

find a hotel there. Holden consolidates his funds, grabs his suitcases, and heads out. His parting shot to his sleeping schoolmates is "Sleep tight, ya morons!"

Canasta "'Listen,' I said, 'do you feel like playing a little Canasta?'" (47). Canasta was just becoming popular in the late 1940s. It is a partners card game that is best for four players, two to a team, though it is possible for just two to play. Canasta requires two full decks of cards, including the four jokers. The game originated in Montevideo, Uruguay, around 1940, and from there it migrated to Argentina, the U.S., and elsewhere. It was especially fashionable in the 1950s. The term "canasta" is a Spanish term meaning "basket"— apparently referring to the tray that the cards were kept in.

Ely's bed "'Hey,' I said, 'is it okay if I sleep in Ely's bed tonight?'" (47). This reference to Ely as Ackley's roommate is a curious inconsistency, since Holden had told us earlier (19) that Herb Gale was Ackley's roommate.

wished I was dead "I felt so lonesome, all of a sudden. I almost wished I was dead" (48). Holden's statement reflects the language in chapter 1 of *The Adventures of Huckleberry Finn*, where Huck, alone is his room, tells us, "I felt so lonesome I most wished I was dead" (quoted from p. 3 of the Ballantine Ivy edition, 1996). Huck wishes for death other times, as well. For example, near the end of chapter 16, he says, "I got to feeling so mean and so miserable I most wished I was dead" (p. 109). At other places Huck, like Holden after him, thinks about his own death and shows envy of those who are dead. There is no absolute evidence that Salinger knew Mark Twain's famous novel, but almost no one doubts that he did.

jumping out the window "Every time I thought about it, I felt like jumping out the window" (48). Holden's suicidal thoughts anticipate his later reference to James Castle's having jumped out the window to his death (170).

joining a monastery "'What's the routine on joining a monastery?' I asked him. [. . .] 'Do you have to be a Catholic and all?'" (50). We don't know much about Holden's religion, but this and other lines suggest a certain naivete about religious matters. We are probably to assume that Holden is not a practicing Catholic, though we find out later that his father had once been a Catholic (112). Salinger's daughter Margaret reports that, according to her mother Claire, at the time he was finishing *The Catcher in the Rye*, her father "was seriously considering becoming a monk." He was at that time interested not in joining a Catholic monastery, however, but a Buddhist one: "He had become friends with Daisetz Suzuki and meditated, he told her, at a Zen center in the Thousand Islands" (*Dream Catcher* 11).

Kolynos "There was this empty box of Kolynos toothpaste outside Leahy and Hoffman's door" (51). Kolynos was a toothpaste widely advertised in the 1940s.

Gladstones "I packed these two Gladstones I have" (51). Gladstones, named for William Everett Gladstone, British politician under Queen Victoria, were expensive leather suitcases or hinged carrying bags. Gladstones are mentioned again later (see 53–54). Holden mentions the importance of suitcases again on 108–09. Carol and Richard Ohmann see in Holden's discussion of suitcases evidence of "the novel's critique of class distinction" ("Reviewers, Critics, and *The Catcher in the Rye*," *Critical Enquiry* 3 [1976]: 30).

Spaulding's "I could see my mother going in Spaulding's and asking the salesman a million dopy questions—and here I was getting the ax again" (52). Spaulding's was a sportswear and sports equipment store with outlets nationwide.

Holden goes to Manhattan (chapters 8-14)

Chapter 8: On the train with Mrs. Morrow

Since it is too late for a cab, Holden walks in the snow to the train station, washes the blood from his face with some snow, and catches a train for New York. A middle-aged woman gets on the train at Trenton and they begin talking. She turns out to be the mother of a classmate named Ernest Morrow, a boy Holden does not like. Holden lies about who he is—he tells her his own name is Rudolf Schmidt— and tells her all sorts of flattering but untrue stories about what a great guy her son is. When she asks why Holden is going home from Pencey early, he tells her that it is because he has to have a small brain tumor removed. She gets off at Newark.

guys named David "One of those stories with a lot of phony, lean-jawed guys named David in it, and a lot of phony girls named Linda or Marcia that are always lighting all the goddam Davids' pipes for them" (53). There may be some humor or irony in Salinger's selection of the name David— his own middle name—which he is said to have disliked because it sounded too Jewish.

Trenton "All of a sudden, this lady got on at Trenton and sat down next to me" (54). Trenton, New Jersey, is a regular stop on the train lines between Philadelphia and New York. Penn Station in New York would have been at least an hour's train ride from Trenton.

telephone "She should've carried a goddam telephone around with her" (54). The telephone, of course, would have been useless. Cell phones were not invented until much later.

Vogue "She started reading this *Vogue* she had with her" (58). *Vogue* was a leading women's fashion magazine. It is interesting that the December 1949 issue contained a story by Thomas W. Phipps, "Joe Carter and the Ducks," about a lawyer who goes on a duck hunt wearing a cap with ear flaps.

Gloucester, Massachusetts "[S]he invited me to visit Ernie during the summer, at Gloucester, Massachusetts" (58). Gloucester is a seaside town north and east of Boston.

Newark "She got off at Newark" (58). Newark is in New Jersey not far from New York. It would almost certainly have been the last stop on the west side of the Hudson River before Penn Station.

Chapter 9: On the phone with Faith Cavendish

Holden gets off the train at Penn Station [A] *takes a cab, but forgets that he intends to "shack up in a hotel" and gives the cabby his home address. After a bit, as they drive north, he tells the cabby to take him back downtown to the Edmont Hotel* [B]. *On the way he asks the cabby about the ducks in Central Park. He takes a room at the Edmont. Across the court from his room he sees an older man getting dressed in women's clothes, then a younger man and woman squirting liquid on each other. Though he finds these people to be "perverts," their actions fascinate him. He thinks of calling Jane Gallagher, but, feeling "pretty horny," he instead calls a prostitute named Faith*

Cavendish. She says it is too late for an "engagement" and, besides, her roommate is sick. So they say good-by.

Penn Station "The first thing I did when I got off at Penn Station, I went into this phone booth" (59). Penn Station, the terminus for trains coming from the Philadelphia area, is still between Seventh and Eighth avenues and between 31st and 33rd streets. The actual station building that Holden would have visited in the late 1940s, however, was torn down in 1963 and replaced. For a fascinating account, with illustrations, of the construction of Penn Station in the first decade of the twentieth century, see Jill Jonnes's *Conquering Gotham—Gilded Age Epic: The Construction of Penn Station and Its Tunnels* (New York: Viking, 2007). To get a sense of the magnificent structure that served as Holden's entrance to Manhattan, see especially her illustrations on pp. 279, 281, and 291.) **See Figure 17 for a map of Holden's Manhattan, with encircled letters showing most of the places he visits on his journey. The key to the letters is on the facing page.** Not all of the places are specified exactly in the text, so some locations are generalized. Holden visits some places more than once—the Edmont, Grand Central Station, and Central Park—so they have more than one letter. By tracing the letters from **A** (Penn Station) to **V** (the carrousel in Central Park), readers can follow Holden's circuitous journey around Manhattan. In a *New York Times* article published just after Salinger's death, James Barron converted my map into an interactive version in which readers could click on the various places Holden visits ("Taking a Walk through J. D. Salinger's New York," January 20, 2010).

my **regular address** "I'm so damn absent-minded, I gave the driver my regular address, just out of habit and all" (60). Holden's statement is interesting in part because it suggests that he really wants to go home, not to a hotel, but in part because the address he gives the driver takes him up the west side of Manhattan—not the direction where later information suggests that he lives. Are we to assume that Holden forgets where he lives or, more likely, that Salinger changed his mind as he worked on the novel and let this minor inconsistency stand? Salinger's daughter Margaret reports that Salinger's own original home was on the Upper West Side until, after he finished the eighth grade, his family moved to a Park Avenue neighborhood east of Central Park (*Dream Catcher* 29–30). Paul Alexander gives the address of the original home as West 82nd Street, and the later home in a more posh neighborhood at 91st Street and Park Avenue (*Salinger* 33–34).

Ninedieth Street "'This here's a one-way. I'll have to go all the way up to Ninedieth Street now'" (60). The cab driver is heading from Penn Station north, perhaps up the West Side Highway, a fast but limited-access north-south artery along the Hudson. Alternatively, he might be going up Tenth Avenue (Amsterdam Avenue). Either way, it is puzzling why the driver would refer to 90th Street, since there is no exit from the West Side Highway or transverse road across Central Park at 90th Street. A few lines later Holden refers to coming "out of the park at Ninetieth Street" (60). Perhaps Salinger or Holden meant 96th Street, where there is both an exit ramp from the West Side Highway and a transverse road across the park. Apparently the cab then took Holden back south on the east side of the park, probably on Fifth Avenue, which is one-way south.

those ducks "'You know those ducks in that lagoon right near Central Park South? That little lake? By any chance, do you happen to know where they go, the ducks, when it gets all frozen over?'" (60). Holden later asks a similar question of

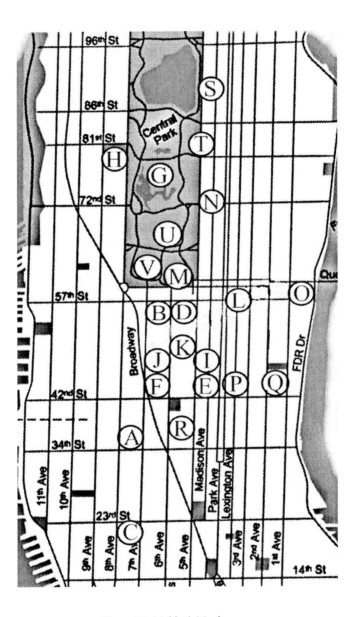

Figure 17: Holden's Manhattan

A. Penn Station: "I got off at Penn Station" (59).

B. Edmont Hotel: "We got to the Edmont Hotel" (61).

C. Ernie's: "Ernie's is this nightclub in Greenwich Village" (80).

D. Edmont Hotel: "I walked all the way back to the hotel" (88).

E. Grand Central Station: "I told the driver to take me to Grand Central Station" (107).

F. Broadway: "I started walking over toward Broadway" (114).

G. Central Park: "I took a cab up to the park" (118).

H. Museum of Natural History: "I walked [. . .] over to the Museum of Natural History" (119).

I. Biltmore: "All I did [. . .] was get a cab and go down to the Biltmore" (122).

J. Theater: "We horsed around a little bit in the cab on the way over to the theater" (125).

K. Radio City ice rink: "'Let's go ice-skating at Radio City!'" (128).

L. Wicker Bar: "[H]e'd meet me for a drink [. . .] at the Wicker Bar over on 54th" (137).

M. The lake: "I started walking over to the park [. . .] by that little lake" (153).

N. Home: "So I got the hell out of the park, and went home" (156).

O. Antolini's: "Mr. and Mrs. Antolini had this very swanky apartment over on Sutton Place" (180).

P. Grand Central: "I [. . .] took the subway down to Grand Central" (194).

Q. Restaurant: "I started walking way over east, where the pretty cheap restaurants are" (196).

R. Fifth Avenue: "I left and started walking over toward Fifth Avenue" (196).

S. Phoebe's school: "I [. . .] started walking fast as hell up to her school" (199).

T. Metropolitan Museum of Art: "I just went over to the museum" (202).

U. Zoo: "I started walking downtown toward the zoo" (208).

V. Carrousel: "[W]e kept getting closer and closer to the carrousel" (210).

Horwitz, another taxi driver (81–82). What Holden calls the "lagoon" is the crescent- or horseshoe-shaped body of water in the southeast corner of Central Park (see Figure 18). It is labeled simply "The Pond" on most maps of the park. Holden's question about the ducks is never answered in the novel, but Thomas Beller closes his July 22, 2001, *New York Times* article on "Holden's New York" with the answer given him by Henry J. Stern, Commissioner of Parks for New York, who gets several *Catcher*-inspired queries about the ducks every year. He gives this answer: "'The ducks generally go to the middle of the lake, which is the least likely to freeze. If that freezes over they have been seen in the Hudson and East rivers. Ducks travel much less than they used to. It's really much easier for the ducks than it was in 1951'"—the year *The Catcher in the Rye* was published (p. CY 8). In a more recent article, James Barron quotes Sara Cedar Miller: "I have no idea what J. D. Salinger was thinking. I've worked for the park for twenty-six years, and I've always seen ducks. I photographed them sitting on the ice" ("Taking a Walk through J. D. Salinger's New York," *New York Times*, January 20, 2010). The ducks are mentioned several times in the novel (see especially 13, 81–83, 153–54). Most scholars assume that Holden is concerned about who will take care of the ducks in the winter because he is worried about who will take care of *him* this winter when he is feeling so rootless, homeless, and directionless.

the Taft, the New Yorker "'Do you happen to know whose band's at the Taft or the New Yorker, by any chance?'" (60). The Taft Hotel is on Seventh Avenue between West 50th and 51th streets. The New Yorker Hotel is close to Penn Station, at Eighth Avenue and 34th Street.

Figure 18: This view of the lagoon, looking northeast, shows the ducks that Holden worries about. Where do they—where does he—go in the winter?

the Edmont "'Well—take me to the Edmont then'" (60). The
Edmont Hotel is a made-up name for a hotel, since none by
that name exists or existed in Manhattan. Because it is in
this hotel that Holden sees "perverts" and later encounters a
pimp and a prostitute, it is likely that Salinger did not want
to use the name of a real hotel. Holden does not specify
the street location of this fictional hotel, but it is apparently
not far from Central Park, perhaps one of the several hotels
around 53rd and 55th streets—a few blocks south of the
park. I have two reasons for this guess. First, because he
twice mentions the ducks in Central Park when he is in a
taxi going to or from the Edmont, the location may have
reminded him of the ducks in the nearby park. Second,
when he walks back from Ernie's nightclub (at an unspecified
location in Greenwich Village) to the Edmont, he says
he walked "[f]orty-one gorgeous blocks" (88). If Ernie's is
somewhere near the upper boundary of Greenwich Village
(14th Street), that would make 55th Street about right. If
Ernie's was further south in the Village, the Edmont would
likewise be further south. Of course, we are not meant to
know the exact location of either place.

B.M. "'B.M., where she went'" (63). B.M. is possibly an
abbreviation for the Bryn Mawr School, a girls' prep school
in Baltimore. See my reference to **B.M.** and to **Shipley** in
the explanatory notes to chapter 4, above.

Stanford Arms Hotel "Her name was Faith Cavendish, and
she lived at the Stanford Arms Hotel on Sixty-fifth and
Broadway" (63–64). There is no such hotel in Manhattan.
Since it houses a prostitute and is what Holden calls a
"dump, no doubt" (64), Salinger would not have wanted
to use the name of a real hotel. The name was perhaps
reminiscent of a pleasant hotel named the Pickwick Arms
on East 51st Street.

Chapter 10: Three witches from Seattle

After thinking about his sister Phoebe, Holden goes down to the Lavender Room, a nightclub off the lobby of the Edmont. Buddy Singer and his band are playing. Holden orders a Scotch and soda, but the waiter won't serve him alcohol without proof that he is twenty-one, so he orders a soft drink. He joins three tourist women from Seattle— Bernice, Marty, and Laverne—buys them drinks, and dances with them. He gets depressed when they tell him they are going to go to bed because they want to get up early in the morning to see the first show at Radio City Music Hall.

still pretty early "It was still pretty early. I'm not sure what time it was, but it wasn't too late" (66). Actually, it must be quite late. Holden, Ackley, and Brossard get back to the Pencey dorm from Agerstown "about a quarter to nine" (37). Holden finishes Stradlater's composition "around ten-thirty, I guess" (39). After his fight with Stradlater, Holden tries to get Ackley to play canasta "around eleven, eleven-thirty'" (47). After that he has to pack and, since it is too late to call a cab, walk into Agerstown to the train station, wait ten minutes for the next train, take it to Penn Station, take a cab clear up to 90th Street and back to the Edmont, where he checks in and finds his room. It must be at least two a.m. on Sunday morning, perhaps later. After his other adventures that night—dancing with the three women from Seattle, going to Ernie's in Greenwich Village, walking forty-one blocks back to the hotel, encountering Maurice and Sunny—it is not surprising that "it was getting daylight outside" (98).

crossing over Fifth Avenue "I watched her once from the window when she was crossing over Fifth Avenue to go to the park" (67). That sentence suggests that the Caulfields lived on or very near Fifth Avenue, or Holden would not have been able to see her from the window of their apartment. An apartment overlooking Central Park would have been very expensive indeed.

the Lavender Room "They had this night club, the Lavender Room, in the hotel" (66). The room, like the Edmont Hotel, is fictional, though of course some hotels did have night clubs.

Buddy Singer "The band was putrid. Buddy Singer. Very brassy, but not good brassy—corny brassy" (69). There was no such actual band in New York City.

The Baker's Wife "D.B. and I took her to see this French movie, *The Baker's Wife*, with Raimu in it" (67). This farcical comedy, directed by Marcel Pagnol (1939, see Figure 19), is about a middle-aged French baker whose lovely young wife flirts with and runs off with a handsome shepherd. Raimu is the chubby actor who plays the role of the kindly but naive baker. At first the baker refuses to believe what is obvious to others, that his much younger wife, bored with being the wife and bakery-assistant of an aging village baker, has been unfaithful to him. When the truth hits home, he becomes distraught and attempts to hang himself, but the other villagers, including the mayor, the village priest, and the school teacher, dismayed at the thought of losing the skills of the only baker in town, band together to bring the baker's wife back so that they can have fresh bread again. On the face of it, *The Baker's Wife* seems a strange movie to take a little girl like Phoebe to see. It is in no sense pornographic, but it is a talky film, in French with English subtitles, with little that would appeal to a child. The humor, such as the argument that the priest and the school teacher have about whether Joan of Arc actually heard or only thought she heard voices, would have gone over the heads even of precocious children like Phoebe. Holden tells us that she is "ten now" (68), which would have made her at most eight or nine when she saw the movie, at least a year earlier.

The 39 Steps "Her favorite is *The 39 Steps*, though, with Robert Donat. She knows the whole goddam movie by heart, because I've taken her to see it about ten times" (67). This 1935 mystery (see Figures 20–22), directed by Alfred Hitchcock, stars Robert Donat and Madeleine Carroll. It concerns an innocent man drawn into a plot that involves murder, spying, danger, pursuit, and of course romance.

Figure 19: From *The Baker's Wife* (Films Marcel Pagnol, 1939), starring Raimu as the baker and Ginette LeClerc as his unhappy wife. Holden tells us that young Phoebe loved it: "It killed her" (67). Courtesy Photofest.

Figure 2(: From Alfred Hitchcock's *The 39 Steps* (1935, re-released by Diamond Entertainment in 1995), starring Robert Donat, who is here handcuffed to Madeleine Carroll. This movie was one of Phoebe's (and Salinger's) favorites. Holden says that he had taken young Phoebe to see it often. Courtesy Photofest.

The scene in which the hero asks "Can you eat the herring?" comes near the start of the film when the handsome central character seeks lodging in a Scottish shepherd's cottage. The German spy who "sticks up his little finger with part of the middle joint missing" (68) is the mastermind villain of the

Figure 21: The scene outside the Scottish farmhouse in *The 39 Steps.* The farmer asks Robert Donat, "Can you eat the herring?" (67)—a favorite line of Phoebe's.

film. It is puzzling why Phoebe likes the film so much that she has memorized all "the talk," but it does take on a kind of campy tone, easily laughed at by those who have seen it before.

Salinger's daughter Margaret writes of the difficulty in being compared always to the fictional Phoebe and of the need she felt to be her father's "perfect Phoebe" (*Dream Catcher* 236–37). She remembers the time her father took

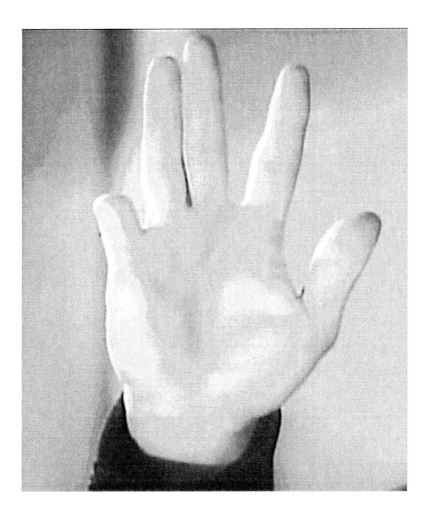

Figure 22: The scene in *The 39 Steps* where the German spy "sticks up his little finger with part of the middle joint missing" (68). At this point in the movie Phoebe would stick her little finger up in front of Holden's face in the dark.

her and her brother Matthew to Scotland to meet a teenaged girl he had been corresponding with: "We planned to drive through Scotland with her in search of where my father's beloved *39 Steps* was filmed." He was disappointed at the homeliness of his young pen pal, but as they drove through Scotland, he "was absolutely delighted by a flock of sheep in the road. That was how, in *The 39 Steps*, the hero and heroine were able to escape, handcuffed to each other, from their captor's car" (*Dream Catcher* 261–62).

three witches "I started giving the three witches at the next table the eye again" (70). By the term "witch" Holden probably just refers to their lack of beauty—"The whole three of them were pretty ugly" (69)—but he may have been thinking of the three witches in Shakespeare's *Macbeth* who stir up "toil and trouble" for Macbeth.

grools "The other two grools nearly had hysterics" (70). The word "grools" is apparently a slang neologism, made up of a combination of "girls" and "ghouls." Elsewhere in this chapter Holden refers to the three women from Seattle as "witches," "morons," "stupid girls," and "dopes."

some dancer "The blonde was some dancer. She was one of the best dancers I ever danced with" (70). Joyce Maynard reports that "Jerry is an expert ballroom dancer. As little as he's told me about his own teenage years, I know he attended dancing classes in his Upper West Side and (later) Park Avenue adolescence" (*At Home* 172). Holden's—and Salinger's—knowledge of dancing is revealed later when Holden dances with Phoebe: "She stays right with you. You can cross over, or do some corny dips, or even jitterbug a little, and she stays right with you. You can even tango, for God's sake" (175).

"Just One of Those Things" "Buddy Singer and his stinking band was playing 'Just One of Those Things' and even *they* couldn't

ruin it entirely" (71). The lyrics to this famous song were
written by Cole Porter. The first two stanzas run,

> It was just one of those things,
> Just one of those crazy flings,
> One of those bells that now and then rings,
> Just one of those things.
>
> It was just one of those nights,
> Just one of those fabulous flights,
> A trip to the moon on gossamer wings,
> Just one of those things.

Marco and Miranda "'[D]id you ever hear of Marco and
Miranda?'" (71). Marco and Miranda are apparently a dance
team—possibly Flamenco dancers—in the 1940s, not
otherwise identified. Their names, like that of Buddy Singer,
are apparently made up.

Peter Lorre "'I and my girl friends saw Peter Lorre last night,' she
said. 'The movie actor. In person. He was buyin' a newspaper.
He's *cute*'" (71). Peter Lorre (1904–1964), a Hungarian Jew
raised in Vienna, left Germany not long after Hitler rose
to power. He is most famous for playing sinister villains. In
his first film as a speaker of English, he played a terrorist in
Alfred Hitchcock's 1934 thriller *The Man Who Knew Too
Much*. He became an American citizen in 1941. See Figure
16 above for a photograph of him in a 1944 movie.

Seattle "'Seattle, Washington,' she said" (72). Seattle is about
as far as they can be from New York and still be from the
United States. One scholar, Robert P. Moore, thinks that the
woman is a "blonde pickup" who lies to him when Holden
asks where they are from. According to Moore, Holden sits
with the three women "naively believing that they are really
from Seattle, indignantly believing that they are going to
bed early so that they can get up and see the first show at
Radio City Music Hall, too youthfully obtuse to see what
they were and what they thought of him" ("The World of

Holden," *English Journal* 54 [1965]: 163). I see no reason to doubt that the three are the naive ones, and that they really have come across the country to New York hoping to see a movie star.

the Stork Club, El Morocco "They probably thought movie stars always hung out in the Lavender Room when they came to New York, instead of the Stork Club or El Morocco and all" (73). The famous Stork Club, on East 53rd Street, dating from the late 1920s, drew such celebrities as Joe DiMaggio, Marilyn Monroe, J. Edgar Hoover, Frank Sinatra, and even John and Jackie Kennedy. Joyce Maynard says that Salinger had once been "a young man about town in Manhattan, taking Eugene O'Neill's beautiful daughter, Oona, to places like the Stork Club" (*At Home* 172). El Morocco was a restaurant on East 54th Street known for its north African and Middle Eastern cuisine. In the 1940s and on through the early 1960s, El Morocco was famous for its jazz music.

Gary Cooper "So I told her I just saw Gary Cooper, the movie star, on the other side of the floor" (74). Gary Cooper (1901–1961), who acted in more than a hundred movies, won the best actor Academy Award for his role in *High Noon*—produced in 1951, the same year *The Catcher in the Rye* came out. Earlier, Gary Cooper had played the lead in two films based on Hemingway novels, *A Farewell to Arms* in 1932 (see Figure 23) and *For Whom the Bell Tolls* in 1943. Cooper was a close friend to Hemingway for twenty years, though it is probably a coincidence that Hemingway shot himself a month after Cooper's death.

Tom Collins "She and old Marty were drinking Tom Collinses— in the middle of December, for God's sake" (74). A Tom Collins is a sweetish summer thirst-quencher made with gin, sour mix, soda, and ice, garnished with an orange slice and a cherry, served in a tall glass. There are several theories

Figure 23: From the film adaptation of Hemingway's *A Farewell to Arms* (Paramount, 1932), starring Gary Cooper as Lt. Frederic Henry, the American ambulance driver, and Helen Hayes as Catherine Barkley, his nurse-lover. Courtesy Photofest.

about how it got its name. One is that it was invented by an Irish bartender named Tom Collins. Another is that it was made originally with "Old Tom Gin"—a brand name for a sweet gin. The point here is that the three Seattle women are pretty unsophisticated or they would not have ordered Tom Collinses in the winter time.

ice-cold hot licks "[S]he thought Buddy Singer's poor old beat-up clarinet player was really terrific when he stood up and took a couple of ice-cold hot licks" (74–75). In jazz terminology, a "hot lick" is an instrumental solo, probably improvised by the player. A "cold hot lick" is a solo by someone trying to sound good, but failing miserably—because of bad music, bad improvisation, or bad performance. Clearly, Holden is less impressed with the improvisation than Marty is.

licorice stick "She called his clarinet a 'licorice stick'" (75). A "licorice stick" is an old-fashioned slang term for a clarinet. Marty is trying to use "with it" jargon, but she is failing, at least in Holden's view.

Radio City Music Hall "They said they were going to get up early to see the first show at Radio City Music Hall" (75). Radio City has been a famous institution in New York since it was built in mid-town Manhattan (between 50th and 51st streets just east of Sixth Avenue). The twelve-acre complex known as Rockefeller Center was developed between 1929 and 1940 by John D. Rockefeller, Jr. One of the first tenants of the complex was the Radio Corporation of America (RCA), hence the name Radio City and Radio City Music Hall. Until the 1970s, it presented both a movie and a stage show as part of the same program. Holden seems more upset about the fact that the three Seattle tourists want to see "the first show"—he mentions it three times on this page—than that they imagine Radio City to be a purveyor of great movies. Perhaps the first show would have catered mostly to families with small children.

Chapter 11: Thinking of Jane Gallagher again

Holden goes back out to the lobby of the Edmont and sits down, thinking about Jane Gallagher and how he got to know her one summer in Maine, where his mother's summer place was next door to hers. He remembers Jane's dog and playing golf, tennis, and checkers with her. He never really necked with her, though they came close one rainy afternoon when her stepfather caused her to weep when she and Holden were playing checkers. Holden mostly just held her hand, though he remembers one "pretty" time when, in a movie, she put her hand on the back of his neck. When he starts thinking again about what she and Stradlater may have done in Ed Banky's car, he gets upset and decides to go down to Ernie's [C] in Greenwich Village.

Doberman pinscher "The way I met her, this Doberman pinscher she had used to come over and relieve himself on our lawn" (76). Originally bred to be a guard dog, the Doberman has energy and strength. It is usually not vicious, but it can be. For Jane to have a Doberman—or any brand-name dog— would have indicated, once again, a certain level of wealth.

the club "Then what happened, a couple of days later I saw Jane laying on her stomach next to the swimming pool, at the club" (76). The country club is further evidence of the privileged life Holden has led, with a series of expensive private schools and summers spent at exclusive country clubs in New England.

good golfer "I'm a very good golfer. If I told you what I go around in, you probably wouldn't believe me" (77). This passage about Holden's prowess as a golfer does not coordinate well with other things we know of his life as a sportsman. He is, after all, the manager of the fencing team, not a fencer, and he shows almost no interest in the football game against Saxon Hall. His interest in baseball is mostly confined to the poems on his brother's baseball mitt. More important, he

smashed his hand after Allie died, and so may be presumed
to have trouble gripping a golf club properly: "My hand
still hurts me once in a while, when it rains and all, and I
can't make a secure fist any more—not a tight one, I mean"
(39). If he can't make a tight fist, how successfully could
he grip a golf club? On the other hand, we find out that
Holden "started playing golf when I was only ten years old"
(38), so perhaps he has enough skill that he has learned to
compensate for an uncertain grip.

muckle-mouthed "She was sort of muckle-mouthed" (77).
Holden's description of Jane means that she has an
unconventionally large and expressive mouth. The reference
may be to the proverbial Scottish lass named "Muckle-
Mouthed Meg," who grinned widely when she was
introduced to her husband-to-be. "Muckle" (and its variant
"mickle") usually means "large." Holden's own description in
the next sentence suggests what he meant: "her mouth sort
of went in about fifty directions" (77).

LaSalle convertible "Jane used to drive to market with her mother
in this LaSalle convertible they had" (77–78). The LaSalle
was a pricey, upscale Buick, in prestige and cost just under
the Cadillac, which was also produced by General Motors.
For the Gallaghers to own such a car would have indicated
(along with references to private schools, to being a member
of the country club, to spending summer vacations in Maine
and on Cape Cod, and so on), that Jane Gallagher, like
Holden, comes from a wealthy family. The car was named
for a French explorer of America, René Robert Cavelier,
Sieur de LaSalle, or more simply, Robert de LaSalle.

newsreel "The newsreel was on or something, and all of a sudden
I felt this hand on the back of my neck" (79). Movies in the
1940s and 1950s, especially before the advent of television,
usually were preceded by short subjects, like a cartoon and a

"newsreel" clip showing film shots of current sports, military, or political events.

first base "I knew she wouldn't let him get to first base with her" (80). This baseball metaphor is well-known, though the interpretive details could vary. Getting to first base involved making out, probably including French kissing; getting to second base involved heavy petting; third base involved digital or oral sex; getting to home base or hitting a home run meant "going all the way," or having genital sex.

Ernie's "I went down in the elevator again and got a cab and told the driver to take me down to Ernie's" (80). Both the name of the night club and its namesake owner are fictional.

Greenwich Village "Ernie's is this night club in Greenwich Village that my brother D.B. used to go to quite frequently" (80). Greenwich Village is one of the oldest communities in lower Manhattan. It lies between Broadway on the east, the Hudson River on the west, Houston Street on the south, and 14th Street on the north. At its center is Washington Square. Its narrow and winding street layout was not altered to fit the square grid of most of the rest of the city. It is famous for its relatively recent reputation as a bohemian community with a culture of coffeehouses, night clubs, and literary, musical, artistic, and cultural innovation.

Chapter 12: Greenwich Village

Holden asks Horwitz, the taxi driver who takes him to Ernie's, if he knows what happens to the ducks when the lagoon in Central Park freezes over. Horwitz, who seems to get pretty defensive, answers that just as Mother Nature takes care of the fish when the lagoon freezes solid, so she takes care of the ducks. Ernie's is crowded, even so late, but Holden is given a tiny table behind a post. He observes Ernie showing off playing the piano, and he listens to the conversations of the couples around him. Lillian Simmons, his brother D.B.'s old girlfriend, invites him to join her and her Navy-guy date at their table, but Holden dislikes her and says he must meet someone. He leaves Ernie's, not sure what to do next.

frozen Daiquiris "I ordered a Scotch and soda, which is my favorite drink, next to frozen Daiquiris" (85). A Daiquiri is a cocktail typically made with rum, lime juice, and sugar, though other fruits can be used, like strawberries or pineapples pureed in a blender. Frozen Daiquiris are made either with crushed ice or with frozen fruit chunks, whipped until smooth in a blender. The Daiquiri is named for the village and iron mines of Daiquiri near Santiago, Cuba, where the cocktail probably originated around 1900.

Tattersall vest "On my right there was this very Joe Yale-looking guy, in a grey flannel suit and one of those flitty-looking Tattersall vests" (84). Tattersall refers to the fabric and the brightly colored cross-bar pattern, not to a brand name. The term "flit," of course, is Holden's term for gay or homosexual men.

Yale, Princeton "My father wants me to go to Yale, or maybe Princeton, but I swear I wouldn't go to one of those Ivy League colleges, if I was *dying*" (84). Holden mentions two of the most expensive and exclusive private universities in the country. Of course, there is irony in Holden's statement that he wouldn't go to either one, since by flunking out of Pencey Prep he has all but ruined his chances of being accepted. Salinger's daughter Margaret reports that her father had firm opinions about the whole notion of "getting into a good college" and that he once said that he would "'break out with a strange and hideous rash' at the mere mention of anything Ivy League" (*Dream Catcher* 35).

Chapter 13: Encounter with Sunny

Holden walks the forty-one blocks back to the Edmont [D], wishing he had the gloves that someone at Pencey had stolen. He wishes he had had the nerve to stand up to the thief, if he knew who it was, but he knows he is too yellow to punch him. At the hotel, the elevator boy Maurice offers to send him a prostitute for five dollars, and he accepts, insisting only that she be a young one. When Sunny comes in and takes her dress off, the nervous Holden suddenly decides that he is not interested in "doing it." He makes up a lame medical excuse and pays her the five dollars. Annoyed, she tells him that the cost is ten dollars, not five. He refuses to pay the extra five dollars. Sunny puts her dress back on and leaves.

five bucks "'Five bucks a throw. Fifteen bucks the whole night'" (91). Adjusted for inflation, five dollars would be at least $75 in 2010 dollars.

book "I read this book once, at the Whooton School, that had this very sophisticated, suave, sexy guy in it" (92–93). The supposed novel about a Casanova- or James Bond-type main character is apparently one Salinger made up. No novel matching the plot outline that follows, or that has a main character named Blanchard, has been identified. Of course, it may be that Holden, very tired and fairly drunk by now, misremembers a real novel he has read. The point, of course, is that Holden wishes he were more like the fictional Blanchard and wants to be more "sophisticated, suave, sexy" than he is. His plan to become more confident in his dealings with women by hiring a prostitute, of course, fails miserably.

château, Riviera "He had this big château and all on the Riviera, in Europe" (93). A château is a castle or country estate-house. The Riviera is a coastal resort area along the

Mediterranean Sea in southern France and northwestern Italy.

like a violin "He said, in this one part, that a woman's body is like a violin and all, and it takes a terrific musician to play it right" (93). The general similarity of the hourglass shape of a violin to the physical shape of a young woman, with the violin bow being the phallic instrument that can "play it right," is both commonplace and sexist.

polo coat "She had a polo coat on, and no hat" (93). Sunny is wearing a loose-fitting overcoat, probably with a belt, and probably of camel's hair or a similar material.

Sunny "'Sunny,' she said" (95). It is interesting that for much of his youth Salinger was called "Sonny" at home. In selecting a homonym of his own childhood name for a Hollywood prostitute, might Salinger have been thinking of his own recent bad experience in selling the movie rights to "Uncle Wiggily in Connecticut" to a Hollywood film maker?

Hollywood "'Hollywood,' she said" (95). If Sunny is telling the truth, we are perhaps to imagine that she came to New York to pursue a career in acting, but is having trouble getting started. She would, in any case, along with D.B., be another Hollywood prostitute.

clavichord "'On my wuddayacallit—my clavichord'" (96). Perhaps caught up in the image of the violin, Holden here confuses medical and musical terminology. He means, of course, his clavicle, a bone in the upper chest, often known as the collar bone. A clavichord is a small, portable, piano-like early keyboard instrument having strings struck by tangents attached directly to the key ends.

a guy in the movies "'You look like a guy in the movies. You know. Whosis'" (97). Sunny's reference here is to the 1937 film *Captains Courageous*, starring Spencer Tracy as Manuel, a

Portuguese fisherman who befriends and helps to educate a young spoiled brat who falls off an ocean liner. For discussion of the film and a still from the movie showing young Harvey (Figure 4), see above in my introductory essay, the section on **Holden Caulfield's appearance.**

The film version of *Captains Courageous* bears a number of suggestive parallels with *The Catcher in the Rye:* a smart but very spoiled rich kid is expelled from an expensive private boys school in New York; he has trouble getting along with some of his classmates; his father has a meeting with a principal and a teacher about what to do about the lad; he has issues with his neglectful father; he has growing-up and manhood issues; he finds a mentor (Manuel, vaguely parallel to Antolini?); he heads west at the end. Since young Harvey Cheyne is indeed young in the movie—merely ten years old—Sunny apparently thinks of Holden as immature, perhaps because he is so nervously inexperienced about women and sexual performance. Are we to see a parallel between Holden's fake "limping like a bastard" (158) and young Harvey's faking a limp when he lies to his father about an incident at school?

It is interesting that the film writer introduced sweeping changes when he adapted Kipling's 1897 novel to the movies. There is no solid evidence that Salinger had read *Captains Courageous*, but it is possible. If he had, that might explain some of the ways his own novel is closer to the novel than to the film. In the novel, Harvey Cheyne is fifteen, almost Holden's age, not ten as in the film. Harvey is being sent alone on the ship to an exclusive British private school, not so different from Holden's Pencey Prep, rather than accompanying his father on a business trip as in the film. Harvey's mother, like Holden's, is still alive, not dead as in the film. And Harvey in the novel version even wears "a red flannel hat on the back of his head" (New York; Signet

Classic, 1964, p. 8). But there are lots of differences between the novel and the film version of *Captains Courageous* that do not support a connection with Salinger's novel. For example, Harvey in the novel is sick from smoking a cigar when he falls off the ship, whereas in the movie he is sick from drinking six ice cream sodas. The captain's son Dan (played by Mickey Rooney) has a much more important role in novel than in the film, and the Portuguese fisherman Manuel (played by Spencer Tracy) has a much more important role in the film than in the novel. In the novel Manuel does not die but goes off to see a young woman, whereas in the film he dies in a storm at sea in front of Harvey's grieving eyes.

Chapter 14: Encounter with Maurice

Unable to sleep, Holden sits and smokes until he hears a loud knock on the door. It is Maurice and Sunny, there to collect the extra five dollars they say Holden owes them. He feels silly confronting them in his pajamas, but he refuses to give them the money. Maurice threatens to get rough, but Sunny tells him to leave Holden alone and takes the five dollars out of Holden's wallet. When Holden insults Maurice, Maurice punches him in the stomach and leaves with Sunny. Holden gets up and staggers into the bathroom, imagining himself the tough-guy hero of a movie, with Jane Gallagher coming to help him recover from his bullet wound—or perhaps to ease his dying moments. He fantasizes shooting Maurice six times in his fat belly, then takes a bath, goes to bed, and finally falls asleep.

Lake Sedebego "Bobby and I were going over to Lake Sedebego on our bikes" (98). There is no such lake in Maine, though there is in southern Maine a Sebago Lake, known for its land-locked salmon. Sebago Lake has several camping areas and recreational facilities.

pray "I can't always pray when I feel like it" (99). This line
is reminiscent of Huck Finn's famous line when his
"conscience" tells him to turn Jim in: "You can't pray a lie—
I found that out" (p. 241 in the Ballantine Ivy Book edition,
1996). Holden says, a little later, "I couldn't pray worth a
damn" (100).

Disciples "Take the Disciples, for instance. They annoy the hell
out of me" (99). A disciple is a pupil or devoted follower, but
Holden is here referring to the original twelve men whom
Jesus selected as his core followers, men he particularly
wanted to help him spread his word: Simon, Andrew, James,
John, Philip, Nathaniel (also called Bartholomew), Matthew,
Thomas, James (son of Alpheus), Simon the Zealot, Judas
(son of James), and Judas Iscariot.

that lunatic "If you want to know the truth, the guy I like best in
the Bible, next to Jesus, was that lunatic and all, that lived in
the tombs and kept cutting himself with stones" (99). In the
King James version of Mark 5:1–20 we read:

> 1 And they came over unto the other side of the sea, into
> the country of the Gadarenes.
>
> 2 And when he [Jesus] was come out of the ship,
> immediately there met him out of the tombs a man with an
> unclean spirit,
>
> 3 Who had his dwelling among the tombs; and no man
> could bind him, no, not with chains:
>
> 4 Because that he had been often bound with fetters and
> chains, and the chains had been plucked asunder by him, and
> the fetters broken in pieces: neither could any man tame him.
>
> 5 And always, night and day, he was in the mountains,
> and in the tombs, crying, and cutting himself with stones.
>
> 6 But when he saw Jesus afar off, he ran and worshiped
> him,
>
> 7 And cried with a loud voice, and said, What have I to
> do with thee, Jesus, thou Son of the most high God? I adjure
> thee by God, that thou torment me not.

8 For he [Jesus] said unto him, Come out of the man, thou unclean spirit.

9 And he asked him, What is thy name? And he answered, saying, My name is Legion: for we are many.

10 And he besought him much that he would not send them away out of the country.

11 Now there was there nigh unto the mountains a great herd of swine feeding.

12 And all the devils besought him, saying, Send us into the swine, that we may enter into them.

13 And forthwith Jesus gave them leave. And the unclean spirits went out, and entered into the swine: and the herd ran violently down a steep place into the sea (they were about two thousand), and were choked in the sea.

14 And they that fed the swine fled, and told it in the city, and in the country. And they went out to see what it was that was done.

15 And they come to Jesus, and see him that was possessed with the devil, and had the legion, sitting, and clothed, and in his right mind: and they were afraid.

16 And they that saw it told them how it befell to him that was possessed with the devil, and also concerning the swine.

17 And they began to pray him to depart out of their coasts.

18 And when he was come into the ship, he that had been possessed with the devil prayed him that he might be with him.

19 Howbeit Jesus suffered him not, but saith unto him, Go home to thy friends, and tell them how great things the Lord hath done for thee, and hath had compassion on thee.

20 And he departed, and began to publish in Decapolis how great things Jesus had done for him: and all men did marvel.

Perhaps the most important verses are numbers 2–5, where Jesus encounters the man Holden calls "that lunatic and all" who is possessed by diabolical spirits; number 13, where

Jesus sends the evil spirits into a large herd of swine who then destroy themselves in the sea; and numbers 19–20, where Jesus shows compassion to the purged madman and sends him home. Holden may see himself as a lunatic who lives in the tomb of his brother Allie, and who needs to have himself purged of evil spirits and sent home—as perhaps he is at the end of the novel after his time in the sanitarium. It is interesting that Holden thinks of this man as a positive contrast with the twelve disciples, who annoyed him because Jesus picked them "at *random*" (99). The cured lunatic, on the other hand, had earned the right to be a disciple and spread the word of Jesus' good deeds because, having suffered and been specifically cured by Jesus, he was a more authentic disciple. For slightly different versions of this story, but not as close as the one in Mark, see also Luke 8:26–39 and Matthew 8:28–33.

Not many critics have discussed the possible relevance of this passage, but James Lundquist thinks that "Holden is the lunatic in the tombs. [. . .] Like the lunatic, he is possessed not by one demon, but many [. . .] the demon of fate and death, the demon of emptiness and meaninglessness, the demon of guilt and condemnation, the demon of despair, the demon of jealousy. The casting forth of these evil spirits is what his story ultimately comes down to" (*J. D. Salinger* [New York: Ungar, 1979], p. 42).

Quaker "Old Childs was a Quaker and all" (99). Quakers, or members of the Society of Friends, are a Christian sect known for their simplicity, their devoutness, and their pacifism. In the purest form, a Quaker service (known as a "silent meeting for worship") has no minister and no hymns. Instead, members of the congregation, if they feel moved to do so, sometimes speak out briefly to the gathered worshipers.

Judas "I said I'd bet a thousand bucks that Jesus never sent Judas to Hell" (100). Judas Iscariot carried the disciples' money box. He betrayed Jesus for a bribe of thirty pieces of silver by identifying him to the Roman soldiers with a kiss—the "kiss of Judas." After Jesus was arrested, the guilt-ridden Judas returned the bribe and comitted suicide.

different religions "In the first place, my parents are different religions, and all the children in our family are atheists" (100). We learn in the next chapter that Holden's father had once been a Catholic. The implication is that the "different religions" are Christianity and Judaism, but Holden never quite tells us that. Salinger's daughter Margaret reports that her aunt Doris, "Sonny" Salinger's older sister, had told her that she and her brother had grown up thinking that they were Jews:

> When Doris was nearly twenty, shortly after Sonny's bar mitzvah, their parents told them that they weren't really Jewish. Their mother, Miriam, was actually named Marie, and she had been "passing" as a Jew since her marriage to Sol.
>
> Until that moment, I never knew that my father grew to adolescence believing both of his parents were Jews. He has often told me that he writes about half-Jews because, he says, that's what he knows best. (*Dream Catcher* 20)

Some scholars have assumed, with no clear evidence, that Holden is a "WASP" or White Anglo-Saxon Protestant. See, for example, Mary Suzanne Schriber's "Holden Caulfield, C'est Moi," in *Critical Essays on Salinger's The Catcher in the Rye*, ed. Joel Salzberg (Boston: G. K. Hall, 1990), pp. 227, 233. That reading assumes that the different approaches to Christianity are "different religions" rather than just different sects or branches of the same religion.

movies "The goddam movies. They can ruin you" (104). The tough-guy hero he pretends to be does not seem to reflect the exact plot of any specific movie, but it seems that Holden has seen some westerns or perhaps some Humphrey Bogart films. John Seelye, in "Holden in the Museum" in Jack Salzman, ed., *New Essays on* The Catcher in the Rye (Cambridge: Cambridge University Press, 1991), pp. 23–33, writes in general terms about Salinger's possible allusions to Bogart films.

Holden wanders Manhattan (chapters 15-20)

Chapter 15: Breakfast with two nuns

Holden is hungry when he wakes up. He calls Sally Hayes and makes a date to take her to a matinee later that day. Then he leaves the Edmont and takes a cab to Grand Central Station [E], locks his suitcases in a luggage depository there, and goes into a sandwich bar for breakfast. He strikes up a conversation with two nuns and talks about Romeo and Juliet *with one of them. Just as he is embarrassed that his suitcases are more expensive than those of a friend, so he is embarrassed to have eaten eggs when the nuns have only toast and coffee. He makes a ten-dollar contribution to their cause, glad that they have not asked whether he is a Catholic.*

Mary A. Woodruff "I gave old Sally Hayes a buzz. She went to Mary A. Woodruff, and I knew she was home" (105). There is no actual Mary A. Woodruff School, but it is clearly a private school. In Salinger's earlier story, "Slight Rebellion Off Madison" in the *New Yorker*, for December 1946, we find it referred to on p. 82 as "the Mary A. Woodruff School for Girls ('Special Attention to Those Interested in Dramatics')."

Biltmore "I told her to meet me under the clock at the Biltmore at two o'clock" (106). The Biltmore, on Madison Avenue between 43rd and 44th streets, was an elegant landmark and an easily recognized place to meet. When it was gutted in 1981 and renovated as the Bank of America Plaza Building, the old clock was repositioned in the lobby.

Grand Central Station "I told the driver to take me to Grand Central Station" (107). This large train terminal is between 42nd and 44th streets on Vanderbilt Avenue. Holden goes back later to retrieve his bags (194).

lawyer "He's a corporation lawyer. Those boys really haul it in" (107). Salinger's own father, Sol Salinger, was an importer of meats and cheeses from Europe, but he also "hauled it in."

H. V. Caulfield "It isn't much, but you get quite a lot of vitamins in the malted milk. H. V. Caulfield. Holden Vitamin Caulfield" (107–08). We never learn what the V. actually stands for, or even if that is Holden's true middle initial. On p. 82 of Salinger's story "Slight Rebellion Off Madison," he is referred to as "Holden Morrisey Caulfield." Although the middle name "Vitamin" is a joke, Salinger is known to have been deeply—almost fanatically—interested in nutrition. Joyce Maynard talks at some length in *At Home in the World* about "Jerry's" ideas concerning foods, cooking, and homeopathic medicine. See, for example, pages 110–11, 136–38, 173–75.

Mark Cross "Mine came from Mark Cross, and they were genuine cowhide and all that crap" (108). The Mark Cross company was a seller of upscale leather suitcases, briefcases, and handbags. It is not clear whether the suitcases Holden had at Elkton Hills are the same Gladstones he had referred to earlier (51–54).

bourgeois "He kept saying they were too new and bourgeois" (108). To be bourgeois, at least in this context, was to be ostentatiously middle or mercantile class, demonstrating petty or materialistic values. It suggested the crassness of lower-class people wanting to appear upper-class. Several Marxist critics focus on this long paragraph as a critique of capitalism and the damaging pretensions of the wealthy classes. Carl Freedman, for example, sees this paragraph as showing that "Holden, while perched near the top of capitalist America's class hierarchy, is nonetheless capable of understanding how much misery class relations cause" ("Memories of Holden Caulfield—and of Miss Greenwood," *Southern Review* 39 [2003]: 416).

Beowulf, and old Grendel, and Lord Randal My Son "Well, most of the time we were on the Anglo-Saxons. Beowulf, and old Grendel, and Lord Randal My Son, and all those things" (110). These are standard British literature anthology pieces. In the ninth-century epic *Beowulf*, the monster Grendel fights the hero Beowulf. *Lord Randal* is a ballad of much later date—probably seventeenth century—about a young man who gradually reveals to his mother that he has been poisoned. The last two of the twenty lines in the ballad are,

> Oh yes, I am poisoned. Mother, make my bed soon,
> For I'm sick at the heart, and I fain wald lie down.

Romeo and Juliet* and *Julius Caesar "I read [. . .] *Romeo and Juliet* and *Julius*—" (110–11). These are two tragedies by William Shakespeare. The first is the story of two young star-crossed lovers. *Julius Caesar* is a play about a Roman leader whose lust for power is his undoing.

Mercutio "I mean I felt much sorrier when old Mercutio got killed" (111). Mercutio is connected to the Montague clan. When the lovesick Romeo declines to fight the Capulet hothead Tybalt, Mercutio challenges Tybalt himself. When Romeo impulsively interrupts the sword fight, Tybalt takes advantage and kills Mercutio. Mercutio, then, is another good man whose death, like that of Allie and James Castle, troubles Holden.

Irish "[M]y last name is Irish" (112). The Caulfield family was probably among the English Protestant families sent as homesteaders to Ireland in the seventeenth century to settle on lands seized by Queen Elizabeth, but many of them would eventually have become Catholics. We may probably assume that Allie's and Phoebe's red hair comes through their Irish father.

Catholic "As a matter of fact, my father was a Catholic once. He quit, though, when he married my mother" (112). Holden never tells us what his mother's religious orientation was. Salinger's own mother, Marie, was a Catholic, but gave Catholicism up, became a practicing Jew, and took the name Miriam when she married Sol Salinger, a Polish Jew. Margaret Salinger speculates about why her father would reverse the situation in his novel: "Reading my father's work recently, I wondered, Why the disguise? Why would the central character of his first book, which he had told friends would be an 'autobiographical novel,' not be half-Jewish?" She notes that Salinger's sister Doris had told her that "I think he suffered terribly from anti-Semitism when he went away to military school" (*Dream Catcher* 24). It does not appear that religion was a major issue in J. D. Salinger's upbringing. He became interested in Zen Buddhism as an adult.

Forest Hills "He told me he went to the Nationals at Forest Hills every summer, and I told him I did too" (112). Holden refers here to the West Side Tennis Club, which has hosted many U.S. Open tennis championships. The West Side Complex, on fourteen acres on Long Island, is just twenty minutes from midtown Manhattan. It is referred to again as the club where Holden played tennis with the Antolinis (180–81).

smoke in their face "I blew some smoke in their face" (113). For a man to blow cigarette smoke into a woman's face was sometimes seen as a seductive signal meaning anything from "Hey, I like you" to "Hey, I'd like to sleep with you." Even to hint at such a message to two nuns would have been especially embarrassing to Holden. There was in the 1930s a Camel cigarette ad in which a pretty woman says, "Blow some in my direction."

Chapter 16: Remembering the Museum of Natural History

Having a couple of hours to kill before the play starts, Holden walks over to Broadway [**F**]. *At a music store he buys a record of "Little Shirley Beans" to give to Phoebe, and then watches a little boy walking in the street near the curb singing "If a body catch a body coming through the rye." He buys two theater tickets to* I Know My Love, *thinking about how much he hates actors. He takes a cab up to Central Park* [**G**] *to try to find Phoebe and give her the record. When he doesn't find her, he reminisces about the Museum of Natural History* [**H**], *which he likes because nothing changes there. He starts to go into the museum, then suddenly changes his mind and takes a cab down to the Biltmore to meet Sally Hayes.*

"Little Shirley Beans" "There was this record I wanted to get for Phoebe, called 'Little Shirley Beans'" (114). No record or song by that name has been identified or located. Holden is unusually specific about it, reporting the contents of the song ("about a little kid that wouldn't go out of the house because her two front teeth were out"), the date of the record ("about twenty years ago"), and the way Estelle Fletcher (see next item) sang it ("very Dixieland and whorehouse"). All such details are fictional, made up either by Holden or by Salinger for Holden. The record is mentioned again when Holden buys it (116) and when he breaks it in Central Park (154). A psychoanalytic scholar named James Bryan, analyzing the attraction Holden feels for his sister Phoebe, has speculated on the possible significance of the record and Holden's smashing it:

> One wonders if the accident wasn't psychically determined. If the Shirley Beans affair were a subject of dream analysis, the missing teeth, the shame, and the translation through "whorehouse" jazz by a singer who "knew what the hell she was doing" would conventionally suggest the loss of virginity. ("The Psychological Structure of *The Catcher in the Rye*," *PMLA* 89 [1974]: 1070)

It may be relevant that a song written by Donald Gardner in 1944 and recorded by Spike Jones and His City Slickers in 1948 became very popular in 1949, the year *The Catcher in the Rye* is set. The most famous lines of the song—usually sung with a lisp for the s-sounds—are

> All I want for Christmas is my two front teeth,
> My two front teeth, see my two front teeth.
> Gee, if I could only have my two front teeth,
> Then I could wish you "Merry Christmas."

Estelle Fletcher "It was a very old, terrific record that this colored singer, Estelle Fletcher, made" (114). There is no record of such a singer, but it is possible to speculate that Salinger selected that name as one that would make readers think of Ella Fitzgerald (1917–1996), the famous African-American jazz artist. Note that the two singers share the initials "E. F."

Dixieland "She sings it very Dixieland" (114–15). Dixieland jazz is usually associated with New Orleans and a kind of improvisation known as the blues. Although Dixieland originated in Louisiana, it quickly spread to Memphis, St. Louis, Texas, Detroit, San Francisco, and so on.

"If a body catch a body" "He was singing that song, 'If a body catch a body coming through the rye'" (115). The lines are a misremembered segment of a famous poem by the Scottish writer Robert Burns (1757–1796). The little boy walking along the curb on Fifth Avenue mistakes "meet" for "catch." Holden does not seem to recognize the error, though later Phoebe points it out to him (173). The boy is singing a modernized version where the Scottish "gin" is translated "if." Here are the first two stanzas of five in Burns's original dialect, along with the chorus, meant to be repeated after each stanza ("a'" is here a contraction for "all"):

> O, Jenny's a' weet, poor body,
> Jenny's seldom dry:
> She draigl't a' her petticoatie,
> Comin thro' the rye!
>
>   Chorus:
>   Comin thro' the rye, poor body,
>   Comin thro' the rye,
>   She draigl't a' her petticoatie,
>   Comin thro' the rye!
>
> Gin a body meet a body
> Comin thro' the rye,
> Gin a body kiss a body,
> Need a body cry?

Peter Shaw speculates on why Holden replaces "meet" with "catch":

> The phrase "meet a body" conjures up not only a meeting between a lad and a lass, but because of the suggestiveness of "body" [. . .], the phrase implies the coming together of male and female bodies. The next line of the song—"If a body kiss a body, need a body cry"—makes explicit the romantic/sexual context of the first. This is why Holden catches only the one line, and that one imperfectly. Unconsciously suppressing the word "meet," he avoids the very matter of his relations with girls, which he has been unable to resolve. ("Love and Death

in *The Catcher in the Rye*," in Jack Salzman, ed., *New Essays on* The Catcher in the Rye [Cambridge: Cambridge University Press, 1991], pp. 104–05)

Paramount, Astor, Strand, Capitol "Everybody was on their way to the movies—the Paramount or the Astor or the Strand or the Capitol or one of those crazy places" (115). The four theaters Holden lists were all in the theater district centered around Broadway and Times Square. Several of them have since been demolished.

I Know My Love "So what I did was, I went over and bought two orchestra seats for *I Know My Love*. It was a benefit performance or something" (116). S. N. Behrman's play, copyrighted 1949, played at the Shubert Theater (on 44th Street just west of Broadway) starting November 2, 1949, and ending, after 247 performances, on June 3, 1950. It starred the famous acting couple Alfred Lunt (1892–1977) and Lynn Fontanne (1887–1983) in their twenty-first play together. Interestingly, in Salinger's "Slight Rebellion Off Madison" (*New Yorker*, December 21, 1946), the play to which Holden takes Sally Hayes is *O Mistress Mine*, also originally starring the Lunts. That play had a longer run (452 performances) starting January 23, 1946. Salinger redid some of the incidents from that story for *The Catcher in the Rye*. He apparently felt the need to update the play referred to, while still keeping the same lead actors. In any case, the specific mention of *I Know My Love* tells us that the events of the novel probably take place in late December, 1949. For the plot of the play see Holden's summary of it on pp. 125–26 of the novel, and my note to those pages.

An interesting side note is that the author of *I Know My Love*, S. N. Behrman, published in the *New Yorker*, vol. 27, for August 11, 1951, pp. 64–68, a highly favorable review of Salinger's novel. Entitled "The Vision of the

Innocent," the review refers to *The Catcher in the Rye* as a "brilliant, funny, meaningful novel" (p. 64). Behrman makes no direct reference to Salinger's mention of the play that Holden and Sally see, but he does refer to Holden's "expedition" through mid-town New York with Sally Hayes, which included *I Know My Love*, as "one of the funniest expeditions, surely, in the history of juvenlilia" (pp. 67-68).

spoils it "[I]f any actor's really good, you can always tells he knows he's good, and that spoils it" (117). Joyce Maynard reports a conversation in which Salinger had told her his view of Olivier in *Hamlet*: "'He's brilliant, of course,' Jerry tells me. 'Still, when you're watching him, you can't helping being aware of how brilliant he is. Something rotten about it'" (*At Home* 93).

Hamlet "You take Sir Laurence Olivier, for example. I saw him last year in *Hamlet*" (117). The reference here is of course not to the Shakespeare play, a stage production, but to the film version (see Figure 24). Holden's two specific references make that certain. The first is the scene early in the movie where Ophelia (played by Jean Simmons) jokes with her brother Laertes while their pompous father Polonius gives him a parting sermon of fatherly advice (see Figure 25). It is perhaps the only bit of humor in an otherwise dour tragedy, with the possible exception of the gravedigger's grim humor in the Yorik scene. The second is the very brief bit of a scene in the movie—the only bit that Phoebe liked—in which Hamlet, while talking to the troop of actors, pats on the head their dog walking on its hind legs (see Figure 26). It is perhaps the only scene where Hamlet does a spontaneously human act. Neither of those actions was scripted in the play, but were specific to this film version, which came out in 1948—a year that jibes well with the "last year" reference if the "present" is December 1949. By the end of the film,

Figure 24: From the 1948 film version of Shakespeare's *Hamlet*, directed by and starring Sir Laurence Olivier in the title role. It may be a pose like this that led Holden to say of him that Olivier's Hamlet "was too much like a goddam general, instead of a sad, screwed-up type guy" (117). Courtesy Photofest.

all of the principles are dead: the king, the queen, Polonius, Ophelia, Laertes, and Hamlet. The film version, which announces itself in the opening frames as "the tragedy of a man who couldn't make up his mind," won several Academy Awards for 1948, including best picture and best actor. One scholar finds it "suggestive" of Holden's sexual attraction to Phoebe that Holden particularly enjoys and remembers this

Figure 25: From Olivier's 1948 *Hamlet*, showing Ophelia, played by Jean Simmons, "horsing around" with her brother Laertes, played by Terence Morgan, while their father Polonius, played by Felix Aylmer, lectures him. Holden liked this scene: "I got a big bang out of that" (117).

Figure 26: Also from Olivier's 1948 *Hamlet*, showing Hamlet patting the head of a dog before talking with the actors. This is the only part of the movie Phoebe liked: "She thought that was funny and nice, and it was" (117).

Ophelia-Laertes scene (see James Bryan, "The Psychological Structure of *The Catcher in the Rye*," *PMLA* 89 [1974]: 1070).

the Mall "I kept walking over to the Mall anyway, because that's where Phoebe usually goes when she's in the park" (118). The Mall, a wide walkway promenade in the south-central part of Central Park, is the most popular gathering place in the park. In pleasant weather it is teeming with New York residents and tourists.

bandstand "She likes to skate near the bandstand" (118). Holden refers to the Naumburg Bandshell on the eastern edge of the Mall. Skaters are often seen on the lake just to the west of the bandshell.

Seventy-first Street "'Phoebe Caulfield. She lives on Seventy-first Street'" (118). We learned earlier that Holden had "watched her once from the window when she was crossing over Fifth Avenue to go to the park" (67), and we learn later that she lives east of the park. We can assume then, that Holden and Phoebe live on or near the corner of Fifth Avenue and East 71st Street in an apartment overlooking the park. That corner, a dozen or so blocks up from the lower end of Central Park, was in one of New York's most desirable and expensive residential locations.

Museum of Natural History "I walked all the way through the park over to the Museum of Natural History" (119). This famous museum is contiguous to the park, just across Central Park West between 77th and 81st streets. Some of the exhibits that Holden mentions were still there in 2006. Although Holden does not go into the museum this time, he has many memories of what it was like when he visited it with school groups (see Figure 27).

war canoe "Then you'd pass by this long, long Indian war canoe" (120). What he calls a war canoe was actually a Haidu canoe from the Northwest, used, according to the description on the display, to take the Indians to a potlatch, not a war engagement (see Figure 28).

three goddam Cadillacs "[A]bout as long as three goddam Cadillacs in a row, with about twenty Indians in it" (120). The Cadillac was at the time *the* prestige car in America. It was manufactured by General Motors and was famous

Figure 27: Photograph of the 77th Street entrance to the American Museum of Natural History, taken in 1976. Courtesy American Museum of Natural History.

for its size, comfort, sleek styling, and expense. To own a Cadillac was to have arrived financially. This prestige car is referred to again later: "'It's full of phonies, and all you do is study so that you can learn enough to be smart enough to be able to buy a goddam Cadillac some day'" (131). In fact, the canoe he refers to is around seventy feet long—actually a bit longer than three Cadillacs end to end—and it had only a dozen Indians in it.

Figure 28: Photograph of the large Haidu canoe, taken in 1910. Holden mistakenly remembers it as a war canoe. Courtesy American Museum of Natural History.

a squaw "Then you'd pass by this big glass case, with Indians inside it rubbing sticks together to make a fire, and a squaw weaving a blanket" (121). The big glass case is, of course, a diorama. In the actual diorama, the "blanket" is more likely a reed mat than a blanket (see Figure 29). Another section

Figure 29: Diorama of an Indian woman weaving a mat, with her hanging papoose-cradle in foreground. Photo taken in 1916. Courtesy American Museum of Natural History.

of this diorama shows the Indian woman to whom Holden calls special attention (see Figure 30).

Figure 30: Close-up of the woman Holden calls a "squaw [. . .] sort of bending over and you could see her bosom and all. We all used to sneak a good look at it" (121). Photo taken in 2006. Courtesy American Museum of Natural History.

this Eskimo "[Y]ou passed this Eskimo. He was sitting over a hole in this icy lake" (121). There was such a diorama, and the fish he has already caught were visible (see Figure 31).

Figure 31: Diorama of the ice-fishing Eskimo, photographed in 1929, with the fish he has caught beside the hole. Courtesy American Museum of Natural History.

deer "Boy, that museum was full of glass cases. There were even more upstairs, with deer inside them drinking at water holes" (121). Holden does not mention snow in connection with the deer in the glass case, but he apparently refers to the winter-scene diorama that was in 2006 still on display at the American Museum of Natural History (see Figure 32).

Figure 32: Photograph of the diorama of three deer, taken in 2006. Holden remembers the deer "drinking out of that water hole, with their pretty antlers and their pretty, skinny legs" (121). Courtesy American Museum of Natural History.

birds "[A]nd birds flying south for the winter" (121). That particular diorama has been dismantled, but a photo is available in the Museum archives (see Figure 33).

Figure 33: Photograph of the case showing birds in flight, taken in 1949, not long after Holden would have seen it. Courtesy American Museum of Natural History.

Chapter 17: A date with Sally Hayes

Holden waits in the lobby of the Biltmore [I] *and watches the pretty girls. He feels sorry that they will someday marry "dopey guys." When Sally comes they set off for the play, "horsing around" in the taxi on the way. In the theater* [J] *they watch the Lunts in* I Know My Love. *During the intermission they talk with George, an Andover guy who annoys Holden. After the play Sally wants to go to Radio City ice rink* [K] *to skate. They go, but neither is any good at it. They have a soft drink in the bar there. Holden rants for a while about how much he hates school and just about everything else in his life, and asks her if she will run off with him and get married and live in the woods beside a brook somewhere in rural New England. When she questions that plan he tells her that she gives him "a royal pain in the ass," then leaves the skating rink bar without her.*

"Tin Roof Blues" "He could take something very jazzy, like 'Tin Roof Blues,' and whistle it so nice and easy" (124). The instrumental song "Tin Roof Blues" was written by members of a group called the New Orleans Rhythm Kings, who recorded it in 1923.

Saturday Evening Post "All that crap they have in cartoons in the *Saturday Evening Post* and all" (124–25). A weekly magazine, the *Saturday Evening Post* was probably the most popular weekly in the United States until the 1950s. It published cartoons, fiction, travel articles, personality profiles, and so on. When television became popular the *Post* started to fade. It was closed down in the late 1960s, then was reconstituted under new management as a bimonthly devoted largely to medical issues and nostalgia.

five hundred thousand years "It was about five hundred thousand years in the life of this one old couple" (125).

Holden is referring to the play *I Know My Love*, and of course he exaggerates, since it covers only slightly more than fifty years in the lives of Thomas and Emily Chanler (played by Alfred Lunt and his wife Lynn Fontanne). It opens in 1888 before they marry against the wishes of the bride's father, then moves to 1902, then 1918, then 1920, and finally to the couple's golden wedding anniversary in 1939. It has a large cast—over twenty—and there is, as Holden says, a lot of coming and going out of the living room that is the setting for all five scenes. The changing age of the Chanlers is indicated by changes in dress, makeup, and hair color. Theirs has been a satisfying but at times trying marriage, as Emily struggles to keep together a relationship strained by her husband's womanizing. They have lots of money and servants to ease the pain.

Several features of the play might have interested Holden. Most obviously, Holden might well have identified with Richard Chanler, younger brother to Thomas Chanler, the male protagonist of the play. Richard appears only in the second scene of the first act, where we learn that he has, though brilliant, behaved in such a way that he is expelled from Harvard. He has an unrealistic and idealistic plan to run off to Italy to become an artist. His older brother thinks he lacks discipline and wonders why he doesn't grow up. The scene ends with Richard, helplessly thwarted by unrequited love, committing suicide by throwing himself under the hoofs of a passing team of horses. Other bits might have interested Holden, as well, such as the pre-Christmas setting of the first act where one of the characters is trimming the tree, two references to crushed hands, and the handsome cad Felix sneaking off to Hollywood to become an actor. An interesting side note is that the part of Nicola, the rebellious granddaughter of the Chanlers, was played by an actress named Betty Caulfield in that 1949 production.

Andover "His name was George something—I don't even remember—and he went to Andover" (127). Founded in 1778, Phillips Academy, better known as Andover, is an exclusive and expensive coeducational private high school of around a thousand students. It is situated on a hilltop in Andover, Massachusetts, about twenty miles north of Boston.

Radio City " 'Let's go ice-skating at Radio City' " (128). Part of the Radio City Music Hall complex (referred to in my note to the earlier reference on page 75 of the novel) is a below-street-level outdoor skating rink. Some people go there to skate, some to be *seen* skating.

Brooks "[A]nd guys fitting your pants all the time at Brooks" (130). This is almost certainly a reference to the chain of stores, usually referred to as Brooks Brothers, that sold upscale expensive men's clothing.

a horse " 'I'd rather have a goddam horse. A horse is at least *human*, for God's sake' " (131). Holden may not realize it, but this kind of talk connects his thinking with that of Gulliver in Jonathan Swift's classic *Gulliver's Travels* (1726). In the fourth part of that famous work, Gulliver comes to understand that the rulers are all horses (their name for themselves, "Houyhnhnms," means "the perfection of nature"), while certain animalistic and ugly creatures ("Yahoos") are, though human-like in some ways, base and repulsive. Gulliver becomes a member of a horse's household where he admires and emulates the Houyhnhnms. He rejects the Yahoos as subhuman because of their lack of reason and their foul habits.

Book-of-the-*Month* Club "Even the guys that belong to the goddam Book-of-the-*Month* Club stick together" (131). Subscribers to the national Book-of-the-Month Club agree to buy a certain number of books from a group of books selected by the organizers. Ironically, *The Catcher in the Rye* was picked as one its selections, and the exposure helped to make the novel "catch" on all across the United States.

Chapter 18: Thoughts about war

Holden tries to telephone Jane Gallagher, but no one answers. He calls Carl Luce and makes a date to meet him at ten that night at a bar. To kill time until then, he goes to the show at Radio City Music Hall, including the pre-movie live performance by the Rockettes. He describes the movie he sees in some detail, a romantic story about a duke who loses his memory in the war and has no idea who he is, who his family is, or even that he had been engaged to a woman named Marcia. After the movie Holden starts walking down to the Wicker Bar to meet Carl Luce, but the movie makes him think about war and his brother D.B.'s experience as a soldier in World War II. Holden says that if there is another war, they can execute him in front of a firing squad. He imagines volunteering to sit on an atomic bomb when it goes off.

Choate "She was dating this terrible guy, Al Pike, that went to Choate" (135). Begun in the 1890s in Wallingford, Connecticut, Choate was a small private school that later merged with another small private school to become what is now called Choate Rosemary Hall.

Lastex "He wore those white Lastex kind of swimming trunks" (135). Lastex was the trade name for an elastic, two-way-stretch textile woven from the fine thread of Latex, a chemically modified rubber. This synthetic fiber was introduced about 1925 and was quickly incorporated into bathing suit fabric to give it stretch and body-hugging flexibility. We are apparently to envision Al Pike's trunks as revealing the contours of his body.

Wicker Bar "[H]e said he couldn't make it for dinner, but that
he'd meet me for a drink at ten o'clock at the Wicker Bar,
on 54th" (136–37). The name of the bar is made up. There
was never, so far as I can tell, a Wicker Bar on 54th Street,
or anywhere else in Manhattan for that matter. In his
"Holden's New York" (*New York Times* for July 22, 2001, p.
CY 8), Thomas Beller says that he was not successful either
in finding the bar in the Seton Hotel or in finding anyone
there who remembered it. There is more on the Seton Hotel
below in my notes for chapter 19.

Rockettes "The Rockettes were kicking their heads off, the way
they do when they're all in line with their arms around each
others' waist" (137). Starting in 1933, Radio City Music
Hall featured new movies accompanied by a lavish stage
production starring the Rockettes, a troupe of thirty-six
female dancers choreographed to make exactly the same
coordinated kicks and steps, so that they all moved as if
they were one dancer. Everything from the costumes to the
specific steps was kept identical.

"Come All Ye Faithful" "All these angels start coming out [. . .]
singing 'Come All Ye Faithful' like mad" (137). The song,
originally written in Latin (*Adeste Fidelis*), was translated
into English by John Wade in the eighteenth century. It
celebrates the birth of Jesus. The first stanza and the refrain
run thus:

> O come, all ye faithful, joyful and triumphant,
> O come ye, O come ye, to Bethlehem.
> Come and behold Him, born the King of angels.
>
> Refrain:
> O come, let us adore Him,
> O come, let us adore Him,
> O come, let us adore Him,
> Christ the Lord.

the goddam picture "After the Christmas thing was over, the goddam picture started. It was so putrid I couldn't take my eyes off it" (138). The plot summary that follows tracks somewhat with the 1942 film *Random Harvest*, directed by Mervyn LeRoy (see Figure 34). *Random Harvest* is the romantic but unlikely story about a shell-shocked veteran of World War I who has lost all memory of who he is or what his life or family had been. He takes the name of John Smith ("Smithy"). At the start of the story Smithy (played by Ronald Colman) wanders away from the mental asylum where he has been incarcerated. He is helped by a music-hall actress named Paula (played by Greer Garson). They fall in love, marry, move to a country cottage, and have a son. On a trip alone to Liverpool to take up a job as a newspaper writer, Smithy is involved in a freak accident. His memory of earlier events returns, but he now remembers nothing at all about his new life as a married man. Puzzled, he returns to his original home at Random Hall, soon becomes a successful industrialist, and is even elected to Parliament. The rest of the story involves his wife Paula's efforts to bring back his memory. Unable to tell him directly for fear of disturbing his delicate mental condition, she becomes his secretary. He does not remember anything about her. She is devoted to him, and of course is deeply saddened and conflicted when he appears to fall in love with, and then becomes engaged to, a pretty young socialite. The story has a happy ending.

The plot Holden gives is different in many ways. In it the main characters have different names (Alec and Marcia), they meet on a bus, not a tobacconist's shop. The soldier is an industrialist, not a duke, the girl a dancer, not a publisher. There is no mention of Dickens or *Oliver Twist*, of the alcoholic surgeon brother, of the blind mother, or of the

Figure 34: From the film version of *Random Harvest* (Metro-Goldwyn-Mayer, 1942), which may have been one of the movies Salinger was thinking of when he created the plot summary for the movie Holden sees at Radio City. Ronald Colman plays the soldier who has lost his memory, Greer Garson the dance-hall girl who befriends him. Courtesy Photofest.

Great Dane with puppies. Besides, no 1942 film, no matter how good—*Random Harvest* won Academy Awards for Best Picture and Best Actor—would have been showing in Radio City Music Hall as late as 1949. For the record, the movie showing at Radio City from December 8, 1949, through the beginning of January, 1950, was the musical *On the Town*, with Frank Sinatra and Gene Kelly. All in all, we should conclude that Salinger mostly made up or pasted together from several movies (see next item) the plot of the "putrid" movie he describes but never names.

Alec "It was about this English guy, Alec something" (138). Salinger or Holden may have been thinking of David Lean's production of Noel Coward's *Brief Encounter*, released in 1945. It is about two married English people, each with a spouse and two children, who chance to meet in a railroad station café and, in that and subsequent weekly meetings, fall deeply in love. Played by Trevor Howard, a physician named Alec is on his way to do weekly service at a nearby hospital. Played by Celia Johnson, a housewife named Laura is reading a book (not specified as to author or title) during their first meeting. *Brief Encounter* has little in common with the movie Holden describes beyond the name and nationality of the male lead, the sudden falling in love with a stranger met at a public transport station, the mention of a book, and the mention of a doctor.

Charles Dickens "[T]hey go upstairs and sit down and start talking about Charles Dickens. He's both their favorite author and all" (138). Dickens was a well-known nineteenth-century British author (1812–1870) of many novels, including *David Copperfield* (see above, pp. 74–75), mentioned on the first page of *The Catcher in the Rye*.

Oliver Twist "He's carrying this copy of *Oliver Twist*, and so's she" (138). This famous novel by Dickens is about a boy, Oliver Twist, who becomes an orphan when his unmarried mother dies right after he is born. The novel is about his growing up in an orphanage and a workhouse, and then becoming an apprentice pickpocket in London. He eventually discovers that he is the son and heir of a wealthy upper-class gentleman.

D-Day "My brother D.B. was in the Army for four goddam years. He was in the war, too—he landed on D-Day and all" (140). The war, of course, is World War II, and D-Day was June 6, 1944, the day Allied forces, many of them Americans, landed at Normandy in northern France, to scale the cliffs and gain a beachhead in Nazi-occupied Europe. It was the largest air, land, and sea operation undertaken before or since. It involved over 5,000 ships, 11,000 airplanes, and 150,000 servicemen. When the day was over, more than 4,000 Allied troops were dead, but they had gained a beachhead that marked the beginning of the liberation of Europe. Salinger himself was on the D-Day landing at Utah Beach. Interestingly, however, Salinger makes Holden's writer-brother D.B. play the role of the soldier. Holden would have been around eleven—"I was practically a child at the time" (140)—but Holden's description of D.B.'s experiences in the invasion and his reaction to the war and the Army may in some ways reflect Salinger's own reactions.

Rupert Brooke "He made Allie go get his baseball mitt and then he asked him who was the best war poet, Rupert Brooke or Emily Dickinson" (140). Rupert Brooke (1887–1915) was born in Rugby, England. He attended Cambridge and was a poet before he went off to be a soldier in World War I. He did not see any real action, but before he went to do battle he wrote the fifteen-line patriotic poem he is most famous for, "The Soldier." Its prescient opening lines are:

> If I should die, think only this of me:
>> That there's some corner of a foreign field
> That is forever England. There shall be
>> In that rich earth a richer dust concealed;
> A dust whom England bore.

Brooke died of septicemia as a result of a mosquito bite (or perhaps food poisoning) on a hospital ship off the Greek island of Scyros on April 23, 1915. Not yet thirty, Brooke was buried on the island.

Emily Dickinson "Allie said Emily Dickinson" (140). Emily Dickinson (1830–1886) was born in Amherst, Massachusetts, to a family known for educational and political activity. She was educated at Amherst Academy (1840–1847) and Mount Holyoke Female Seminary (1847–1848). Somewhat like Salinger after her, she became a reclusive New England writer seeking neither fame nor fortune in her lifetime. She almost never left Amherst, so she knew of the Civil War only indirectly. Still, she wrote with considerable eloquence about it, as in this 1863 poem, written when she was in her early thirties. I give only the first eight of its twenty lines:

> It feels a shame to be Alive—
> When Men so brave—are dead—
> One envies the Distinguished Dust—
> Permitted—such a Head—
>
> The Stone—that tells defending Whom
> This Spartan put away
> What little of Him we—possessed
> In Pawn for Liberty—

Boy Scouts "I was in the Boy Scouts once, for about a week" (140). The Boy Scouts of America, started in 1910, was set up to help boys develop athletic and survival skills while they did community service work. There is no record of Salinger's joining the Boy Scouts, but in his story "The Laughing Man" (published in the *New Yorker* in 1949), the narrator talks about his having joined a somewhat similar organization called the Comanche Club. The "Chief" of the club had been an Eagle Scout and takes the boys in the club on various outings.

atomic bomb "Anyway, I'm sort of glad they got the atomic bomb invented. If there's ever another war I'm going to sit right the hell on top of it. I'll volunteer for it" (141). Developed from 1939 to 1945 for use in World War II, the atomic bomb was tested at the Los Alamos testing ground in New Mexico. Not long after, atomic bombs were dropped on the Japanese cities of Hiroshima and Nagasaki. In 1949, when *The Catcher in the Rye* is set, the atomic bomb was a relatively recent invention. Holden's desire to be blown up is somewhat reminiscent of Huck Finn's statement when he decides to tell the truth to Mary Jane Wilks: "I'll up and tell the truth this time, though it does seem most like setting down on a kag of powder and setting it off just to see where you'll go to" (*The Adventures of Huckleberry Finn* [Ballantine Ivy edition, 1996], p. 213).

A Farewell to Arms "What gets me about D.B., though, he hated the war so much, and yet he got me to read this book *A Farewell to Arms*" (141). Ernest Hemingway's novel, published in 1929, is about an ambulance driver on the Italian front during World War I. There is some account of the horrors of war, as when Lieutenant Henry is wounded in the head and leg, but most of the story is about the ill-fated romance between Lieutenant Henry and the lovely British nurse Catherine Barkley. Much of the novel is based on Hemingway's own life as an ambulance driver on the Italian front. Salinger, who was directly involved in the D-Day offensive against Germany in 1944, may have found *A Farewell to Arms* to be both tame and unrealistic as a novel that purported to be about the real experience of real soldiers in war. I cannot agree, then, with Robert P. Moore, who argues that Holden finds *A Farewell to Arms* to be a "phony book, because it is about war, and war is wrong as violence is wrong as force is wrong as any crude, animal-like actions are wrong on the part of man" ("The World of Holden," *English Journal* 54 [1965]: 162). Holden questions the novel not because it is about war, but because it is not enough about war and because it shows a romantically phony side to war.

Salinger's daughter Margaret tells us that while her father was in Europe he met Hemingway, then a war correspondent: "Their visit was, apparently, a warm one. Hemingway asked to see my father's most recent work, and he showed him 'Last Day of the Last Furlough.' Hemingway had read it and said he liked it very much" (*Dream Catcher* 60). Margaret Salinger believes that her father's post-war trauma is "displaced" onto the fictional Holden: "While the traumas of war and death and dislocation are displaced in *The Catcher*—Nazis are replaced by 'phonies' as the enemy—their ability to destroy lives and to wreak emotional havoc upon the survivors diminishes not a whit" (*Dream Catcher* 75). We must, of course, be careful about assuming that any of Holden's opinions are also those of Salinger. If the sixteen-year-old Holden is skeptical about Hemingway's novel, that does not mean that Salinger was. Salinger, after all, like D.B., had been to war, so we might well surmise that Salinger would have been more approving of D.B.'s point of view on *A Farewell to Arms* than of naive Holden's that Lieutenant Henry is a "phony."

Ring Lardner "I don't see how he could like a phony book like
    that and still like that one by Ring Lardner" (141). See **a
    book by Ring Lardner** in my explanatory notes to chapter 3
    of *The Catcher in the Rye*, p. 94 above.

The Great Gatsby "I was crazy about *The Great Gatsby*. Old
    Gatsby. Old sport" (141). Holden does not give the name
    of the author, but it was of course F. Scott Fitzgerald
    (1896–1940), an American writer born in St. Paul,
    Minnesota. *The Great Gatsby* (1925), his most famous
    novel, is about a man eager to be financially successful so
    that he can win the love of Daisy, a woman who is married
    to the wealthy and aristocratic but brutal Tom Buchanan.
    Its first-person narrator, Nick Carraway, is in some ways the
    central character in the novel. He and Holden both are able
    to describe with some clarity of vision the corrupt ways of
    the rich country-club set who lord it over those who, like
    Gatsby, have had fewer advantages.

      There are a number of other similarities, some of them
    probably intentional, between *The Great Gatsby* and *The
    Catcher in the Rye*. Most obvious is the one Holden himself
    refers to, Gatsby's repeated epithet "old sport" for people
    he knows. Gatsby uses it most often for Nick, but does so
    for others, also. Holden uses the adjective "old" often: "old
    Phoebe," "old Thurmer," "old Ackley," "old Luce," and so on.
    Gatsby and Holden share certain other qualities, as well,
    such as a romantic tendency to put the women they like on a
    pedestal, and a perverse refusal to accept change.

      Both novels are set in and around New York City.
    Nick, like Holden, refers to specific places in the city, such
    Penn Station and Madison Avenue, as well as to the names
    of songs popular at the time. Fitzgerald's Tom Buchanan was
    perhaps in some ways a model for the handsome, athletic,
    but insensitive and mean-spirited Ward Stradlater, as Daisy

was in some ways a model for Jane Gallagher, for whose affection Holden sees himself as Stradlater's rival, just as Gatsby saw himself as a rival to Tom for Daisy's affection.

Certain other parallels, though possibly coincidental, may suggest influence. For example, the distraught George Wilson wandered around Long Island and "bought a sandwich that he didn't eat and a cup of coffee" (New York: Scribner Paperback Fiction, 1995, p. 168), an incident that may have suggested the one in which the distraught Holden, upset by what he takes to be a "flitty" pass by Mr. Antolini, orders doughnuts and a cup of coffee but can't eat the doughnuts (196). The scene in which Gatsby's body is buried, almost unattended, in the rain (see p. 183 in the Scribner edition) may have suggested the scene in which family visitors to Allie's grave run for cover when it begins to rain (155–56).

We may even find in *The Great Gatsby* a scene that could have suggested to Salinger the scene where Holden tries to erase the obscene words in Phoebe's school. Near the very end of Fitzgerald's novel Nick Carraway goes for one last look at Gatsby's mansion before he leaves West Egg:

> On the white steps an obscene word, scrawled by some boy with a piece of brick, stood out clearly in the moonlight and I erased it, drawing my shoe raspingly along the stone. Then I wandered down to the beach and sprawled out on the sand. (Scribner edition, pp. 188-89)

Those brief sentences might have flowered into this more extended paragraph in *The Catcher in the Rye*:

> But while I was sitting down, I saw something that drove me crazy. Somebody'd written "Fuck you" on the wall. [. . .] I hardly even had the guts to rub it off the wall with my hand, if you want to know the truth. I was afraid some teacher would catch me rubbing it off and would think I'd written it. But I rubbed it out anyway, finally. Then I went up to the principal's office. (201)

Chapter 19: Cocktails and conversation with Luce

Holden arrives at the Wicker Bar [L] well before Carl Luce does and has a couple of drinks alone, listening to "two French babes" play the piano and sing. He observes what he thinks is the "flitty" behavior of some young men at the other end of the bar. When Luce joins him, they have a conversation in which Holden asks Luce about his sex life and Luce tells Holden to "grow up." Luce then reluctantly describes his relationship with a middle-aged Chinese woman from Shanghai. When Holden admits that his sex life is lousy, Luce suggests, for the second time, that Holden ask a psychoanalyst to help him to "recognize the patterns of your mind." Then Luce leaves. Holden stays, alone and lonesome, in the bar.

Seton Hotel "In case you don't live in New York, the Wicker Bar is in this sort of swanky hotel, the Seton Hotel" (141). There is a Seton Hotel in New York, but it is on East 40th Street, not 54th Street, where Holden places the Wicker Bar. The Seton Hotel on 40th Street has no Wicker Bar, and apparently never did have one. It is possible that Holden—or Salinger—was confused. Radio City is on 50th Street, so to walk to 54th from there would have meant walking uptown. Holden tells us, however, "After the movie was over, I started walking *down* to the Wicker Bar" (140, emphasis added).

"Vooly Voo Fransay" "'And now we like to geeve you our impression of Vooly Voo Fransay'" (142). I have found no song by that name. The expression "voulez-vous français" means "do you want French?" There may be an echo in the name of the song of the brief interchange between Huck and Jim in *Huckleberry Finn*:

> "Spose a man was to come to you and say *Polly-voo-franzay*—what would you think?"

"I wouldn' think nuff 'n; I'd take en bust him over de head. Dat is, if he warn't white. I wouldn't 'low no nigger to call me dat."

"Shucks, it ain't calling you anything. It's only saying, do you know how to talk French." (Ballantine Ivy edition [1996], p. 86)

story of a leetle Fransh girl "'Eet ees the story of a leetle Fransh girl who comes to a beeg ceety, just like New York, and falls een love wees a leetle boy from Brookleen.' [. . .] [S]he'd sing some dopey song, half in English, half in French" (142). Perhaps Holden was thinking of the song "Parlez-Vous Français?" ("Do you speak French?" I have not been able to find information about its composer, lyricist, or date of first publication.) The lyrics run, in part:

> *Parlez-vous français?*
> *Je suis* sad.
> *Parlez-vous français?*
> I feel bad.
>
> How do you say
> "*Ce soir vous êtes si belle*"?
>
> I only know
> A word or so,
> Like "Cat" and "School"—
> *Je suis* fool.
>
> *Parlez-vous français?*
> Please say "*oui.*"
> *Parlez-vous français?*
> Speak to me.

Martini "Then he ordered a dry Martini. He told the bartender to make it very dry, and no olive" (144). A standard martini cocktail is a mixture of gin and vermouth, with an olive. The less vermouth there is, the "dryer" it is.

Shanghai "'She happens to be from Shanghai'" (146). Carl Luce's girlfriend apparently left China just before the revolution in which Mao Zedong defeated the forces of Chiang Kai-shek and declared mainland China an independent Communist nation with himself as its leader. Actual Independence Day was October 1, 1949—the official beginning of the People's Republic of China. Assuming that she left shortly before that date, her arrival in the U.S. "a few months ago" (146), jibes well enough with a date of mid-December 1949 for the setting of the primary events of *The Catcher in the Rye*.

Eastern philosophy "'I simply happen to find Eastern philosophy more satisfactory than Western'" (146). Although Salinger does not portray Carl Luce as a particularly attractive man, it is interesting that he himself at about this time was beginning to feel more and more drawn to Eastern philosophy, particularly Zen Buddhism.

Chapter 20: Imagining dying

Holden has more drinks and, as he gets drunker and drunker, starts to fantasize about having a bullet in his guts. Several people tell him to go home and go to bed—Sally Hayes when he calls her again, the pianist in the men's room, the hat-check woman—but he decides to walk to Central Park to see if he can find the ducks in the lake [M]. He finds the lagoon but not the ducks, and he almost falls into the lagoon wandering around to see if he can find them nesting or sleeping in the grass. Then he sits shivering on a bench wondering if he is going to die of pneumonia and imagining all his relatives coming to his funeral, as they had to Allie's. He thinks about Allie in a graveyard. He is glad that Phoebe is too young to come to his funeral if he does die of pneumonia, then decides to walk home to see her.

walked around "I walked around the whole damn lake" (154). The lagoon in the southeast corner of Central Park is not large. Staying on the paved pathways, walking around it takes ten minutes or so. It would have been much more difficult, and taken much longer, to try to follow the water's edge around the lake, lined as it is with trees, rocks, and brambles. If Holden tried that, drunk and at night, he could scarcely not have fallen in.

fell in "I damn near fell in once" (154). Biographer Ian Hamilton reports that as a boy Salinger once did fall into the lagoon (*In Search* 15).

Detroit "My grandfather from Detroit, that keeps calling out the numbers of the streets when you ride on a goddam bus with him" (154–55). Margaret Salinger tells the family story about her father's grandfather: "One story was about the time his grandfather from Chicago came to visit them in New York and my father, then a young boy, nearly died of embarrassment as his grandfather called out each street number on the Madison Avenue bus they were riding. 'Forty-*feef* Street, Forty-*seex* Street,' my father would call out in a loud voice with a heavy Yiddish accent as he told the story" (*Dream Catcher* 22).

home "So I got the hell out of the park, and went home" (156). Since we have been told that Phoebe lives at Fifth Avenue and 71st Street (see 67 and 118), it appears that Holden would have had to walk a dozen or so blocks.

Holden goes home
(chapters 21-26)

Chapter 21: Creeping home to see Phoebe

Holden goes home [N], *lies to the elevator boy about who he is, sneaks into his apartment, and tiptoes down the hallway to Phoebe's room, where she is sleeping. He looks at some of the books and notebooks on her desk, then wakes her up. She tells him about her day and the play she has a big part in. She says that their parents are out at a party, then guesses that Holden has been kicked out of Pencey. "Daddy'll kill you," she tells him. When she hides her head under her pillow, he goes out to the living room to get some cigarettes.*

south eastern Alaska "Why has south eastern Alaska so many *caning factories?*" (160). Phoebe's sentence, of course, is flawed. She should have written "southwestern" and "caning" needs an extra "n."

Benedict Arnold "'A Christmas Pageant for Americans.' It stinks, but I'm Benedict Arnold" (162). Benedict Arnold fought bravely and with distinction for the American cause at the start of the Revolutionary War, but later betrayed his countrymen by joining the British. His name is now almost synonymous with the term "traitor." The name of the pageant, "A Christmas Pageant for Americans," is apparently entirely fictional. I am aware of no play, for children or adults, by that name.

Norwalk "'They went to a party in Norwalk, Connecticut'" (162). Norwalk is not far north of New York on the southwest tip of Connecticut.

The **Doctor** "'The Doctor,' old Phoebe said. 'It's a special movie they had at the Lister Foundation'" (162). No real movie, either a documentary or a fiction-film, that matches the plot summary Phoebe describes has ever been found, nor is there any evidence that something called the Lister Foundation existed. It appears that Salinger made the movie up—both the title and the plot summary. It does seem, on the face of it, an unlikely movie for small children. Would anyone really want to take two little girls to see a movie in which a doctor smothers a little crippled girl, or that seems to come out in favor of child euthanasia?

The presence of *The Doctor* in *The Catcher in the Rye* has drawn some critical commentary that connects the movie to Holden Caulfield's personal problems. Bernard S. Oldsey connects the doctor with Holden:

> This summary of *The Doctor*, with its central problem of euthanasia, underscores Holden's own problem. Like the doctor in the movie, he, too (though by different means), wishes to protect the young from the cruelties and indignities of the world. For their pains, the doctor goes to prison, Holden to a mental hospital. ("The Movies in the Rye," *College English* 23 [1961]: 212)

Psychoanalytic scholar James Bryan, seeing a connection between killing and sexuality in *The Catcher in the Rye*, finds a different significance in the plot of *The Doctor*:

> This suggestive plot points to a horrible psychological possibility for Holden. He may "kill" Phoebe, pay his penalty agreeably, and even receive the gratitude of his victim. If interpretation here seems hard to justify, especially the

implications of Phoebe's having suggested all this to Holden, consider the climax of the chapter in which Phoebe puts "the goddam pillow over her head" and refuses to come out. ("The Psychological Structure of *The Catcher in the Rye*," *PMLA* 89 [1974]: 1071)

radio "'We have a radio in it now!'" (163). Although portable battery-operated radios were available for use in cars in the 1930s, it was not until the 1940s that automotive technology made radios available in new cars. In 1948 researchers at Bell Laboratories invented the transistor, which made it much easier to install efficient radios in cars. In 1949 a car radio would have been, if not quite a luxury item, at least something to brag about.

Annapolis "'He may have to stay in Hollywood and write a picture about Annapolis'" (164). Annapolis is a seaport in Maryland, perhaps most famous as the location of the United States Naval Academy (established 1845). Biographer Ian Hamilton reports that after the successful release of *My Foolish Heart* (based on a Salinger story), producer Samuel Goldwyn "invited [Salinger] out to the West Coast to pen a story of young love in a naval academy" (*In Search* 107). Holden's response to the possibility of D.B.'s staying in California to write such a script may well reflect Salinger's own indignation at Goldwyn's invitation:

> "What's D.B. know about Annapolis, for God's sake? What's that got to do with the kind of stories he writes?" I said. Boy, that stuff drives me crazy. That goddam Hollywood. (164)

It is interesting, but probably irrelevant, that four years after *The Catcher in the Rye* was published, director John Ford produced a Hollywood film about West Point. *The Long Gray Line* (1955) is the story, based on the life of a real person, an Irish immigrant who becomes a U.S. Army officer and then spends the rest of his life working at the United States Military Academy at West Point.

kill "'Daddy'll *kill* you!' she said" (165). Margaret Dumais Svogun
has suggested that in making this prediction Phoebe is
serving as Phoebus Apollo, the Delphic oracle who made
predictions to those who came to see her ("Salinger's *The
Catcher in the Rye*," *Explicator* 61 [2003]: 110–12). I'm not
so sure the suggestion works, however. Phoebe's prediction
is, in any case, wrong. Mr. Caulfield does not appear in the
novel and does not kill Holden. If we are to connect Phoebe
with the Delphic oracle, the connection is surely meant
ironically. The oracle had predicted that Oedipus would
murder his father; Phoebe predicts that Holden's father
will murder him. Phoebe does not, of course, mean the
term "kill" literally.

ranch in Colorado "I know this guy whose grandfather's got a
ranch in Colorado. I may get a job out there'" (165). The
"guy" is not specified, here or elsewhere, and it may be that
Holden is making the whole thing up to mollify Phoebe.

Chapter 22: Talking with Phoebe

*Phoebe asks Holden why he got kicked out of Pencey Prep. Holden
replies that he hated lots of things about Pencey. She remarks that he
hates pretty much everything. When he denies that, she asks what he
likes. Holden can't "concentrate" well enough to answer the question.
He thinks of James Castle as someone he likes, but doesn't mention
him to Phoebe. He tells her finally that he likes being there talking to
her and he likes Allie. She asks what he wants to be. What he'd really
like, he says, is to be a catcher in the rye, keeping little kids, playing
in a field of rye, from falling off a cliff. She corrects him about Robert
Burns's poem and says again that his father will kill him. Holden
decides to call Mr. Antolini, his old teacher at Elkton Hills, who now
lives and teaches in Manhattan.*

that goddam military school "'The worst he'll do, he'll give me hell, and then he'll send me to that goddam military school'" (166). The referent for "that" is not specified, but presumably it is a school like Valley Forge Military Academy—further evidence, if any was needed, that Pencey Prep is *not* a military school, just an ordinary private prep school. Military school was the next step. Holden does not tell us in the last chapter "what school I'm supposed to go to next fall" (213), but it may be "that" military academy.

Veterans' Day "They have this day, Veterans' Day, that all the jerks that graduated from Pencey around 1776 come back and walk all over the place" (168). The reference here is apparently to a kind of alumni day or homecoming day in which former graduates of the school are invited to return to the campus for class reunions, for the chance to relive old memories, and of course for the inevitable fund-raising. It would not have referred to the national holiday known now as Veterans' Day (formerly Armistice Day—the day honoring the end of World War I on November 11, 1918). Veterans' Day was not the official name of the national holiday until it was made so by an act of Congress on May 24, 1954—several years after *The Catcher in the Rye* was published.

jumped out the window "Finally, what he did, instead of taking back what he said, he jumped out the window" (170). According to Henry Anatole Grunwald, "One of Salinger's fellow cadets at his military academy did commit suicide by jumping from a window, like James Castle in *Catcher in the Rye*" (*Salinger: A Critical and Personal Portrait* [New York: Harper, 1963], p. 20).

somebody's dead "'If somebody's dead, and everything, and in Heaven, then it isn't really—'" (171). Phoebe has just challenged Holden to name something he likes, and all he can think of to tell her is Allie, his dead brother. Margaret Salinger reports that "My father has, himself, on many occasions told me the same thing, that the only people he really respects are all dead" (*Dream Catcher* 47).

rye "'Anyway, I keep picturing all these little kids playing some game in this big field of rye and all'" (173). Rye is a cereal grass, the seeds of which are used for making rye flour, for feeding livestock, and for making whiskey.

N.Y.U. "He took this job teaching English at N.Y.U." (173). New York University is a large public university that comprises schools, colleges, and divisions in five major centers in Manhattan. Teaching there would have been a step up from teaching in a private preparatory high school and suggests that Mr. Antolini had probably by now earned his doctorate in English.

Chapter 23: Dancing with Phoebe

Holden goes into the living room to call Mr. Antolini, who invites him to come over. Holden then goes back and dances with Phoebe to music from the radio, then smokes a cigarette. When his parents come home he snubs the cigarette out and hides in the closet. Phoebe lies to their mother to cover for Holden, saying she had been smoking. Before he leaves, Holden borrows some money from Phoebe, weeps, then gives her his hunting hat. Almost hoping that his parents find him at home, he walks down the stairs of the apartment building and heads to the Antolinis.

one of those Yogi guys "She was sitting smack in the middle of the bed, outside the covers, with her legs folded like one of those Yogi guys" (174–75). A Yogi is a person who practices Yoga, a method of breathing, movement, and meditation designed to give heightened peace and self-understanding to those who practice it. The term Yoga means "to join or yoke together," the idea being to bring the body and mind together into one harmonious experience. Sitting cross-legged is one of the standard Yoga poses for meditation.

jitterbug "You can cross over, or do some corny dips, or even jitterbug a little, and she stays right with you" (175). The jitterbug is a strenuous dance, to fast music, involving twirls and jiggling, often with minimal physical contact between the partners. It became popular during the 1940s.

tango "You can even *tango*, for God's sake" (175). The word "tango" is thought to come from the Spanish word *tangere* meaning "to touch." Dancing the tango, unlike dancing the jitterbug, usually involves close and sometimes even borderline-obscene, physical contact. The tango apparently originated in turn-of-the-century bordellos in Buenos Aires, Argentina, and was said to refer originally to the emotionally ambiguous relationship between a prostitute and her pimp. After decades of political repression in Argentina, the tango revived in the late 1930s when the Argentinean masses, having regained a measure of their political freedom, celebrated their social rise with the tango. It began to be danced elsewhere in the world after that, and when Juan Perón rose to power in 1946—just a few years before the events of *The Catcher in the Rye*—the tango again became popular in Argentina and elsewhere, as both Perón and his wife Evita embraced it wholeheartedly.

Lexington Avenue "'I walked all over Lexington Avenue'" (177). Lexington is a north-south avenue three blocks east of Central Park.

Chapter 24: Talking with Mr. Antolini

It is very late at night when Holden gets to the swanky Antolini apartment in Suttton Place [O], where Mrs. Antolini has fixed him some coffee and Mr. Antolini drinks highball after highball. Mr. Antolini talks to Holden about his life choices, his future, and his immaturity. Much of what Mr. Antolini says makes sense, but Holden is feeling too sick and too tired to understand much of it. Not long after Holden falls asleep, he wakes up to find Mr. Antolini "petting me or patting me on the goddam head." Horrified and frightened, Holden hastily dresses and leaves the apartment with Mr. Antolini calling him "a very, very strange boy." Holden says "perverty" stuff like that has happened to him often, ever since he was a child.

Sutton Place "Mr. and Mrs. Antolini had this very swanky apartment over on Sutton Place" (180). Sutton Place is a large area of Manhattan in the midtown east section, from 42nd Street to 59th Street, from Fifth Avenue to the East River. Holden probably refers here to Sutton Place "proper," a smaller location only a few blocks long, between 57th and 59th streets, one block east of First Avenue.

West Side Tennis Club "I used to play tennis with he and Mrs. Antolini quite frequently, out at the West Side Tennis Club in Forest Hills, Long Island" (180–81). An exclusive, members-only tennis club on fourteen acres across the East River on Long Island, the West Side Tennis Club is perhaps best known for hosting the U.S. Open tennis championships. It has a large Tudor-style clubhouse, along with a junior Olympic pool complex. For Holden and his friends to play there would have suggested wealth and leisure. The club is referred to earlier on p. 112 of the novel.

a day-old infant "'I expected to see a day-old infant in your arms. Nowhere to turn. Snowflakes in your eyelashes'" (181). Mr.

Antolini is making, apparently, a witty literary allusion to
some novel he has read, though I cannot identify the exact
one. The reference suggests several nineteenth-century
novels. In George Eliot's *Silas Marner*, for example, a young
man, the son of a landowner, has secretly married a woman
regarded as below him in status, and has fathered her
daughter. The woman, whom he has neglected, has resolved
to expose him in order to get help for herself and the child.
She sets off through the snow and wind but dies some
distance from the manor-house of her delinquent husband.
The child wanders into the cottage of Silas Marner, a solitary
weaver and miser. In Dickens's *Oliver Twist*, the mother of
the central character barely makes it to a workhouse before
she dies. Neither of these novels quite fits the reference. It is
interesting that Mr. Antolini wittily casts Holden in the role
of a desperate parent with a baby in his (her?) arms.

highball "He had on his bathrobe and slippers, and he had a
highball in one hand" (181). A highball is whiskey with
something else mixed with it, usually water, soda, or ginger
ale, to dilute the whiskey.

Buffalo "'We've been entertaining some Buffalo friends of Mrs.
Antolini's . . . Some buffaloes, as a matter of fact'" (182).
Buffalo is a large city in western New York State. Mr.
Antolini's supposed wit indicates a lack of respect for his
wife and her subhuman friends.

Richard Kinsella "But there was this one boy, Richard Kinsella.
He didn't stick to the point too much, and they were always
yelling 'Digression!' at him" (183). The name Richard
Kinsella is apparently a made-up name, but a novelist
named W. P. Kinsella gives us a main character in the novel
Shoeless Joe (Boston: Houghton Mifflin, 1982) who is named
Ray Kinsella. Ray claims to have a twin brother named
Richard. For a longer discussion of *Shoeless Joe* and Salinger's

connection to it, see section 6 in my introductory essay, pp. 42–43 above.

polio "'[H]is uncle got polio and all when he was forty-two years old'" (184). Since 1955 when a polio vaccine became available, polio (technically called poliomyelitis) has not been a serious health threat in the U.S., but in the 1940s it was a highly contagious and potentially devastating disease. It could take several forms, the most serious causing muscle paralysis. In this form, which could result in death, the polio virus could affect the nerves governing the muscles in the limbs and the chest muscles necessary for breathing, causing respiratory difficulty and paralysis of the arms and legs. Contemporary readers of Salinger's novel might well have been reminded, in this reference to a grown man having polio, of the most famous such victim, Franklin Delano Roosevelt. Roosevelt suffered a severe attack of poliomyelitis in 1921, when he was thirty-nine years old. He died in 1945, just a few years before the events of the novel take place. Although the disease resulted in paralysis of both legs, Roosevelt was elected president of the U.S. in 1932 and served as president until his death, at the start of his fourth term.

pretty old "She looked pretty old and all" (185). Holden's description of Mrs. Antolini is somewhat reminiscent of the surprise that young Philip Carey, the protagonist of Somerset Maugham's *Of Human Bondage*, felt on first seeing his lover Miss Wilkinson in her boudoir in chapter 35: "He reckoned out her age again, and he did not see how she could be less than forty. It made the affair ridiculous. She was plain and old. His quick fancy showed her to him, wrinkled, haggard, made-up" (New York: Modern Library, 1999, p. 146). Holden earlier mentions having read *Of Human Bondage*.

Wilhelm Stekel "'It was written by a psychoanalyst named
 Wilhelm Stekel'" (188). Wilhelm Stekel (1868–1940) was
 an Austrian psychoanalyst who, after a troubled childhood,
 became a physician and then a pupil of Freud. He eventually
 quarreled with Freud, divorced his wife after a series of
 arguments, and drove away many of his acquaintances. He
 fled Vienna when Hitler invaded Austria and, like many of
 his Jewish compatriots, settled temporarily in England. But
 he was in ill health, and in 1940 he committed suicide.

mark of the immature man "'The mark of the immature man is
 that he wants to die nobly for a cause, while the mark of the
 mature man is that he wants to live humbly for one'" (188).
 Salinger's ascription of this quotation to Stekel has made it
 the most famous quotation by Stekel, but ironically Stekel
 apparently never said it or wrote it. Carl F. Strauch has read
 widely in Stekel, but finds no such quotation, though he
 reports vaguely that he has found some that "hit off the same
 idea" in Stekel's autobiography ("Kings in the Back Row,"
 Wisconsin Studies in Contemporary Literature 2 [1961]: 30,
 note 7). *The Autobiography of Wilhelm Stekel* (New York:
 Liveright, 1950) has several features that Salinger might
 have found interesting, but nothing like the maxim Mr.
 Antolini attributes to him here. Just as we went to press
 with this second edition, I discovered the source of the
 quotation in Stekel's *Psychoanalysis and Suggestion Therapy:
 Their Technique, Applications, Results, Limits, Dangers, and
 Excesses,* trans. James S. Van Teslaar (London: Kegan Paul,
 Trench, Trubner, 1923). On p. 93 we find: "His highest ideal
 was at first to die gloriously for something; now his ideal is
 the supreme one: to live humbly for something." I have in
 preparation a short article in which I discuss Stekel's own
 source for the quotation (a novella by Oteto Ludwig), the
 changes Salinger made in adapting it to its place in his novel,
 and the extent to which it fits Holden.

valuable records "'I do say that educated and scholarly men [. . .]
tend to leave infinitely more valuable records behind them
than men who are *merely* brilliant and creative'" (189). It is
possible that Holden, in writing the story of his three-day
journey, is picking up on Mr. Antolini's suggestion—or
is it a challenge?—about leaving behind a written record.
For a somewhat different view of Holden as an incipient
author, see A. Robert Lee, "'Flunking Everything Else
Except English Anyway': Holden Caulfield, Author" in Joel
Salzberg, ed., *Critical Essays on Salinger's* The Catcher in the
Rye (Boston: G. K. Hall, 1990), pp. 185–97.

petting or patting "[H]e was sort of petting me or patting me
on the goddam head" (192). The ambiguous implications
of this scene have led to many interpretations. Most critics
assume, with Holden, that there is something either mildly
or seriously inappropriate in Mr. Antolini's late-night patting
of Holden's head, but not all do. Patrick Costello defends
Mr. Antolini's actions toward Holden as the innocent
expression of an Italian man for a disturbed young man for
whom he feels fatherly concern and affection: "Is there any
one who has known Italians, who hasn't seen a father kiss
his son, regardless of the son's age, on greeting and parting?
The Italian does not place the same restrictions on his
natural, legitimate inclinations as does the Anglo-Saxon"
("Salinger and 'Honest Iago,'" *Renascence* 16 [1964], p. 173).
David J. Burrows focuses also on Mr. Antolini's emotions:
"When Holden awakes to find the teacher stroking his
head, it is not, as the boy fears, a perverted pass; rather it is
Antolini's gesture of mourning for his own loss of integrity
and youthful purpose" ("Allie and Phoebe: Death and
Love in J. D. Salinger's *The Catcher in the Rye*," in *Private
Dealings: Modern American Writers in Search of Integrity*, ed.
David J. Burrows, et al. [Rockville, MD: New Perspectives,

1974], p. 108). Others focus on what the incident with
Mr. Antolini tells us about Holden himself. For William
Glasser, it symbolizes Holden's awakening: "Holden is
later awakened by Mr. Antolini patting him on the head,
an act which is apparently meant to signify the awakening
of Holden's intellect" (*The Catcher in the Rye*," *Michigan
Quarterly Review* 15 [1976]: 448). For Duane Edwards,
Holden "is projecting his desire for homosexual expression
onto Antolini. This does not mean that Holden is himself
a homosexual but that he has not yet made a sexual choice"
("Holden Caulfield: 'Don't Ever Tell Anybody Anything,'"
ELH 44 [1977]: 561). Peter Shaw speculates that Salinger
merely botched Holden's encounter with Mr. Antolini:
"Salinger sensed something wrong with the scene, and tried
to correct it by later undercutting Antolini. But evidently
because he was patching things up rather than writing out of
a more purely creative impulse, he did so rather crudely by
discrediting Antolini as a homosexual" ("Love and Death in
The Catcher in the Rye," in Jack Salzman, ed., *New Essays on*
The Catcher in the Rye [Cambridge: Cambridge University
Press, 1991], p. 111). Perhaps we are safest not trying to
be overly specific about Mr. Antolini's motives or Holden's
suspicions. Joyce Rowe reminds us that Mr. Antolini is
akin to many other adults in the novel: "[T]hese adults are
profoundly ambiguous figures whose seeming beneficence
it is dangerous to trust. All are effectively epitomized in
the teacher Mr. Antolini, whose paternal decency may be
entwined with a predator's taste for young boys" ("Holden
Caulfield and American Protest" in Jack Salzman, ed., *New
Essays on* The Catcher in the Rye [Cambridge: Cambridge
University Press, 1991], p. 89).

Chapter 25: In the Museum of Natural History

Holden starts the final day of his odyssey by going to Grand Central Station [**P**], *where he sleeps for a couple of hours on a hard bench. He is feeling so sick that he can't eat the doughnuts he orders in a restaurant* [**Q**]. *He wanders around Manhattan a bit before heading up Fifth Avenue* [**R**]. *He hatches a silly plan to hitchhike to the far West and build a cabin, but he wants first to say good-by to Phoebe and return to her the money he has borrowed. He walks to her school* [**S**], *leaves a message for her there, then goes and waits for her at the Metropolitan Museum of Art* [**T**]. *While waiting, he escorts a couple of boys down to the Egyptian mummy tomb, but soon gets dizzy and faints. Then he meets Phoebe on the steps of the museum, surprised that she has a suitcase with her. When she asks to join him on his journey to the West, he refuses but instead takes her to the zoo* [**U**] *and the amusement park where Phoebe rides the carrousel* [**V**]. *The chapter ends with Holden sitting in the rain in his red hunting hat watching her ride around and around.*

Grand Central "So finally all I did was I walked over to Lexington and took the subway down to Grand Central" (194). Grand Central is the train terminal between 42nd and 44th streets on Vanderbilt Avenue, referred to earlier in the novel (107).

this sore "I'd had this sore on the inside of my lip for about *two weeks*. So I figured I was getting cancer" (196). Holden probably has a canker sore, a small ulcer caused by a virus. Such ulcers last for ten or so days. In his depressed vulnerability, perhaps exacerbated by sleeplessness, he gives in to the paranoia of imagining—wishing?—that he has a disease that will kill him. Sores in the mouth that do not heal are possible indicators of oral cancer, particularly among tobacco users. In Holden's day, of course, there was no known link between smoking and cancer, so Holden would have had no reason to link smoking with cancer. Indeed, many people believed that smoking prolonged life.

Salvation Army "All those scraggy-looking Santa Clauses were standing on corners ringing those bells, and the Salvation Army girls, the ones that don't wear lipstick or anything, were ringing bells too" (197). Begun in 1865 in England by a Methodist minister and his wife, the Salvation Army was at first an evangelical group dedicated to preaching among the people living in the poverty in London's East End. In addition to preaching, the workers in the "Army" provided food, shelter, and rehabilitation to the aged, the hungry, and the homeless. The Salvation Army is now a worldwide organization involving more than a hundred countries. Holden had referred to the Salvation Army earlier (109).

Bloomingdale's "We had a helluva time. I think it was in Bloomingdale's" (197). This famous store was founded in New York City in 1872 by Lyman and Joseph Bloomingdale. There were many branch stores around the nation, but Holden almost certainly refers to the huge store, opened in 1927, on Third Avenue between 59th and 60th streets. Offering fashionable clothing, jewelry, and home furnishings, it is sometimes now affectionately known as Bloomie's. It is interesting that Salinger's sister Doris worked as a buyer in Bloomingdale's.

charged "We finally bought a pair of moccasins and charged them" (197). Holden's parents would have had a store charge account at Bloomingdale's. Individual carry-along credit cards had not been invented yet.

the zoo "I know I didn't stop till I was way up in the Sixties, past the zoo and all" (198). Holden is still walking north on Fifth Avenue, which above 59th Street marks the east border of Central Park. The Central Park Zoo is on the east side of the park, on five acres between 63rd and 65th streets (see Figure 35).

Holland Tunnel "I'd go down to the Holland Tunnel and bum a ride" (198). Two tunnels head into and out of the west side of Manhattan, the Lincoln Tunnel at 39th Street and the Holland Tunnel further south below Greenwich Village, at Canal Street. It is not clear why Holden would have selected the one so much further from his home. Of course, Holden is not thinking clearly about much of anything, particularly in planning his trip out West.

Figure 35: This sign in Central Park announces the presence of its zoo. And, yes, it had—and still had in 2006—a sea lion pool and bears, as referred to by Holden later (209).

deaf-mute "I'd pretend I was one of those deaf-mutes" (198).
   Holden's fantasy may reflect the scheme of "the duke" in
   Huckleberry Finn. The duke pretends to be a deaf-mute who
   can communicate only by writing notes. It is all part of a
   dishonest scheme to rob the Wilks girls of their inheritance.
   Holden's motives, of course, are quite different since his
   plans involve marrying a deaf-mute woman and having
   children. Some critics have seen a connection between
   Holden's wanting to be an isolated deaf-mute and Salinger's
   in effect being one by isolating himself in New Hampshire,
   refusing to speak to reporters, and refusing to listen to
   almost anyone.

a little cabin "I'd build me a little cabin somewhere with the
   dough I made and live there for the rest of my life" (199).
   Salinger's daughter Margaret thinks it "uncanny [...] the way
   Cornish would appear as if in response to Holden's dream of
   a little cabin somewhere right at the edge of a forest" (*Dream
   Catcher* 79). In any case, with the first money he made from
   The Catcher in the Rye, Salinger purchased the run-down
   house in the woods near Cornish, New Hampshire. He
   moved in on his thirty-fourth birthday, January 1, 1953.
   That property and, after his divorce, a nearby one, became
   his primary residence ever since. His daughter Margaret
   describes the small green-painted concrete-block building
   where for a long time Salinger did much of his writing (see
   the very end of chapter 8 of *Dream Catcher*, especially p.
   136). Holden's dream of building a small, private, secluded,
   rural cabin for himself is, of course, reminiscent of Henry
   David Thoreau's *Walden*.

her school "I knew where her school was, naturally, because I
   went there myself when I was a kid" (199). At age nine (in
   1928), Salinger moved with his parents into an apartment

at 221 West 82nd Street, and for a time he attended Public
School 109, which is located at 410 East 100th Street. It
is possible that he was thinking of that school when he has
Holden visit his old school.

Museum of Art "'Meet me at the Museum of Art near the door
at quarter past 12 if you can'" (200). Holden sends Phoebe
to the Metropolitan Museum of Art on the east edge of
Central Park between 80th and 84th streets (see Figure 36).

Pharaoh's tomb "To get to where the mummies were, you had
to go down this very narrow sort of hall with stones on the
side that they'd taken right out of this Pharaoh's tomb and
all" (203). The Metropolitan has a sizeable and important
collection of Egyptian art, including the limestone Tomb of
Perneb, an Egyptian pharaoh or emperor who dates from
around 2350–2323 B.C.E. It is presumably to this tomb
that Holden leads the two little boys, who are apparently
playing hooky from school (see Figure 37).

the mummies "[T]hese two little kids came up to me and asked
me if I knew where the mummies were" (202). According to
A Brief Guide to the Egyptian Collection in the archives of the
Metropolitan Museum of Art, a new Egyptian display was
opened in 1946, so it would have been unfamiliar to Holden
in 1949 when he tried to find it for the two little boys. The
mummies in question are probably the Hawara mummy and
the mummy of Artemidora, both from the late first century,
and both still in their original wrappings (see Figure 38).

school "Her school was practically right near the museum, and
she had to pass it on her way home for lunch anyway" (200).
It is not clear to what extent Holden's life reflected Salinger's
own, but in the fall of 1932, when Salinger was thirteen, he
moved with his parents to 1133 Park Avenue, on the corner

Figure 36: The steps leading up to the main entrance to the Metropolitan Museum of Art, near where Holden watches for Phoebe: "I went out the doors and started down these stone stairs to meet her" (205).

Figure 37: Perneb's tomb, from a photo taken in 1946. Courtesy Department of Egyptian Art, Metropolitan Museum of Art.

of 91st Street, a half-dozen blocks north of the Metropolitan Museum of Art. We are not told exactly where Phoebe's school is, but since she had to pass the museum on the way home for lunch, it must have been north of the museum, probably on Fifth Avenue, since she lives further south, on 71st Street (118). Holden tells the school secretary that he had "gone there to school, too" (202). Salinger is locating the Caulfield family on the prosperous Upper East Side not far from where he himself had spent his teenage years—that is, when he was not off at boarding school.

pants open "The one little kid, the one that asked me, had his pants open" (202). One scholar sees in Holden's reference here evidence of "his voyeuristic tendencies" (Duane Edwards, "Holden Caulfield: 'Don't Ever Tell Anybody Anything,'" *ELH* 44 [1977]: 559).

Figure 38. One of the mummies near Perneb's tomb, from a photo taken in 1946. Courtesy Department of Egyptian Art, Metropolitan Museum of Art.

glass part "It was written with a red crayon or something, right under the glass part of the wall, under the stones" (204). To protect the stones, the inscriptions, and the art work from possible defacement or other damage, parts of the Egypt collection are kept behind glass (see Figure 39).

diarrhea "I sort of had diarrhea, if you want to know the truth" (204). This statement may be a clue to the nature of Holden's illness. Warren French, however, connects the diarrhea with the "Fuck you" signs that Holden sees: "After seeing the third of those signs Holden has a bowel movement (a rather literal symbol of catharsis) and then faints" (*J. D. Salinger* [New York: Twayne, 1963], p. 121).

Figure 39: In the Egyptian collection, below a glass case like this one, Holden sees a "Fuck you" sign. Photograph taken in 1946. Courtesy Department of Egyptian Art, Metropolitan Mustum of Art.

carrousel "It was on the way to the carrousel" (210). A carrousel —now usually called a merry-go-round—is a park or carnival amusement ride in which music plays while the passengers ride around on toy horses, some stationary, some moving up and down. Thomas Beller, in "Holden's New York" (*New York Times*, July 22, 2001), reports that a 1950 fire in the amusement park in Central Park probably destroyed the carrousel that Phoebe would have ridden on, but that another has replaced it (see Figure 40). In fact, it burned on November 8, 1950, further evidence, if any were needed, that the events of the novel take place in December of 1949, not 1950. By December of 1950 the carrousel would have been destroyed for a month and could not have been replaced so quickly. It is interesting to speculate that as he completed *The Catcher in the Rye*, Salinger read this article in the *New York Times* and was influenced by some of its features: the nostalgic memories of fun on the carrousel; the little red-haired ten-year-old patron; the brass ring; the songs:

CARROUSEL BURNS
IN CENTRAL PARK

Pre-Dawn Fire Ruins Ride That Had Been
Dear to Young New Yorkers Since 1871

"Probably Beyond Repair"

Owner Sadly Reflects on the Impossibility of Replacing
44 Hand-Carved Horses

By LAURIE JOHNSTON
The Central Park carrousel, dear to the hearts of small New Yorkers since 1871, was ruined by fire before dawn yesterday. Its forty-four gaudy wooden steeds were charred

into black immobility, while fire and water combined to halt its mechanism and silence its carnival music.

The blaze was discovered at 5:30 A.M. by passers-by on Central Park West and Fifth Avenue. Six engine companies and four hook and ladder companies responded. But Myron Lomberg, owner of the carrousel, said it was damaged "probably, beyond repair." Cause of the fire was still under investigation. A short circuit was considered most likely. [. . .]

A Day of Disappointment

All day there was disappointment, and round-eyed wonder, too, as pleasure-bent children arrived clutching the necessary seven cents for a three-minute ride. "Who would start a fire like this?" an orange-haired former patron, aged 10, inquired of the world at large. "Some day it'll be fixed, won't it, Butchie?" asked a young lady who said she was Delores and that she was 4½.

"It'll be hard on the youngsters," the grown-ups told each other, clustering in little circles. But there were indications that, at the moment at least, it was harder on the grown-ups.

An elderly man who preferred anonymity said the carrousel building was the first he had really looked at when he arrived in New York in 1894 and, fresh from the country, headed straight for Central Park's greenery. "I've been coming back ever since," he said. "It was one place you could always see somebody having fun."

Patrolman Thomas Crawford, who has patrolled the area every working day for ten years, was busy answering mothers' questions and shepherding children from the unsafe structure. But he was busy with his own memories, too.

Recalls the Good Old Days

"I used to ride the carrousel here when I was a boy," he said. "Must have been about 1900—I'm 60 years old—and it cost us 3 cents then. It wasn't the same carrousel, of course. Back in those days it was powered by a team of mules on a circular track below it. The music came from a three-wheeled hand organ and a man who ground it. Sometimes you could stretch three cents into two rides by grabbing the brass ring."

Mr. Lomberg was a shaken man as he prowled the black and smoky-smelling wreckage, with its dark puddles. "Those horses were every color under the sun," he said. "They were so gorgeous it'd frighten you. And that organ played every song you ever heard—'In the Good Old Summertime,' 'New York Town,' 'Sweet Rosie O'Grady.' New ones, too. You can't just keep throwin' the same tunes at people." [. . .]

For seventeen years Mr. Lomberg's brother-in-law, Max Sesky, who lives with him at 53 East Ninety-sixth Street, has operated the carrousel. Known to thousands of youngsters as "Uncle Max," he said he had given rides to the children of many well-known persons, including Ethel Merman and Jack Demsey, and the grandchildren of the late President Franklin

Figure 40: The carrousel in Central Park, still in operation in 2006. This one replaced the actual one that Phoebe would have ridden on, but it was in the same location.

D. Roosevelt.

Mr. Lomberg and Park Department officials agreed it was too soon to say whether carrousel horses would ever prance their circular course around the old building again. Patrolman Crawford hoped they would reach a decision soon.

"This whole day, everybody's asking me are they going to rebuild it," he said. "A park isn't a park with [*sic*] it has a carrousel." (*New York Times*, November 9, 1950, p. 35; quoted with permission.)

Edgar Branch sees this carrousel as evidence of Holden's resistance to growing up: "The carrousel, bearing the beautiful child and playing the songs of Holden's childhood, goes round and round, going nowhere—a dynamic moment of happy, static immaturity eternalized in his mind" ("Mark Twain and J. D. Salinger: A Study in Literary Continuity," *American Quarterly* 9 [1957]: 149). Robert M. Slabey says that for Holden the carrousel is "an unchanging and undefiled point in the midst of chance and corruption: Holden's visit to it is almost like a return to the womb" ("*The Catcher in the Rye*: Christian Theme and Symbol," *CLA Journal* 6 [1963]: 176–77). Clinton W. Trowbridge, on the other hand, connects the carrousel more optimistically to Salinger's interest in Zen Buddhism: "Salinger means us to see the carousel as symbolic of the wheel of life, the constantly changing pattern of the Eternal One" ("Salinger's Symbolic Use of Character and Detail in *The Catcher in the Rye*," *Cimaron Review* 4 [1968]: 11).

"Oh Marie" "It was playing 'Oh Marie.' It played that same song about fifty years ago when I was a little kid" (210). I have found lyrics to at least two songs called "Oh Marie!" I give below the opening stanzas of the most likely one (I have not been able to find either its author or its date of first publication):

Oh Marie, oh Marie,
In your arms I am longing to be.
Oh baby, tell me you love me.
Kiss me once while the stars shine above me.

Oh Marie, oh Marie,
In your arms I am longing to be.
Oh baby, tell me you love me.
Oh Marie, oh Marie.

Of course, it is probable that the music was played without the lyrics. When I visited the carrousel in Central Park in April, 2006, they played among other songs "Lara's Theme" from the movie *Dr. Zhivago* and "Georgie Girl." None of the songs I heard that day was played with lyrics.

"Smoke Gets in Your Eyes" "There were only about five or six other kids on the ride, and the song the carrousel was playing was 'Smoke Gets in Your Eyes'" (211). This song has had a long life. It was originally composed by Jerome Kern (music) and Otto Harbach (lyrics) for the musical *Roberta* in 1933. The opening two stanzas are:

They asked me how I knew
My true love was true.
I of course replied, "Something here inside,
Cannot be denied."

They said, "Some day you'll find,
All who love are blind.
When you heart's on fire, you must realize,
Smoke gets in your eyes."

the gold ring "All the kids kept trying to grab for the gold ring, and so was old Phoebe" (211). In some early carrousels, the riders on the outer row of horses could reach out to try to take steel rings as they came down a little chute. Perhaps one in a hundred was a gold ring—though of course it was brass or painted steel, not real gold. A rider who got the special ring won a small reward of some sort, typically a free ride. The procedure was potentially dangerous, since the riders had to hold on to a carrousel pole with one hand and lean out to grab for the ring with the other. It was possible to fall off, or to get a finger caught in the chute. Such games are mostly illegal now, and in any case insurance companies will refuse to insure carrousel owners who try to use them. Phoebe could not reach for the gold ring if she were riding the carrousel in Central Park today.

soaking wet "I got pretty soaking wet, especially my neck and my pants" (212). Perhaps Salinger was thinking of psychoanalyst Wilhelm Stekel's experiences: "Once I was caught in a chilly rain without the proper clothing for such weather. The result was an attack of pleurisy. [. . .] I had to stay in bed for more than three weeks. [. . .] Suddenly a vision of the ocean, of sunshine, flashed before me. I said to myself, 'You will overcome this disease by getting out in the sun'" (*The Autobiography of Wilhelm Stekel* [New York: Liveright, 1950], p. 108). Stekel then went to a sunny area near an ocean, where he soon recovered. The similarities may well be entirely coincidental, of course, but if Salinger did read Stekel's autobiography as he was completing *The Catcher in the Rye*, he was perhaps thinking that Holden may have gotten "an attack of pleurisy" and been sent to sunny coastal California for recovery. Pleurisy is a painful disease of the membrane that surrounds and protects the lungs. It is a viral condition sometimes associated with pneumonia, tuberculosis, or other diseases of the lung.

so damn happy "I felt so damn happy all of a sudden, the way old Phoebe kept going around and around" (213). In her memoir Margaret Salinger talks about the times her father took her to New York to the Museum of Natural History, the lagoon and the zoo in Central Park, and even the carrousel: "Daddy always took me for a ride on the carrousel. I remember how happy my father looked, how he stood there grinning from one big ear to the other, waving to me each time I came around on my horse" (*Dream Catcher* 185).

Chapter 26: Missing them

Holden says that he did go home after the carrousel experience with Phoebe, but he really doesn't feel like talking about that now, or feel like speculating about how he'll do when he goes to school in September. He thinks he will do all right, but he just doesn't know. His brother D.B. visits and asks him what he thinks about telling the story of what happened, but Holden really doesn't know what to think. All he knows is that telling about it makes him miss the people he told about, even Stradlater, Ackley, and Maurice.

psychoanalyst guy "A lot of people, especially this one psychoanalyst guy they have here, keeps asking me if I'm going to apply myself when I go back to school next September" (213). A number of scholars have assumed, on the basis of this brief reference to a psychoanalyst, that Holden is in a mental institution. For example: "he's a severely depressed adolescent telling the story of his youth while in a mental institution" (Duane Edwards, "Holden Caulfield: 'Don't Ever Tell Anybody Anything,'" *ELH* 44 [1977]: 555); "The narrative, after all, was written in a mental hospital" (James Bryan, "The Psychological Structure of *The Catcher in the Rye*," *PMLA* 89 [1974]: 1065). See also **this crumby place** in my notes to chapter 1, pp. 78–79 above. Some readers, of course, think that Holden is in a sun-belt sanitarium recovering from pneumonia or tuberculosis (see, for example, Robert P. Moore, "The World of Holden," *English Journal* 54 [1965]: 159–65). It would not have been unusual for such a medical hospital to have on call a staff member who could treat patients' mental stress.

telling "D.B. asked me what I thought about all this stuff I've been telling you about" (213). Edwin Haviland Miller reads the whole novel as

> the chronicle of a four-year period of the life of an adolescent whose rebelliousness is his only means of dealing with his inability to come to terms with the death of his brother. Holden Caulfield has to wrestle not only with the usual difficult adjustments of the adolescent years in sexual, familial and peer relationships; he also has to bury Allie before he can make the transition into adulthood. ("In Memoriam: Allie Caulfield in *The Catcher in the Rye*," *Mosaic* 15 [1982]: 128)

Miller reads the closing reference to telling his story as proof of Holden's successful transition: "telling is precisely what he has been doing and in the process Holden has finished mourning. Allie now rests in peace" (p. 140).

miss everybody "About all I know is, I sort of miss everybody I told about. Even old Stradlater and Ackley, for instance. I think I even miss that goddam Maurice" (214). Holden's closing lines may reflect Huck Finn's lines in chapter 33, when he sees the scoundrel king and duke deservedly tarred and feathered and run out of town on a rail: "Well, it made me sick to see it; and I was sorry for them poor pitiful rascals, it seemed like I couldn't ever feel any hardness against them any more" (*The Adventures of Huckleberry Finn* [Ballantine Ivy edition, 1996], p. 259). Many scholars see in Holden's missing his old antagonists evidence that he begins to see things from their point of view, that he is less self-centered than he was, and that he is now on his way to a more forgiving and mature attitude.

Glossary for ESL and EFL Readers

"ESL," English as a Second Language, is a pedagogical term usually referring to the linguistic needs of people who live in an English-speaking country but whose native language is not English. "EFL," English as a Foreign Language, refers to the linguistic needs of people who live in countries where English is not the native language. I am grateful to Marcela B. Gamallo, a native of Argentina and an EFL teacher, for providing me with an initial list of the expressions she thought some ESL and EFL readers of *The Catcher in the Rye* might have most trouble understanding.

The Catcher in the Rye is read not only in the United States but around the world, often in English rather than in one of its many translations. Indeed, the novel is often assigned in ESL and EFL courses as a way to encourage non-native speakers of English to learn about American culture and colloquial expressions. The words and phrases listed below may be difficult for such readers because of their nonstandard spelling, their unusual method of forming contractions, their slang origins, or their idiomatic nature. Recognizing that context always helps us to understand meanings, I show each word or phrase in its context in the novel, then give a brief definition or explanation.

I do not list below all of the words and phrases that appear to be in nonstandard English, since readers can easily enough figure out as they read through the novel, by common sense or from context, that "c'mon" (5) means "come on," "m'boy" (8) means "my boy," "willya?" (23) means "will you," "oughta" (32) means "ought to," "wanna" (47) means "want to," "gotta" (47) means "got to," "gonna" (49) means "going to," "helluva" (97) means "hell of a," "awready" (103) means "already," "G'night" (151) means "Good night," "fella" (157) means "fellow," "G'by" (193) means "Good-by," "gimme" (208) means "give me," and so on. But other forms and expressions deserve special mention. I list them here in alphabetical order, and generally begin with the first instance in which the word appears in *The Catcher in the Rye*, but not always. And in any case, readers who find my explanation puzzling should be sure to consult the full context, not just the sentence I cite. And of course they should be aware that this is a glossary, not a dictionary. That is, I discuss the meanings of the words and phrases as they appear in *The Catcher in the Rye*. In other contexts, they can have quite different meanings.

and all "[How] my parents were occupied and all before they had me" (1). Holden uses this expression as a lazy shortcut that suggests vaguely, "there's more, but I don't want to go into it now." It usually adds little to the meaning, as when Holden says he knocked on Spencer's door "just to be polite and all" (7).

ass "Game, my ass. Some game" (8). One's "ass" is one's buttocks. Holden use the term "my ass" here to show his contempt for the notion that life is a game to be played by the rules. He seems to say, "life is a game about as much as my ass is." In other contexts there is no contempt, as when Holden says, "I moved my ass a little bit on the bed" (10). See **half-assed** below.

attaboy "'Wake 'er up, hey. Attaboy'" (150). This is Holden's slurred way of saying, "That's the boy." Typically used to speak to male children, it is scarcely an appropriate way to speak to Sally's grandmother. Holden is quite drunk when he says this.

backasswards "'You always do everything backasswards'" (41). Stradlater uses this slang synonym for "backwards" to describe Holden as a rebel who refuses to do things in the right or proper way. The more usual way to express the slang term is "ass-backwards."

bang "They got a bang out of things" (6). This slang noun suggests that the Spencers have an ability to enjoy life, to find pleasure in small things that might bore others. We learn later that Holden "really got a bang" (27) from wearing his red hunting hat. Holden sometimes uses the verb form, as in "He banged the hell out of the room" (34). That is, Stradlater left the room noisily, probably slamming the door as he left.

barge in "All of a sudden the door opened and old Stradlater barged in" (25). A "barge" is a large boat used for carrying freight or garbage. To "barge in" is to rush in uninvited and unwelcome, to intrude in a bulky, awkward way. Holden later tells us that Ackley "barged back in" (34) and, later still, that he himself is afraid his parents will "barge in" while he is talking with Phoebe (161).

bawling "I was so mad, I was practically bawling" (45). To "bawl" is to cry, usually out loud, this time in angry frustration at the thought of what Stradlater did to or with Jane Gallagher. Much later Holden says, "I was damn near bawling, I felt so damn happy" (213). In this case Holden is weeping for joy to see his sister on the carrousel, and for relief at having decided to return home.

beat it "I said no, that I'd better beat it" (180). To "beat it" is to leave, go away, usually in a hurry.

belching "'I'm taking belching lessons from this girl, Phyllis Margulies'" (174). Phyllis is teaching Phoebe how to burp—that is, eject gas noisily from the stomach through the mouth. The childish humor of this unladylike activity is obvious.

belongsa "'Who belongsa this?'" (22). This word is Ackley's supposedly clever way of saying "belongs to" or, more precisely, "Who belongs to this"—a nonstandard way to say, "Whom does this belong to?"

between he and I "'Then again, you may pick up just enough education to hate people who say, "It's a secret between he and I"'" (88). As an English teacher, Mr. Antolini would of course know that the proper construction would be "between him and me." Holden sometimes makes such errors himself, as when he says, "I used to play tennis with he and Mrs. Antolini" (180). He should of course say "with him and Mrs. Antolini."

big stink "[M]y mother [. . .] called up Jane's mother and made a big stink about it" (76). That is, Jane's mother complained about the dog's defecating on her lawn. The humor of "big stink" for the dog's smelly deposit is obvious. Holden could have said "made a fuss" or "asked her to keep her dog penned up," but he preferred the humor of "made a big stink."

blue "I just felt blue as hell" (154). In this context, "blue" means sad or depressed.

booze hound "'Her mother was married again to some booze hound'" (32). "Booze" is a slang term for alcoholic beverages, so a "booze hound" means a person who drinks too much. Holden sometimes uses "booze" as a verb, as when he says that a certain movie character "boozes all the time" (138) and when he says that Mr. Antolini "was still boozing" (193).

"Boozing" is a slang term for drinking alcohol. Beer, wine, and spirits are sometimes referred to as "booze."

bore "Harris Macklin [. . .] was one of the biggest bores I ever met" (123). The noun "bore" refers to a person who is tiresome, dull, tedious, and contributes nothing of interest to a conversation. The word is of course closely related to the verb "bore" (as in, he "he bores me") and the adjective (as in, "he was a boring man").

boy "Boy, I rang that doorbell fast when I got to old Spencer's house" (5). "Boy" is a slang expression indicating little more than mild intensity, like "gosh," "golly," or "wow." Holden himself comments on his use of the term: "'Boy!' I said. I also say 'Boy!' quite a lot" (9).

buck "[Y]ou could get members of your family buried for about five bucks apiece" (16). A "buck" is a slang term for a dollar. Soon after, we learn that Holden paid "a buck" (17) for his red hunting hat.

buddyroo "'Be a buddy. Be a buddyroo'" (28). A slang expression for "friend" or "pal." Holden uses the term again in describing the friendship between Sally and George: "Old buddyroos. It was nauseating" (127).

bull "That kind of stuff. The old bull" (13). "Bull" is an abbreviated euphemism for "bullshit," a coarse term for lies or nonsense-talk. Holden later refers to a "bull session" (167) in a school dormitory room—an informal gathering where students talk about things not related to their school work.

bum "I'd go down to the Holland Tunnel and bum a ride, and then I'd bum another one, and another one" (198). Holden means he will be a bum or hobo and hitchhike west. "Bumming" a ride, like "bumming" a cigarette, means begging, taking without paying or intending to pay back.

butt-twitcher "[T]hey gave Sally this little blue butt-twitcher of a dress" (129). The word may be Holden's coinage, but skating dresses were usually short and ruffly, with the ruffles emphasizing the way a woman's bottom moved or "twitched" seductively as she skated.

buzz see **give a buzz**, below.

can "I didn't have anything special to do so I went down to the can" (26). A "can" is usually a cylindrical container, but here it is a slang term for toilet or washroom. In Holden's dormitory the showers are between adjoining bedrooms, while the toilet stalls and the washbowls are in a separate room, or "can," down the hall.

can'tcha "'Can'tcha stick a little rum in it or something?'" (70). A sloppy way for Holden to say "can't you?" Rum, of course, is an alcoholic beverage, which in New York in 1949 could be served only to people over eighteen.

caught a glimpse "Old Mart said she'd only caught a glimpse of him" (74). To "catch a glimpse" is see out of the corner of the eye, or just to see with blurred vision. Holden is amused—"That killed me" (74)—because he had made up the story about seeing Gary Cooper.

chewed the rag "I went down [. . .] and chewed the rag with him" (26). To "chew the rag" is to talk. The term is similar to "chew the fat," as when Holden says that he and Sally Hayes "chewed the fat for a while. That is, she chewed it. You couldn't get a word in edgewise" (106).

chisel "'You're trying to chisel me'" (101). To "chisel" in this context means to cheat or swindle someone. Maurice, of course, denies it: "'Nobody's tryna chisel nobody'" (102). See **tryna** below.

Chrissake "'On the *sub*way, for Chrissake!'" (20). A shortening of "for Christ's sake." For Holden in this context, it is not a seriously blasphemous term.

clique "[E]verybody sticks together in these dirty little goddam cliques" (131). A "clique" is a small group of people that excludes others who are not like them. Holden gives several examples in the next couple of sentences. See **goddam** below.

cockeyed "[A]nd finally some dirty kid would tell them—all cockeyed, naturally—what it meant" (201). "Cockeyed" usually means squinty-eyed or cross-eyed, but here it means, more generally, twisted or wrong. Holden is worried that children will learn too early and from improper sources what the words "Fuck you" mean. Earlier Holden had told us that Phoebe "was in a cockeyed position way the hell over on the other side of the bed" (169). In this context it means that Phoebe is lying slanted, twisted, or contorted, as if she is trying to get as far away from Holden as possible across the bed from him.

corny "I mean if a boy's mother was sort of fat or corny-looking or something, and if somebody's father was one of those guys that wear those suits with very big shoulders and corny black-and-white shoes" (14). The term "corny" originally referred to a country hick or rustic-farmer-type, someone who would be obviously out of place in a city or in a sophisticated setting of any kind. Holden is thinking here of the way the snobbish Mr. Haas would spurn all but the most fashionably-dressed parents. Holden uses the term in a more positive sense when he speaks of Ernie the piano player: "He's so good he's almost corny" (80).

crap "[A]ll that David Copperfield kind of crap" (1). Here the word "crap" refers to useless and boring nonsense, but it often refers specifically to human or animal excrement, as when Holden mentions "dog crap" (118). Clearly, "crap" is a negative term, though not always a deeply derogatory one. When Holden leaves Mr. Spencer, he says we "shook hands. And all that crap" (15). He refers here to the usual niceties of saying farewell—handshakes, hugs, well-wishing, and so on. Later he refers to Ackley's lies about his sexual escapades as "all a lot of crap, naturally" (37) and tells us that when Allie's teachers praised him, "they weren't just shooting the crap. They really meant it" (38). See **shoot the crap** below for a slightly different meaning of that last expression.

crazy "I was standing [. . .] right next to this crazy cannon" (2). Holden does of course not mean literally insane, but rather more generally strange, unusual, outdated, or out of place. See also **mad** and **madman**, below. Sometimes he uses the term "crazy" in a manner closer to its more usual meaning, as when he refers to "that kind of crazy afternoon, [. . .] you felt like you were disappearing every time you crossed a road" (5), when he tells Phoebe to "cut out this crazy stuff" (208), and when he says "that drives me crazy" (10). Sometimes in the negative, "not crazy about" means that the speaker does not like something or someone: "I'm not too crazy about sick people" (7).

creeps "He was the witch doctor. He gave me the creeps" (120). To get the "creeps" is to feel nervous or frightened, especially in the presence of the occult or alien. Holden later talks about "creepy guys that go around having affairs with sheep" (143). There the term means weird or abnormal.

crew cut "I wear a crew cut quite frequently" (6). Sailors on naval vessels were given very short haircuts—sometimes called "buzz cuts" because they were given not with scissors but with buzzing electric clippers. Because these sailors were part of a ship's crew, the haircuts were called "crew cuts." The style caught on, and many men and boys not in the military wore their hair short.

crook "Pency was full of crooks" (4). A "crook" is a slang term for thief or robber.

crumb-bum "'So long, crumb-bum,' she said" (98). The term is usually a vaguely insulting way to describe someone who is acting like a complete jerk. More specifically, a "bum" can be either a homeless vagrant or a term for a person's buttocks. A crumb is the useless residue, as of a cookie. Sunny, insulted that Holden does not want to have sex with her and won't pay the extra fee she demands, by this epithet may want to call him a "crap-bottom." See next item.

crumby "That isn't too far from this crumby place" (1). Holden uses "crumby" as an adjective for almost anything he doesn't like or feels negative about—in this case, the California hospital or sanitarium where he has been recuperating. Later he refers to Ackley's "crumby nails" (23) and to the pimp Maurice's "crumby old hairy stomach" (102).

cut out "'Well, just cut out calling me—'" (25). A slang expression meaning "stop" or "quit." A similar expression appears later when Holden tells Stradlater to "'Cut it *out*'" (43).

damn see **give a damn** and **goddam**, below.

dime "'[A] dime for a cup of coffee'" (103). A dime is a coin worth ten cents or one-tenth of a dollar. In 1949 a dime could still buy a cup of coffee. For other names for coins, see **single** below. Later Holden says that he can't stop crying because "once you get started, you can't stop on a goddam dime" (179). The expression to "stop on a dime" refers to the fact that a dime is the thinnest and smallest of American coins. We are to imagine a car trying to make a stop while running over a dime on the road. It could not stop so suddenly, of course.

doing it "It was the address of this girl that wasn't exactly a whore or anything but didn't mind doing it once in a while" (63). The context makes clear that by "doing it" Holden means to have sexual intercourse.

don'tcha "'Why don'tcha?'" (32). "Why don't you?"

dopey guys "You figured that most of them would probably marry dopey guys" (123). The term "dopey" has nothing to do with drugs or "dope" in the sense of a controlled substance. It refers, rather, to people who are silly or shallow or immature. Holden gives some examples in the next five sentences. He spells the word differently when he refers to his mother's "asking the salesman a million dopy questions" (52).

dorm "He was probably the only guy in the whole dorm, besides me, that wasn't down at the game" (19). The term "dorm" is short for "dormitory"—now usually called a residence hall—where students live. The term derives from its French root, *dormir*, to sleep.

dough "He's got a lot of dough" (1). A slang expression for money. Holden tells us that his brother D.B. is rich. Later he reports that Mr. Ossenburger "gave Pencey a pile of dough" (16)—meaning lots of money.

drooling "I knew old Sally, the queen of the phonies, would start drooling all over the place when I told her I had tickets for that, because the Lunts were in it" (116). To "drool" is to salivate, as a dog does in anticipation of a good meal. Holden does not think that Sally will literally salivate, of course, but he knows that she will be excited. And she is: "'The Lunts! Oh, marvelous!' I told you she'd go mad when she heard it was for the Lunts" (125).

drop a note "'[Y]ou dropped me a little note, at the bottom of the page'" (12). The expression "drop a note" probably derives from "dropping" a letter into a mail slot or mailbox. Spencer uses the term somewhat sarcastically to refer to Holden's writing the short letter at the end of the exam. As he leaves Mr. Spencer, Holden promises to "drop you a line" (15)—meaning a letter or post card. There is no evidence that he keeps the promise.

faggy "[S]crawny and faggy on the Saxon Hall side" (2). A "fag"—
a shortened form of "faggot"—is a derogatory term for a
male homosexual, like "flit" and "queer." Here it refers to the
weak cheering for the visiting team, since so few spectators
came to the game.

falsies "[S]he had on those damn falsies that point all over the
place" (3). "Falsies" are artificially enhanced breasts made by
adding padding inside a woman's brassiere to make her look,
she imagines, more grown up and, thus, supposedly more
attractive to men. Falsies are different from breast implants,
which are surgically inserted inside or under breast tissue.

flitty-looking "On my right there was this Joe Yale-looking guy, in
a gray flannel suit and one of those flitty-looking Tattersal
vests" (85). In Holden's vocabulary, a "flit" is an effeminate
or gay man. Holden talks more specifically about "flits and
Lesbians" (143) when he reports his conversation with Carl
Luce, and he suspects that Mr. Antolini has made "a flitty
pass" at him (194). Compare **faggy** above.

flop "They always flop, though" (107). To "flop" is to fail. The
Broadway plays that Holden's father invests in always close
early, so he loses his investment.

flunking "I was flunking four subjects" (4). To "flunk" a subject is
to fail it. To be failing four of five courses was, of course, to
be in serious academic difficulty.

for the birds "Strictly for the birds" (2). Holden thinks the
advertisements for Pencey Prep are false and misleading, like
garbage or crumbs that scavenging birds will eat.

foyer "It was dark as hell in the foyer" (158). The "foyer" is the
vestibule or entrance hall to a house or an apartment.

freeze "I should've given them the freeze, after they did that" (70).
Holden means that he should have ignored them or, to use
a similar suggestion of iciness, "given them a cold shoulder."

Later, he speaks of the way Jane Gallagher "gave me the big freeze" (77).

galoshes "I was putting on my galoshes" (36). "Galoshes" are heavy rubber boots that fit over one's regular shoes.

get on nerves "'He gets on my nerves'" (164). Phoebe means that Curtis Weintraub, the boy who pushed her down the stairs, makes her nervous or scared—or just plain annoys her.

get sore "She never got sore, though, Miss Aigletinger" (120). To "get sore" is to become annoyed or be short tempered. Miss Aigletinger, apparently, always has a cheerful demeanor when she takes the children to the museum. Holden uses the same term later, in describing "dopey guys" who "get sore and childish as hell if you beat them at golf" (123), Sally Hayes, who "got sore when I said that" (127), and Carl Luce, who "got sore" (147) when people asked him personal questions.

give a buzz "I felt like giving somebody a buzz" (59) and "I went over to the phone and gave her a buzz" (63). To "buzz" someone is to call her or him on the telephone. The term derives from the buzzing sound heard in some telephone receivers. Holden uses this expression often, as in "I damn near gave my kid sister Phoebe a buzz" (66). "I gave [Sally] a buzz" (105), and "'I'm probably gonna give [Jane Gallagher] a buzz tomorrow'" (191).

give a damn "I don't give a damn" (9). Holden's slang expression means "I don't care" or "It doesn't bother me." In fact, though, in this instance it does seem to bother Holden when people comment on his immaturity. See also **goddam** below.

give the time "'What'd you do,' I said. 'Give her the time in Ed Banky's car?'" (43). To "give the time" is a slang for making love. Holden wants to know if Stradlater had sexual intercourse with Jane Gallagher in the coach's automobile.

goddam "I'm not going to tell you my whole goddam autobiography" (1). The term "goddam" is an abbreviated form of "God damn," but Holden does not use it in a blasphemous sense. That is, he does not really want God to condemn anyone or anything to the hell pit. Rather, he uses it as a more general term of minor disgust, like "darn" or "blasted." He sometimes uses the term "damn," but in a similarly uncondemnatory sense: "I was damn near bawling, I felt so damn happy" (213). In expressions like this, "damn" means little more than "very."

goner "With a guy like Ackley, if you looked up from your book you were a goner" (20). A "goner" is a dead man. Holden of course does not mean the term literally. He means that if he paid a little attention to Ackley, he might as well be dead because Ackley would just continue bothering him.

gorgeous "Forty-one gorgeous blocks" (88). The word "gorgeous" means lovely or beautiful in most contexts, but of course on this grim, dark, and cold night, Holden is being sarcastic. Here it means ugly or miserable. Later, when he suspects that he has cancer, Holden tells us that "It certainly didn't make me feel too gorgeous" (196).

go swell "[T]hese dark brown loafers [. . .] went swell with that suit my mother bought her in Canada" (159–60). That is, Phoebe's shoes matched the suit in color and style.

got the ax "So I got the ax" (4). An ax is a tool for cutting wood or trimming branches, but here Holden means that he has been kicked out or expelled from school. Holden uses the expression later: "I hated like hell for her to know I got the ax again" (107).

grand "Grand. There's a word I really hate. It's a phony" (9). "Grand" is a general and nonspecific term like "large," "luxurious," "nice," or "wonderful" that Holden thinks sounds false and pretentious. He uses similar language later, when Sally Hayes uses the word: "*Grand*. If there's one word I hate, it's grand. It's a phony" (106).

guts "[H]e didn't have guts enough not to at least grunt" (26). To have "guts" is a slang expression for having courage. Ackley is afraid not to make some response to Stradlater's question.

half-assed "They got a bang out of things, though—in a half-assed way" (6). One's "ass," of course, is one's butt or bottom. To be "half-assed" is to be somehow incomplete or abnormal. This slang expression usually is meant to be negative, but in Holden's use of it here to describe the Spencers' enjoyment of life, it is an almost endearing term meaning "old-fashioned" or "simple-minded."

halitosis "I have this one aunt with halitosis" (155). Foul smelling breath.

hellja "'Where in the hellja get that hat?'" (22). The term is a sloppy and childishly irreverent way of saying "hell did you"—"Where in the hell did you get that hat?" Ackley does not, of course, really think that Holden got the red hunting hat in hell.

hellya "'What the hellya reading?'" (21). This term abbreviates "hell are you"—"What [in] the hell are you reading?"

hit me "I guess it hasn't really hit me yet. It takes things a while to hit me" (14). "Hit" in this context refers not to physical hitting, but to cognitive awareness. Holden means that he has not yet fully confronted what it means to have flunked out of school.

hollering "'You guys start hollering and fighting in the middle of the goddam—'" (47). To "holler" is to shout or speak loudly.

hoodlumy-looking guys "Now and then you just saw [. . .] a bunch of hoodlumy-looking guys and their dates" (81).

Holden speaks of men who look to him like hoodlums—
that is, gangsters or young thugs.

horny "I was feeling pretty horny" (63). To be "horny," a term
usually referring to men, is to be sexually aroused or desirous
of sexual release. Just after he says this, Holden calls Faith
Cavendish.

horsing around "Then I started horsing around a little bit" (21).
Holden uses this expression with several kinds of meanings,
depending on the context. It usually suggests just having
fun, playing around, bantering, or fooling with. Later, when
Holden says that he "horsed around a little bit" with Sally
Hayes in the taxi, he means that he kissed her: "At first she
didn't want to, because she had lipstick on and all" (125).

hot-shot "They advertise in about a thousand magazines, always
showing some hot-shot guy on a horse" (2). The term "hot-
shot" is usually a negative term for an arrogant, privileged
snob. Holden uses the term again of Stradlater—"You take a
very handsome guy, or a guy that thinks he's a real hot-shot"
(27)—to refer to him as a conceited young man who thinks
he is better than other people. The term, however, is not
always negative for Holden. He speaks later of talking with
Louis Shaney "about certain hot-shot tennis players" (112),
apparently meaning that they are unusually good players.

hunks "[T]he back of my hair, even though I had my hunting
hat on, was sort of full of little hunks of ice" (154). These
"hunks" are small bits, residue from his dipping his head
in the sink before going out into the freezing cold. Holden
later describes the "big hunk of adhesive tape on [Phoebe's]
elbow" (164). Both uses are exaggerations, since a "hunk" is a
large piece or lump of something.

I'd've "I'd've killed him" (43). Contraction for "I would have."

innarested "'Innarested in having a good time, fella?'" (90). This is Maurice's sloppy pronunciation of "interested." On the next page he expands it to "'Y' innarested?'"—for "Are you interested?" "Have a good time" here is a euphemism for "have sex with a prostitute."

jammed out "I jammed out my cigarette on my shoe and put it in my pocket" (176). In this unusual usage of "jammed," Holden tells us that he snuffed or snubbed his cigarette by crushing the lit end against the sole of his shoe.

kicked out "'Don't tell her I got kicked out'" (330). Like "to get the ax," to be "kicked out" is to be expelled from school.

kid the pants off "I think I really like it best when you can kid the pants off a girl" (78). Although Holden speaks here of Jane Gallagher, a young woman he really likes, the context makes clear that this is just a generic expression, not a literal one. That is, he does not really want to kid (that is, joke or banter) Jane's pants off, any more than "those dopes that clap their heads off" (84) when Ernie plays the piano no longer have heads, or than the Rockettes "kicking their heads off" (137) are headless dancers.

killed "The best one in it was 'The Secret Goldfish.' [. . .] It killed me" (1–2). Holden here means that he really, really liked D.B.'s story—so much that the sheer enjoyment almost wiped him out. Discussing his liking for his sister Phoebe, Holden says "She killed Allie, too. I mean he liked her, too" (68). In other contexts, it can have a different meaning, as when Holden responds to Mrs. Morrow's comment that her son is sensitive: "Sensitive. That killed me. That guy Morrow as about as sensitive as a goddam toilet seat" (55). Here the simile "sensitive as a toilet seat" shows Holden's amused contempt for his classmate. Holden uses the phrase "killed" often, usually to suggest extreme amusement, surprise, contempt, enjoyment, or admiration. On the other hand, when Phoebe tells Holden, "'Daddy'll *kill* you!'" (165, 166, 172), she means something quite different. She does not mean, of course, that their father will literally murder Holden, but only that he will be angry and disappointed with Holden and will punish him. The context determines the meaning.

kiss ass "The only way *she* could go around with a basket collecting dough was if everyone kissed her ass for her when they made a contribution" (114). Holden does not mean the term literally, but means that Sally Hayes's mother would do good deeds only if she got a lot of praise and attention.

knocked out "That knocked him out. He started chuckling" (8). Holden means that Mr. Spencer is so pleased with himself that he nearly passes out. Holden sometimes uses the term in reference to Jane Gallagher—"She knocked me out, though" (77)—to suggest that he finds Jane so attractive and fascinating that he nearly passes out. Another time, in a movie, Jane's touching his neck "just about knocked me out" (79). To say, "she knocked me out" is a little like saying, "she made me delirious."

knockers "She had these very big knockers" (86). "Knockers" is a slang term for breasts.

lemme speaka "'Lemme speaka Sally, please'" (150). Holden, now very drunk, slurs his words. He means, "Let me speak to Sally, please."

letcha "'If I letcha up, willya keep your mouth shut?'" "If I let you."

lousy "[W]hat my lousy childhood was like" (1). The term "lousy" derives from the term "louse" (plural "lice"), an annoying insect parasite that bites humans and makes them hurt or itch. The term has come to be used as a slang catch-all for any negative reaction. Here, Holden clearly feels that he had an unfortunate childhood. When Holden tells us that

Mr. Spencer "really felt pretty lousy about flunking me" (12), he means that his teacher's conscience is bothering him because he feels he has failed with Holden. "Lousy" can have alternative negative meanings, according to the context, as when Holden says that he has "a lousy vocabulary" (9), when Ackley says to Holden, "'I'm old enough to be your lousy father'" (25), when Holden tells Carl Luce, "'My sex life is lousy'" (147), when Phoebe tells her mother that her dinner was "'lousy'" (177), and when Holden says that Mrs. Antolini is "lousy with dough" (181). This last means only that she has a lot of money. Phoebe's mother reminds her that her father had asked her not to use "'that word'" since in her view "lousy" is inappropriate vocabulary for a child. Holden rarely uses the noun form, though occasionally he does, as when he says that "the bartender was a louse" (142).

lulu "And there were some lulus, too" (129). "Lulu" is a slang word for something or someone outstanding, unusual, or exaggerated: "It was a lulu of a storm," "He was a lulu of a president," and so on. The term often has negative connotations. Holden means in this case that there were some *really* bad skaters on the rink.

Mac "'I can't turn around here, Mac'" (60). "Mac," like "bud" and "buddy" below on the same page, is the taxi driver's generic nickname for a stranger whose name he doesn't know and doesn't want to bother to learn. It is akin to the name "Jack" (64) that Faith Cavendish calls Holden when he calls her, and "chief," that Maurice the elevator pimp calls him (91, 101–02).

mad "Old Selma [. . .] wasn't exactly the type that drove you mad with desire" (3). "Mad" usually means either angry or crazy, but for Holden it usually is a jocular reference to the latter. His point here is that Selma, while a nice young woman, is not sexually attractive to him. Later he tells us that Sally went "mad" (125) when she learned that Holden bought tickets to a play with the Lunts. Here he means something like "delirious with joy" rather than actually insane. See also **crazy** above and **madman** below.

made out "Phoebe stopped and made out she was watching the sea lions getting fed" (209). To "make out" in this context is to pretend, to make it look as if, she is watching the sea lions. Holden does not seem to use the phrase "to make out" to refer to preliminary sexual activities, like kissing and sexual touching.

madman "I'll just tell you about this madman stuff that happened to me" (1). Holden uses the adjective "madman" here not to mean literally insane, but more like just strange or nutty or weird. Sometimes it has a more literal meaning, as when Holden uses a simile by saying that Spencer "started chuckling like a madman" (8). Of course Spencer is not mad, any more than the snow is insane when Holden says that it "came down like a madman" (35). In its flexibility of meaning, "madman" is for Holden similar to **crazy** (see above).

mercy killer " 'He was a mercy killer' " (163). The doctor Phoebe speaks of apparently believes in euthanasia—the killing of the very sick and the aged to put them out of their supposed misery.

moron "I told him I was a real moron" (12). A "moron" is a derogatory term for someone who lacks basic intelligence. Here Holden is trying to make Mr. Spencer feel better about failing him. Holden later uses the term of Stradlater— " 'You're a dirty stupid sonuvabitch of a moron' " (44)—for which Stradlater beats him up. Still later, Holden shouts as he leaves the dormitory, " '*Sleep tight, ya morons!* ' " (52).

necking "It was the only time old Jane and I ever got close to necking, even" (78). "Necking" is a slang term for the hugging and kissing that sometimes precedes intercourse, but need not. Holden necks a lot with Sally Hayes: "I'd have found it out a lot sooner if we hadn't necked so damn much" (105).

nuts "'You're nuts. I swear to God'" (21). "Nuts" here is a slang word for insane.

offa "'Go ahead. Get *offa* me'" (44). Abbreviated form of "off of." Holden says this to Stradlater, who is sitting on his chest.

oiled up "You could tell he was a little oiled up" (182). That is, Mr. Antolini was, if not drunk, then well on his way to being so. Alcohol is sometimes said to "oil" difficult or embarrassing human relationships. Holden describes Mr. Antolini with a similar expression again: "He was pretty oiled up" (188).

old "Old Selma Thurmer—she was the headmaster's daughter" (3). Holden uses the adjective "old" many times, but rarely to signify anything about a person's age. Often it is a sign of familiar affection, as when he refers to his young sister as "old Phoebe."

oodles "'We'll have oodles of time to do those things. [. . .] There'll be oodles of marvelous places to go to'" (133). A nonspecific but large quantity of anything, roughly synonymous with "lots."

passed out "I sort of passed out" (204). To "pass out" here means to faint.

Pencey Prep "Where I want to start telling is the day I left Pencey Prep" (2). This term is an abbreviation for Pennsylvania Preparatory School. A preparatory school is a high school, usually private and expensive, that "prepares" high school students for college.

pets "Stradlater was one of his pets" (43). "Pet" means a favorite, an abbreviated form of the term "teacher's pet."

phony slob "She probably knew what a phony slob he was" (3). To be "phony"—a word Holden uses a lot, both as a noun and as an adjective—is to be insincere, false, deceptive, or hypocritical. A "slob" is a slang term for a person one does not like. It usually connotes sloppiness, dirtiness, or general slovenliness, but here, referring to the headmaster of the school, it suggests an obnoxious personality. Holden later describes both Ackley and Stradlater as slobs.

pretty "[M]y parents would have about two hemorrhages apiece if I told anything pretty personal about them" (1). While "pretty" often means lovely or beautiful, here and elsewhere it means "very." Holden uses it again when he tells Spencer that his parents will be "pretty irritated about it" (9).

puke "I could puke every time I hear it" (9). "Puke" is a slang term for vomiting or throwing up. Holden often uses such expressions for things he does not like, as in "The band was putrid" (69)—meaning rotten, stinking.

rip off "We tried to get old Marsalla to rip off another one" (17). The term "rip off" can have several meanings—like cheat someone, as in "he ripped me off"—but here it refers to the act of farting. The term in this context is meant to suggest the sound of cloth being torn apart.

rocks "Boy, she was lousy with rocks" (55). "Rocks" is here a slang term for diamonds—in this case diamond rings. The term "lousy" here means simply that there were a lot of them. Mrs. Morrow is apparently quite rich.

rubbering "Old Sally didn't talk much, except to rave about the Lunts, because she was busy rubbering and being charming" (127). This unusual word usage derives from the verb "rubberneck," which means to gawk and look around curiously as if one's neck were made of rubber. Sally likes to look all around to see who she knows or recognizes. Later, at the ice rink, Holden refers contemptuously to "rubbernecks that didn't have anything better to do than stand around and watch everybody falling all over themselves" (129).

rub it off "I tried to rub it off again with my hand" (202). To "rub something off" is to obliterate or erase it. Holden uses the palm of his hand to try to remove the "Fuck you" sign, but as he says, "It wouldn't come off."

sack "'Go home and hit the sack'" (152). The piano player tells Holden to go home and go to bed. Later Holden says that Mrs. Antolini had just recently "arose from the sack" (182)— that is, gotten out of bed.

scraggy "'[Y]ou'll be one of those scraggy guys that come up to you on the street'" (103). "Scraggy" means scrawny or emaciated, here with implications that in begging for coffee money, Maurice will be a homeless and unemployed bum. Later Holden refers to "those scraggy-looking Santa Clauses [. . .] standing on corners ringing those bells" (197). The "real" Santa was supposed to be fat and jolly.

shack up "I completely forgot I was going to shack up in a hotel for a couple of days" (60). To "shack up" is to live temporarily in a place not one's home. Often it suggests living unmarried with a partner, but that is not what Holden is thinking of here.

sharp as a tack "Old Spencer looked like he had something very good, something sharp as a tack, to say to me" (10). A tack is a short nail usually used for attaching carpet or repairing shoes. To be "sharp as a tack" is a slang simile for being bright or incisive or witty. It is like another simile that Holden uses of Mr. Spencer, that he was "hot as a firecracker" (12).

shell out "'I'm sorry—I really am—but that's all I'm gonna shell out'" (98). "Shell out" is a slang term for handing over money, which Holden here refuses to do.

shoot the breeze "Then the old lady that was about a hundred years old and I shot the breeze for a while" (201). To "shoot the breeze" is a slang expression for idle conversation, chatter about things of little consequence. Compare the next two items.

shoot the bull "I was sort of thinking of something else while I shot the bull" (13). There is, of course, no animal-bull being fired upon here. "Shooting the bull," a euphemism or polite alternative to the harsher and more graphic "bull-shitting," means talking or jabbering with others about matters of little consequence.

shoot the crap "I certainly wouldn't have minded shooting the crap with old Phoebe for a while" (67). "Shooting the crap" means talking informally with someone. It is close in meaning to the previous two expressions. It has nothing to do with the term "crap shooting," which is a gambling game involving dice.

show-offy-looking "They were mostly old, show-offy-looking guys with their dates" (69). Holden uses this shortcut term to refer to men who looked as if they were eager to show off their money or clothes or women to others.

single "All I had was three singles and five quarters and a nickle left" (156). A "single" here means a one-dollar bill. A "quarter" is a twenty-five-cent coin—a quarter of dollar. A "nickle" is a five-cent coin. Holden's total cash, then, is $4.30.

sleep like a rock "He slept like a rock" (50). To "sleep like a rock," like to "sleep like a log," means to sleep so soundly that one is virtually lifeless and unwakeable. See **rocks** above for a quite different meaning of the word.

smack "She had her mouth right smack on the pillow, and I couldn't hear her" (169). "Smack" here means "directly" or "tightly against." Later Holden speaks of finding Phoebe sitting "smack in the middle of the bed" (174–75)—meaning exactly in the middle.

snotty "Not snotty, though. She was too charming and all to be snotty" (57). Snot is the unpleasant mucus that drips from the nose when one has a cold. To be "snotty" is to be moody, unpleasant, or snippy—which Mrs. Morrow is not, even when she corrects Holden about having a drink in the club car (the bar). Holden uses the term with some regularity, as of Sally Hayes (130) and his sister Phoebe (167), to mean cold, angry, or arrogant.

so-and-so "'Well, you little so-and so'" (87). Apparently "so-and-so" is a genial euphemism for something worse that Lillian might have said, like "you little bastard" or "you little son of a bitch." But it is genial and friendly, if only because Lillian really does want Holden to give his brother D.B. her message.

sonuvabitch "'I can't stand that sonuvabitch'" (23). "Son of a bitch"—a derogatory slur on Stradlater's mother, suggesting that she is a female dog. It is unlikely, however, that Ackley or any of the others who use the term think of it so literally, any more than "bastard" is meant literally by Holden to suggest illegitimacy. Both are general terms of insult.

soul kiss "'Why don't you go on over and give him a big soul kiss, if you know him?'" (127). By this sarcastic question, Holden tells Sally to go give George an open-mouth, tongue-intertwining kiss, sometimes known as a French kiss.

spooky "He looked sort of spooky in the dark" (46). A "spook" is a ghost or apparition of the dead. With his face smeared in white acne cream, Ackley looks to Holden like a dead man or a ghost. Holden uses the word again to describe the prostitute Sunny: "She was a pretty spooky kid. [. . .] If she'd been a big old prostitute, with a lot of makeup on her face and all, she wouldn't have been half as spooky" (98). Here "spooky" seems to mean just generally "scary," as it does later when Holden refers to the "witch doctor" in the Indian canoe as "a very spooky guy" (120) and when he refers to the Pharaoh's tomb in the museum as "spooky" (203).

spread out "She likes to spread out" (159). That is, she likes to have plenty of room to distribute her clothing, toys, and homework around the room.

stiffs "I can just see the big phony bastard shifting into first gear and asking Jesus to send him a few more stiffs" (17). The noun "stiff" is a slang term for a dead body or corpse, so-named because of the rigor mortis that makes the body rigid.

tail "'Inarrested in a little tail t'night?'" (90). Maurice uses "tail" as a euphemism for "ass" in asking Holden if he wants to purchase the services of a prostitute. See **inarrested** above.

take a leak "Like somebody'd just taken a leak on them" (200). To "take a leak" is a slang term for urinate.

talka "'Wanna talka Sally'" (150). "I want to talk to Sally." Holden, drunk, slurs his speech.

tear "'I have to tear'" (148). Here "tear" (rhyming with "bare"), means to leave or rush off. Carl Luce had started the conversation by telling Holden "he could only stay a couple of minutes" (144).

throw "'Five bucks a throw'" (91). A "throw" in this context is a single sexual encounter—sometimes called a "quickie"—with a prostitute, as opposed to having her spend the entire night.

tiff "'I had a little goddam tiff with Stradlater'" (47). A "tiff" is an argument or fight, usually not a dangerous or prolonged one.

toleja "'Listen. I toleja about that'" (72). Sloppy abridgment of "told you."

tossed his cookies "The cab I had was a real old one that smelled like someone'd just tossed his cookies in it" (81). To "toss one's cookies" as the following sentence makes clear, is to throw up or vomit.

touchy "They're quite touchy about anything like that" (1). To be "touchy" is to be overly sensitive or easily embarrassed.

trimma see **trim the tree** below.

trim the tree "'Are you or aren't you coming over to help me trim the tree Christmas Eve?'" (130). By "trim" Sally means decorate the Christmas tree with ornaments and strings of lights. Later, Holden drunkenly slurs his words by telling Sally that he wants to come over and "trimma tree for ya" (151).

tryna "'I was tryna *sleep*'" (46). Sloppy abridgment for "trying to." Salinger uses this spelling often, as when the taxi driver asks Holden, "What're ya tryna do, bud?" (60), and when Maurice tells him, "'Nobody's tryna chisel nobody'" (102).

up his alley "He wouldn't have understood it anyway. It wasn't up his alley" (13). An alley is a small street, but "not up his alley" means that Mr. Spenser would not have been interested.

up the creek "'I'll be up the creek if I don't get the goddam thing in by Monday'" (28). The full statement of the expression is "up the creek without a paddle"—that is, in dire trouble.

watch on ya "'Ya got a watch on ya?'" (94). Sunny asks if Holden is wearing a wristwatch. Her question is essentially, "What time it is?" Since she is being paid only for "a throw," she wants him to get on with it so she can get back to bed. She asks the same question again on the next page.

wheeny-whiny "She had a tiny little wheeny-whiny voice. You could hardly hear her" (94). Holden's adjective "wheeny-whiny" is his own invention to suggest that Sunny is a young and frail child—perhaps part of the reason he decides not to go through with the encounter. It is probably a conscious rhyme for "teeny-tiny." Holden reminds us later in the chapter of Sunny's "little bitty voice" (98).

whenja "'Whenja get home?'" (161). "When did you get home?"

where'd ya "'[W]here'd ya go with her?'" (42). "Where did you go with her?"

wouldn't've "She wouldn't've cared if I'd woke her up" (59). "Would not have."

wuddaya "'Wuddaya wanna make me do—cut my goddam head off?'" (30). This "word" is a sloppy contraction of "what do you?" Stradlater uses it again when he asks Holden, "'Wuddaya mean *so what?*'" (41), and later Ackley asks Holden, "'Wuddaya mean what the hell am I doing?'" (46).

wuddayacallit "'I had an operation. [. . .] On my wuddayacallit'" (96). A sloppy shortening of "what do you call it?" Since he is lying about his operation, Holden has trouble thinking of what was operated on. He comes up with "my clavichord," a term that humorously shows his ignorance of human anatomy. An alternative form of "wuddayacallit" is Sunny's "wutchamacallit" (102)—"what you may call it."

wudga "'Wudga say?'" (71). "What did you say?"

yella streak "'He's got a yella streak a mile wide'" (204). One of the boys Holden takes to the pharaoh's tomb in the museum accuses the other of being "yellow" or cowardly. To have a yellow streak a mile wide is a slang exaggeration. See **yellow** below.

yellow "I'm one of these very yellow guys" (88). Holden admits here that he is a coward. Later he mentions seeing an actor who "always plays the part of a guy in a war movie that gets yellow before it's time to go over the top" (126). See also **yella streak** above.

Questions for readers
of *The Catcher in the Rye*

In this chapter I give two sets of questions. The first set may help readers of *The Catcher in the Rye* focus on some of the issues that are important in each chapter. They may also help students and teachers begin to frame classroom discussions of the novel. The second set will help users of this volume to find topics for essays on some of the issues raised in my long introductory section to this Companion, "Catching *The Catcher in the Rye*" (pp. 1–72). Implicit in all of the questions is the suggestion that you are to explain and defend your answer.

Discussion questions for readers of *The Catcher in the Rye*

Chapters 1–7: Holden says good-by to Pencey

1. Standing on Thomsen Hill

The second word in the novel is "you"? Who is "you"? Someone in Holden's family? A psychiatrist? A generalized reader? Is it the same "you" that we find on page 68 when Holden says of Phoebe, twice, "You'd like her" and on page 213 when he says "God, I wish you could've been there"? Why does Holden assume that "you" might "want to hear about it"? What is "it"?

Knowing what you know about Holden so far, why do you suppose he might like "The Secret Goldfish," a story about a kid who bought a goldfish with his own money and would let no one look at it?

How does remembering a pick-up football game help Holden "get a good-by"?

2. Playing by the rules

Why does Holden reject the idea that life is a game that we have to play by the rules? Is his problem that he wants to make his own rules? Has he earned the right to make them?

Why does the adjective "grand" make Holden "want to puke"?

How seriously are we to take Holden's statement that the behavior of Mr. Haas at Elkton Hills "drives me crazy. It makes me so depressed I go crazy" (14). Does "crazy" here mean *insane* or something different, like *angry* or just *frustrated*?

3. Robert Ackley

Does Ackley seem like an exaggerated caricature of a repulsive school roommate, or do you believe there are such people? How does Ackley function in the story? Is he, for example, part of the reason Holden leaves Pencey? Is he more like Holden than either would admit? Is he just a foil to Stradlater?

How seriously are we to take Holden's speech to "Mother, darling" (21)? Is he just horsing around or is he, in some sense, really blind?

4. Ward Stradlater and Jane Gallagher

Ackley is a slob. Stradlater is a secret slob. What is the difference, which is worse, and why?

Holden seems to be fascinated with Jane Gallagher. Do you think he is—or was—in love with her? If so, why did he not stay in touch with her? If not, how would you describe Holden's interest in her?

What do you make of Jane's keeping her kings in the back row? Why does Holden ask Stradlater to ask her if she still keeps them there? Is the request supposed to convey a concealed message to her?

Why does Holden not go downstairs to say hi to Jane?

5. Allie's baseball mitt

What does Allie's baseball mitt tell us about Allie? What does Holden's keeping it tell us about him?

What does Holden's decision to write about Allie's mitt tell us about Holden? Does he do it, for example, to pay homage to Allie, or to make trouble for Stradlater, or to assuage his own feelings of guilt, etc.?

When Allie died, Holden broke his hand attacking windows. Why does he break windows rather than, say, books, dishes, car tires, shrubs, flower pots, school water fountains, whatever?

6. Fighting Stradlater

Holden tells us several times in this chapter that he can't remember much of what happened. Is there a pattern to what he forgets? What does his faulty memory tell us about him?

Does Holden pick a fight with Stradlater to punish him, or to be punished by him?

7. Packing up

Why does imagining Jane Gallagher with Stradlater in a parked car make Holden think about jumping out a window? Do such thoughts connect in some way with other windows in the novel?

Three times in this chapter Holden mentions feeling lonesome. What makes him feel that way, and how does it affect his decision to leave Pencey early?

Why does Holden think he wants to join a monastery? What problems would that solve?

Why does getting gifts make Holden feel sad?

Chapters 8-14: Holden goes to Manhattan

8. On the train with Mrs. Morrow

Why is Holden drawn to Mrs. Morrow?

Why does he tell her flattering lies about her son Ernest?

Mrs. Morrow suggests to Holden a perfect reason for going home early—that someone in his family is sick.

Why does he reject that one and claim instead to have a brain tumor?

9. On the phone with Faith Cavendish

Is it of any significance that Holden gives the cab driver the wrong address?

Why does Holden feel the need to give someone "a buzz"? Is it loneliness, horniness, fear, or what?

What does his conversation with Faith Cavendish tell us about Holden? For example, why does he not make an appointment with her, as she suggested, for the next day?

10. Three witches from Seattle

Do you see anything strange or suspect in Holden's admiration of Phoebe?

We hear a lot about what Holden hates—phonies, unfairness, cruelty to children, sexually predatory men, and so on—but in this chapter we learn some of what he likes. Well, what? Do you see any patterns in what he likes?

What are Holden's lies in this chapter, and why does he lie?

11. Thinking about Jane Gallagher again

Can we tell what triggers Holden's thoughts about Jane again?

Again, would you say that Holden is in love with Jane?

What do you think may have happened—if anything—between Jane and Mr. Cudahy? Why does it bother Holden?

12. Greenwich Village

Why does Holden feel so lonesome? If he is lonesome, why does he turn down Lillian's invitation to come to her table? Does he *like* being lonesome?

How do you explain Holden's concerns about the Central Park ducks?

Why does Holden despise Ernie—or doesn't he?

13. Encounter with Sunny

Why would it be easier for Holden to murder an antagonist than to punch him in the jaw?

Holden says he stops when a girl tells him to, but Sunny never tells him to stop. On the contrary, she wants him to go on. Why then does Holden stop with Sunny and dismiss her?

Why does Holden not "tip" Sunny the extra five dollars? At some level, does he *want* to be beaten up by Maurice?

14. Encounter with Maurice

Does that first paragraph about Holden's recollections of Allie grow naturally out of his encounter with Sunny and his sending her away untouched?

Why does Holden like the biblical lunatic more than anyone else in the Bible?

Why does Holden open the door, knowing it is Maurice? Why does he speak so nastily to Maurice?

Why does he then have his movie-fantasy of "plugging" Maurice?

Chapters 15–20: Holden wanders Manhattan

15. Breakfast with two nuns

What does Holden's attitude to suitcases tell us about his values and his sensitivity to the feelings of people with less money?

Why is Holden so generous with the two nuns? Is he somehow making amends for something? Is it connected with his interest in joining a monastery?

What might be said of Holden's reaction to *Romeo and Juliet*? For example, what upsets him about the play, and why?

16. Remembering the Museum of Natural History

What are we to make of the little boy who sings the "If-a-body" song that gives the novel its title.

What are we to make of the little boy's oblivious parents?

Do we learn anything important about Holden from his comment about Sir Laurence Olivier's *Hamlet*?

Why does Holden love the museum?

Why, if he loves it, does suddenly decide not to go inside?

17. A date with Sally Hayes

Holden seems to make a distinction between people who are good at something and people who *know* they are good at it. What is he getting at?

After ice-skating, Holden launches into a list of the things he hates. What *doesn't* he hate? Can you add to the list you started in chapter 10?

Sally, who plays by the rules, thinks that Holden's plan to run off with her and live in a cabin in the woods is impractical. Do you agree with her that Holden's plan is silly?

Holden asks Sally, "Don't you see what I mean at all?" She doesn't. Do you?

18. Thoughts about war

Why does Holden react so violently to the movie he sees at Radio City?

How do you account for the anti-military, anti-war attitudes of Holden, who at age sixteen has had no direct experience of either?

Do you think Holden is serious about volunteering to be blown up by an atomic bomb?

19. Cocktails and conversation with Luce

Who is more obnoxious in this chapter, Holden or Luce?

Are we supposed to think that Luce is a "flit"? What evidence is there either way?

What about Holden's own sexual orientation?

20. Imagining dying

Why does Holden decide to get drunk and then go to check on the ducks?

Is Holden suicidal?

What do we learn about Holden from his imagining being dead, his funeral, others' visits to the cemetery, and so on?

Chapters 21–26: Holden goes home

21. Creeping home to see Phoebe

Why is it so important that Holden sees Phoebe? After all, she's only a ten-year-old kid, and he's sixteen.

How does Phoebe know her brother has been expelled?

Why does Phoebe hide her head under a pillow when she finds out? Does I have anything to do with the film she has just seen, or with her repeated statement that Holden's father will kill him?

22. Talking to Phoebe

What do you think of Holden's answer to Phoebe's question about why he got the ax again?

How accurate is Phoebe's analysis—that Holden doesn't like anything?

What do you think of Holden's desired life's work of saving little kids from falling off a cliff? What events in his life do you think led him to want to do that? How realistic is it?

At one point Holden says he doesn't give a damn if his father does kill him. Do you believe him?

23. Dancing with Phoebe

Is Holden's dancing with Phoebe just "horsing around"?

What triggers Holden's sudden decision to call Mr. Antolini?

Why does Holden cry?

Does Holden really want his parents to "catch" him?

24. Talking with Mr. Antolini

Why does Mr. Antolini think Holden is riding for terrible fall? Do you agree? Is he like a kid playing in a rye field but getting too close to the edge of a cliff?

Is Mr. Antolini right that Holden is "troubled morally and spiritually" (189)?

Does the Stekel quotation about the immature man fit Holden?

Do you think Mr. Antolini makes a "perverty" pass at Holden?

Does it matter whether Mr. Antolini is gay?

25. In the Museum of Natural History

How would you make sense of Holden's symptoms in this chapter: his sweating, his headache, his burning eyes, his nausea, his feeling that he is getting a cold, his inability to swallow, his shortness in breathing, his diarrhea, his dizziness, his passing out?

What do you make of Holden's plan to hitchhike West, work in a gas station, and pretend to be a deaf-mute?

Why does Holden hate it when people say "Good luck" to him?

Is there any significance to Holden's fascination with the ancient Egyptians' methods of preserving dead bodies?

Why does Holden get so angry at the "Fuck you" signs in the school and museum?

Why does Holden change his mind about going West and decide to go home instead?

How do you read Holden's phrase "if I ever die" (204)? For example, why doesn't he say "when I die." Does it matter that he is in a tomb when he says it?

After three days of being pretty miserable, Holden finally feels "so damn happy" (213). What does he have to be happy about? Would you say that the novel has a happy ending?

26. Missing them

Do you think Holden will "apply himself" when he goes back to school in September? In other words, has he changed in the course of the three days he tells us about?

What does it mean that at the very end that Holden misses three men he despised only a short while earlier? Is it a sign of inconsistency, of weakness, of growth, of insanity, of . . . well, what?

Is something missing from the end? For example, would you have liked to see Holden make some reference to his mother, Phoebe, Jane, Sally, or Sunny?

Essay questions keyed to "Catching *The Catcher in the Rye*"

1. Time line of *The Catcher in the Rye*

Do you think Salinger consulted a 1949 calendar in composing *The Catcher in the Rye?*

Does it matter that we work out the time line for Holden's adventures?

2. Biographical references

Why do you suppose Salinger was so reclusive? Was he hiding something or escaping something? Does *The Catcher in the Rye* suggest possible answers?

To what extent did Salinger's reclusiveness make him more fascinating as a subject for biographical research? Is *The Catcher in the Rye* so popular in part because its author has been so famously hermitic?

3. Salinger's life in *The Catcher in the Rye*

How does it matter that Holden is, or is not, a fictionalized self-portrait? Does our decision about its autobiographical nature change our reading or evaluation of the novel?

Pick a chapter from the novel that "sounds" particularly autobiographical and contrast it with one that sounds less so. How are they different?

What does it tell you about Salinger that he so adamantly refused to let anyone put his novel on stage or in film?

4. From the stories to *The Catcher in the Rye*

Does "I'm Crazy" sound like a completed project, or is it clearly just a prelude to more?

What does Holden mean by "crazy"? Does he mean "insane" or something more like "weird" or "impulsive" Does the meaning of "crazy" shift from its use in the story to its use in the novel?

Does the business with Sally Hayes fit in the novel, or does it seem that Salinger just shoe-horned it in because he had it written? Consider Holden's relationship with Jane and Sunny and Phoebe. Is there a place for Sally in this novel?

Why, for the novel, did Salinger want Holden to have two brothers?

In "Slight Rebellion Off Madison" Sally answers the phone herself. Why in the novel did Salinger have Sally's maid and her father talk to Holden before Sally comes on?

5. Holden Caulfield's appearance

Sunny tells Holden looks he looks like the kid "that falls off this boat" in the movie. In describing him thus, does she tell us more about herself than about Holden?

Does it seem to you that Holden thinks he is handsome? Does his handsomeness matter?

6. *The Catcher in the Rye* in other fiction

Read one of the many novels mentioned in this section and decide whether you agree that the author was indeed building on *The Catcher in the Rye*.

If you were to write a novel based on an important sequence of events in your own growing up, do you think you would be able to avoid its being influenced by Salinger's *Catcher in the Rye*? Would you *want* to avoid that influence?

7. *The Catcher in the Rye* in movie and song

What is there about Holden that causes him, more than other literary characters—Huck Finn, Jay Gatsby, Nick Adams come to mind as comparisons—to capture the imaginations of generation after generation of Americans?

Is Holden's influence good or bad for young people? Does it make them better or worse citizens? Is the world a better or worse place because of *The Catcher in the Rye*?

If you were asked to write a story, movie script, or song lyrics about a Holden-like man or woman, how would you start it?

8. The enduring appeal of *The Catcher in the Rye*

Whether or not *The Catcher in the Rye* appeals to you personally, how would you explain its continuing popularity?

How typical of sixteen-year-olds is Holden Caulfield? Were you like that when you were sixteen? If not, how do you explain his popularity as a literary figure?

Which other character in the novel do you find most memorable and appealing?

Refute one of the many explanations of Holden's appeal quoted in this section.

9. The aftermath of J. D. Salinger's death

Challenge one of the statements quoted in this section. For example, do you agree with Adam Gopnik that *The Catcher in the Rye* is "the handbook of the adolescent heart" (p. 68)?

"Jane" reports that Salinger told a visitor in 1975 that *The Catcher in the Rye* "was a silly book when I wrote it twenty-five years ago and it's a silly book today" (p. 70). What do you think he meant by "silly"? Was he being serious or silly when he said that?

Do you agree with the English woman Leslie that Holden is "about a self-absorbed, privileged, ungrateful little snot" (p. 70)? Do you think Salinger would have disagreed, or would he have said, "Yep, Leslie got the point of the novel"?

Index to *The Catcher in the Rye*

This index will help readers of *The Catcher in the Rye* to identify and locate in the novel itself the people and places that Holden refers to. All page numbers are to the Little, Brown paperback edition. Holden Caulfield, of course, is not indexed since, as narrator, he appears on every page of the novel. Note that this index is to the novel itself, not to the *Reader's Companion*. The following index will help readers find references in the *Companion*.

Ackley, Robert, Holden's friend and suite mate at Pencey Prep 19–26, 28–29, 34–37, 39, 46–51, 105, 140, 167, 187, 214

Ackley's babe, with whom he claims to have had sex 37

Agerstown, where Pencey Prep is located in southeastern Pennsylvania 2, 36, 105

Aigletinger, Miss, Holden's grade-school teacher 119–21

alcoholic woman, sells a desk to D.B. 159

Alec, name of character in movie that Holden sees 138–39

Alec's mother, character in movie that Holden sees 139

Allie. *See* **Caulfield, Allie**

Andover, a private prep school in Andover, Massachusetts, not far from Boston 127, 151

Annapolis, city in Maryland, home of the United States Naval Academy 164

Annex, room or building where Jane is waiting for Stradlater 31

Anthony Wayne Avenue, where the Spencers live, just off the Pencey Prep campus 5

Antolini, Lillian, wife of Mr. Antolini 180–85, 194

Antolini, Mr., Holden's English teacher at Elkton Hills 136, 173–74, 180–95

Arnold, Benedict, Revolutionary War traitor, acted by Phoebe in school play 162, 207–08

Astor, movie theater on Broadway 115

Atterbury, Selma, friend of Phoebe 164

aunts, Holden's aunts, one who does charity work, another who speaks at Allie's funeral 114, 155

Banky, Ed, basketball coach at Pencey Prep who lets Stradlater use his car 43, 48–49, 76, 80

bartender, serves Holden at the Wicker Bar 142–43

bellboy, helps Holden find his room at the Edmont 61

Beowulf, hero of Anglo-Saxon epic 10, 110

Bernice, the blonde Seattle woman Holden dances with in the Lavender Room (her last name is "Crabs or Krebs") 69–75

Biltmore, famous hotel where Holden and Sally meet 106–07, 122

Birdsell, Eddie, Princeton man Holden met at a party 64–66

Blanchard, Monsieur, main character in a book Holden has read 93

Bloomingdale's, famous store on Third Avenue between 59th and 60th streets 197

Blop, Commander, misheard name of Navy guy who accompanies Lillian Simmons to Ernie's 86–87

B.M., school where Jane Gallagher may be a student 31, 63

booze hound. *See* Cudahy, Mr.

Broadway, diagonal street in Manhattan best known as the center of the theater district 114–16, 118

Brooke, Rupert, poet whose war poems Allie does not like 140

Brookleen, Janine's French-accented word for Brooklyn, across the East River from Manhattan 142

Brooks, chain of expensive men's clothing stores 130

Brossard, Mal, Holden's friend at Pencey Prep (on wrestling team) 36–37, 51, 105

Buffalo, city in western New York State, home of Mrs. Antolini's friends 181

Burns, Robert, Scottish poet who wrote "Coming Through the Rye" 173

bus driver, takes Holden, Ackley, and Brossard to town 36–37

Cabel, R., and **W. Cabel,** two students at Elkton Hills 171

California, West Coast state where D.B. lives, where Holden's father visits, and where Holden recuperates (*See also* **Hollywood**)

Callon, Miss, Phoebe's teacher 118

Campbell, Paul, Holden's friend at Pencey Prep 4–5

Canada, large country north of the United States where Holden's mother buys a coat for Phoebe 159–60

Cape Cod, expensive Massachusetts resort area where Jane Gallagher used to spend her summers 77

Capitol, movie theater on Broadway 115

Capulets, family in Shakespeare's *Romeo and Juliet* 111

carrousel, merry-go-round in Central Park where Holden watches Phoebe ride 210–13

Castle, James, student at Elkton Hills who leaps from the window to his death 170–71, 174, 195

Caulfield, Allie, Holden's younger brother, now dead 38–39, 67–68, 77, 98–99, 107, 138, 140, 155–56, 171, 198, 210

Caulfield, D.B., Holden's older brother 1–2, 18, 59, 67, 80, 86–87, 117, 140–41, 155, 158–59, 164, 181–82, 205, 210, 213

Caulfield, Mr., Holden's father 1, 8–9, 59, 67–68, 85, 100, 107, 121, 136, 138, 155, 158, 162–63, 165, 172, 176–77, 186

Caulfield, Mrs., Holden's mother 1, 8–9, 51–52, 59, 67–68, 76–78, 89, 100, 107, 114, 121, 138, 155, 158–60, 162–63, 176–78, 185, 191, 205

Caulfield, Phoebe, Holden's younger sister 59, 66–68, 80, 114–19, 122, 155, 156–80, 197–202, 204–13

Cavendish, Faith, loose woman Holden calls from the Edmont Hotel 63–66

Cavendish roommate, whose illness prevents Faith from seeing Holden 64

Central Park, large public park in north-central Manhattan 13, 60, 115, 153–54

Central Park Zoo, small zoo on the east side of the park between 63rd and 65th streets 198, 208–10

Charlene, the deaf-in-one-ear live-in servant who works for the Caulfields 158, 174, 176–77, 206

Chicago, city in Illinois from which the two nuns have arrived 109

Childs, Arthur, Holden's Quaker acquaintance at the Whooton School 99–100

China, large Asian country, original home of Carl Luce's girlfriend 146–47

Chinese sculptress, Carl Luce's girlfriend 145–47

Choate, private school in Wallingford, Connecticut 135

clarinet player, plays in Buddy Singer's band 74–75

Colorado, western state where Holden thinks of living on a ranch 165–66

colored kid, at Phoebe's school, on his way to the bathroom 200

Columbia, university in New York City where Carl Luce is a student 136, 144

Columbus, the so-called discoverer of America 120

Cooper, Gary, actor Holden claims to have seen on dance floor 74

Copperfield, David, character in a Dickens novel 1

Coyle, Howie, Holden's classmate at Pencey Prep, basketball player 29

cross-dress man, wears women's clothes in his Edmont Hotel room 61–62

Cuban-looking guy, comes out of a bar and asks Holden about the subway 90

Cudahy, Mr., Jane Gallagher's "booze hound" stepfather 32, 78–79

Cultz, Jeannette, ice-skating friend of Sally Hayes 129

D.B. *See* **Caulfield, D.B.**

D.B.'s girlfriend. *See* **English babe**

delivery men, unload a Christmas tree in Manhattan 196

Detroit, city in Michigan where Holden's grandfather is from 154

Dickens, Charles, nineteenth-century British novelist 138

Dickinson, Emily, nineteenth-century American poet whose war poems Allie likes 140

Dicksteins, neighbors of the Caulfields in their apartment building 157–59, 180

Dinesen, Isak, Danish author of *Out of Africa* 18

Donat, Robert, actor who plays main character in *The 39 Steps* 68

Edmont Hotel, a made-up name, since no such hotel exists or existed in New York 60–62, 66–75, 88, 90–106

Egypt, Arab country on the Mediterranean in northern Africa 11–12, 203–04

elevator boy 1, in the Edmont Hotel. *See* **Maurice**

elevator boy 2, Pete, the regular elevator boy in Holden's apartment building 157

elevator boy 3, new elevator boy in Holden's apartment building 157, 180

elevator boy 4, in the Antolini's building, 181

Elkton Hills, a school that Holden had attended previously 13, 108, 173, 180

El Morocco, upscale nightclub in Manhattan 73

Ely, Ackley's roommate in whose bed Holden lies 47–50

English babe, the pretty actress that Holden's brother D.B. brings to the California sanitarium 213

Ernie, African-American pianist and nightclub owner in Greenwich Village 80, 83–84, 87, 126

Ernie's, nightclub in Greenwich Village 80, 83–84, 87, 90

Fallon, Bobby, summer neighbor of Holden in Maine 98–99

Fencer, Harry, classmate of Holden at Pencey Prep, elected class president 57

Ferdinand and Isabella, king and queen of Spain who financed Columbus's expedition 120

Fitzgerald, girl whom Stradlater used to date 30

Fletcher, Estelle, singer of "Little Shirley Beans" 114–15

Fontanne, Lynn, stage actress and wife of Alfred Lunt 126

Forest Hills, tennis court complex not far outside New York City 112, 181

funny-looking guy, next to Holden's table at Ernie's 85

funny-looking guy's girl, his date, next to Holden's table at Ernie's 85

Gale, Herb, Ackley's roommate at Pencey Prep 19

Gallagher, Jane, young woman Holden used to know 30–34, 41–44, 48–49, 59, 63, 76–80, 104, 105, 135–36, 150, 191, 202

Gallagher, Mrs., Jane Gallagher's mother (divorced from her father) 32, 76–77

George, boring Ivy League snob at the play, went to Andover 127–28, 130, 151

Goldfarb, Raymond, Whooten student Holden drinks Scotch with 90

Gloucester, Massachusetts, where the Morrows live, at least in the summer 58

Grand Central Station, between 42nd and 44th streets on Vanderbilt Avenue 107, 194

grandfather, Holden's grandfather (which one is not specified) from Detroit 154–55

grandmother, Holden's grandmother (which one is not specified) who sends him money 52

Grant, Cary, film actor whose movie is playing in Agerstown theater 37

Greenwich Village, a section of downtown Manhattan noted for its bohemian culture 80, 126, 132, 145

Grendel, monster in Anglo-Saxon epic *Beowulf* 110

guy at Wicker Bar, tells his date she has aristocratic hands 142

guy who owes Holden ten dollars, former classmate 132

guy whose grandfather has a ranch in Colorado, where Holden dreams of getting a job 165

guy with car, Holden's friend in Greenwich Village from whom he thinks he can borrow a car 132

Haas, Mr., headmaster of Elkton Hills 13–14

Hamlet, lead character in Shakespeare's *Hamlet* 117

Hardy, Thomas, nineteenth-century novelist and author of *The Return of the Native* 19, 110–11

Hartzell, Stradlater's English teacher at Pencey Prep 28

Harvard, prestigious university in Cambridge, Massachusetts 106

Harvard guy, man whom Sally Hayes brags about dating 106

hat-check girl, gives Holden his coat as he leaves the Wicker Bar 153

Hayes, Mr., Sally Hayes's father 105–06, 134

Hayes, Sally, Holden's off-and-on girlfriend 20, 59, 105–06, 113, 122, 124–34, 137, 150–51, 190–91

Hayes's grandmother, answers the phone when Holden calls Sally 150

Henry, Lieutenant, character in Hemingway's *A Farewell to Arms* 141

Hoffman, student at Pencey Prep whose door Holden passes 51

Holland Tunnel, downtown vehicular tunnel at Canal Street 198

Hollywood, the famous section of Los Angeles, California, where movies are made 2, 80, 86, 95, 158, 164

Holmborg, Alice, Phoebe's best friend 163, 176–77

Holmborg, Mrs., Alice's mother, who takes Alice and Phoebe to a movie 163, 177

homey-babe, marries Alec in movie that Holden sees 138–39

homey-babe's brother, alcoholic character in movie that Holden sees 138–39

Horwitz, taxi driver who takes Holden from the Edmont Hotel to Ernie's in Greenwich Village 80–83

ice-skating girl, the bundled-up girl whom Holden asks about Phoebe 118–19

Janine, French singer at the Wicker Bar 141–42, 149

Joe Yale-looking guy, next to Holden's table at Ernie's 85–86

Judas, the disciple who betrayed Jesus 100

Juliet, heroine of Shakespeare's *Romeo and Juliet* 111

Julius Caesar, protagonist of Shakespeare's *Julius Caesar* 111

kettle drummer, plays in Radio City Music Hall 138

kid in cowboy hat, watches the bears at the zoo, asks his father to make them come out 209–10

kid in movie, needs to go to the bathroom but his mother refuses to take him 139–40

kid in street, sings "If a body catch a body" 115

kid with skates. *See* **ice-skating girl**

kids in Museum of Art, two little boys whom Holden takes to the Pharaoh's tomb 202–04

kids on seesaw, Holden sees them on his way to the Museum of Natural History 122

Kinsella, Richard, boy at Pencey Prep in Holden's oral expression class 183–84

Krebs, Bernice. *See* **Bernice**

Lardner, Ring, American author whom Holden admires 18, 141

Lavender Room, nightclub at the Edmont Hotel 66–75

Laverne, one of the three Seattle women Holden talks with in the Lavender Room 69–75

Leahy, student at Pencey Prep whose door Holden passes 51

Levine, Gertrude, grade-school girl who walked with Holden in the Museum of Natural History 120

Lincoln, Abraham, sixteenth president (1861–1865) of the Unites States 49

Lorre, Peter, film actor 71–72

Luce, Carl, a student Holden knew at the Whooton School 59, 136–37, 140, 143–49

Luce, Dr., Carl Luce's father, a psychoanalyst 148

lunatic, insane man in Bible whom Holden likes 99

Lunt, Alfred, famous actor and husband of Lynn Fontanne, plays the male lead in *I Know My Love* 126

Lunts, famous acting couple who have the leads in *I Know My Love* 116–18, 125–27, 151

Macklin, Harris, Holden's roommate at Elton Hills who was a good whistler 123–24

maid 1, answers the phone when Holden calls Sally Hayes 105

maid 2. *See* **Charlene**

Maine, where Holden met Jane Gallagher 77, 98

Mall, large promenade in Central Park where Holden hopes to find Phoebe 119

Marcia, name of character in movie that Holden sees 138–39

Marco and Miranda, two dancers Holden mentions in Lavender Room of the Edmont, not otherwise identified 71

Margulies, Phyllis, friend of Phoebe who teaches her how to belch 174

Marsalla, Edgar, Pencey Prep student who farts in chapel 17

Marty, one of the three Seattle women Holden talks with in the Lavender Room 69–75

Mary A. Woodruff, the school that Sally Hayes attends 105

Maugham, Somerset, British author of *Of Human Bondage*, 18

Maurice, the elevator guy at the Edmont 90–91, 95, 100–04, 106, 140, 214

McBurney School, New York City school that Pencey Prep competes with in fencing 3

Mercutio, character in Shakespeare's *Romeo and Juliet* 111

Montagues, feuding family in Shakespeare's *Romeo and Juliet* 111

Morrow, Ernest, Holden's classmate at Pencey Prep 54–57, 112

Morrow, Mr., father of Ernest Morrow 55

Morrow, Mrs., Ernest's mother whom Holden meets in the train 54–58, 112

mother of boy at movie, weeps at the movie but won't take her son to the bathroom 139–40

movie actor, conceited man in lobby at play intermission 126

movie actor's gorgeous blonde, his date 126

museum guard, speaks nicely to children in Museum of Natural History 120–21

Museum of Art, Metropolitan Museum of Art on the east edge of Central Park between 80th and 84th streets 200–07

Museum of Natural History, just west of Central Park, between 77th and 81st streets 119–22

Nantucket, island off the coast of Massachusetts where Luce lost his virginity 145

Navy guy. *See* **Blop, Commander**

Newark, city in New Jersey across the Hudson River from New York 58

New Yorker Hotel, a hotel mentioned by Holden to a taxi driver 60

Norwalk, town in Connecticut that Holden's parents visit 162

nuns, two pleasant teachers Holden talks with on Sunday morning 108–13, 170, 197

N.Y.U., New York University, in Manhattan 173

old guy, comes back to Pencey Prep on Veterans' Day and asks to see the toilet 168–69

Olivier, Laurence, famous British actor who plays, among many other roles, Hamlet 117

Ophelia, Hamlet's girlfriend in Shakespeare's *Hamlet* 117

Ophelia's brother, Laertes, brother of Hamlet's girlfriend in Shakespeare's *Hamlet* 117

Ophelia's father, Polonius, father of Hamlet's girlfriend in Shakespeare's *Hamlet* 117

Ossenburger Memorial Wing, where Holden's room is at Pencey Prep 16

Ossenburger, Mr., undertaker and benefactor of Pencey Prep 16–17

Oxford, famous old university in England 29

Paramount, movie theater on Broadway 115

Pencey Prep, private academy for boys, usually just called "Pencey" 2–52, 111, 158, 166, 168–69, 202

Penn Station, New York railway terminal between 31st and 33rd streets and between Seventh and Eighth avenues 59

perverts, the cross-dresser and the water-squirters at the Edmont 61–62, 80, 106, 197

Pete. *See* **elevator boy** 2

Philadelphia, large city in southeastern Pennsylvania where D.B. bought a desk 159

Phoebe. *See* **Caulfield, Phoebe**

pianist, the "flitty-looking guy" who plays at the Wicker Bar 149, 152

Pike, Al, Choate student who used to date Jane Gallagher 135

pimpy-looking guys, men Holden sees in the lobby of the Edmont 69

Princeton, exclusive private university in Princeton, New Jersey 63–65, 85

Radio City Music Hall, a large theater between 50th and 51st streets just east of Sixth Avenue 75, 128–34, 136

Raimu, actor who plays baker in *The Baker's Wife* 67

Randall, Lord, poisoned hero of anonymous Scottish ballad 10, 110

Robinson, Bob, Holden gets him a date with Roberta Walsh's roommate 136

Rockettes, dancers at Radio City Music Hall 137

Rocky, imaginary mobster whose mob Holden says shot him 151

roller-skating comedian, performs at Radio City Music Hall 137

Romeo, protagonist of Shakespeare's *Romeo and Juliet* 111

roommate of Roberta Walsh, Holden gets her a date with Bob Robinson 136

Salvation Army women, ring Christmas bells for money 197

Saxon Hall, name of Pencey Prep's rival school 2

Schmidt, Mrs., the janitor's wife 45

Schmidt, Rudolf, the janitor in Holden's dorm whose name he uses as his own in talking to Ernest Morrow's mother 45, 54–55

sculptress. *See* **Chinese sculptress**

Seattle, Washington, Northwest coast city, home to Bernice, Marty, and Laverne 72–73, 75

secretaries at school, take Holden's message to Phoebe 201–02, 205

Sedebego, Lake, fictional lake in Maine, where Holden remembers talking to Allie 98

Seton Hotel, an actual hotel on East 40th Street, located on 54th Street in the novel, supposed home to the Wicker Bar 141

Shaney, Louis, boy at the Whooton School who tried to find out if Holden was a Catholic 112

Shanghai, large city near the east acoast of mainland China 146

Sherman, Anne Louise, a phony girl Holden had necked with 63

Shipley, school that Jane Gallagher may attend 31, 33

shoe salesman, sells Phoebe moccasins at Bloomingdale's 197

Siberia, cold region in far-away Russia 158

Simmons, Lillian, old girlfriend of D.B. whom Holden encounters at Ernie's 86–8

Singer, Buddy, musician whose band (apparently a fictional group) plays in the Lavender Room 69, 71

Slagle, Dick, friend of Holden's at Elkton Hills who had cheap suitcases 108

Smith, Phyllis, a "babe" who was supposed to be Stradlater's date 30

Spencer, Mr., history teacher at Pencey Prep 3–15, 17, 168, 202

Spencer, Mrs., wife of history teacher 5–6, 15, 168

squirters, man and woman who squirt liquid at each other at the Edmont Hotel 62

Stanford Arms Hotel, a fictional hotel where Faith Cavendish stays 64

Steele, Jim, fake name Holden invents for himself 73, 94

Stekel, Wilhelm, Austrian psychoanalyst whom Mr. Antolini quotes 188

Stork Club, upscale nightclub in Manhattan 73

Stradlater, Ward, Holden's roommate at Pencey Prep 18, 23–34, 40–45, 47–50, 61, 76, 80, 103, 109, 140, 153, 169, 187, 214

Strand, movie theater on Broadway 115

Sunny, prostitute whom Maurice sends to Holden at the Edmont 93–98, 101–03

superintendent, in Holden's apartment building 156

Sutton Place, Manhattan east side location where the Antolinis live 180

Taft Hotel, a hotel mentioned by Holden to a taxi driver 60

taxi driver 1, takes Holden from Penn Station to the Edmont 50–61

taxi driver 2. *See* **Horwitz**

taxi driver 3, takes Holden from the Edmont to Grand Central Station 107

taxi driver 4, takes Holden and Sally Hayes from the Biltmore to the theater 125

taxi driver 5, takes Holden from his home to Antolini's 181

terrific-looking girl, with the Joe Yale-looking guy next to Holden's table at Ernie's 85

Thaw, Bud, classmate of Holden who dates Jane Gallagher's roommate 30

Thomsen Hill, hill overlooking football field at Pencey Prep 2–3

Thurmer, Dr., headmaster of Pencey Prep 3–4, 8, 17, 35, 168

Thurmer, Selma, daughter of the headmaster at Pencey Prep 3

Tichener, Robert, Holden's Pencey Prep friend 4–5

Tina, French piano player at the Wicker Bar 141–42, 149

Twist, Oliver, central character in Charles Dickens's novel *Oliver Twist* 138

Tybalt, character in Shakespeare's *Romeo and Juliet* 111

Valencia, singer at the Wicker Bar 149, 152

Village. *See* **Greenwich Village**

Vinson, Mr., Holden's oral expression teacher at Pencey Prep 183–85, 189

visitors to cemetery, who rush away when it starts to rain 155–56

Vye, Eustatia, heroine of Thomas Hardy's *The Return of the Native* 19, 110

waiter 1, man in the Lavender Room who asks Holden for proof of age 69

waiter 2, man in Wicker Bar whom Holden asks to take a message to Valencia 149, 152

waiter 3, man in coffee shop who doesn't charge Holden for the doughnuts 196

Walsh, Roberta, friend of Holden 136

Weatherfield, Hazel, name of fictional character in Phoebe Caulfield's "books" 68, 160–61, 166

Weintraub, Curtis, classmate of Phoebe who pushes her down the steps 164

West Point, United States Military Academy at West Point, New York 106

West Point cadet, Sally Hayes brags about dating him 106

West Side Tennis Club, exclusive club in Forest Hills, Long Island 180–81

Whooton School, school that Holden had attended previously 10, 13, 59, 93, 99, 112, 136, 143–44, 146–47, 149, 206

whory-looking blondes, women in the lobby of the Edmont 69, 80

Wicker Bar, fictional bar on 54th Street where Holden meets Carl Luce 137, 140, 141

witch doctor, fierce-looking Indian in large canoe in the Museum of Natural History 120

Woodruff, Frederick, student at Pencey Prep who borrows, then buys, Holden's typewriter 39, 52

Yale, exclusive private university in New Haven, Connecticut 85

Yellowstone Park, national park in Wyoming 7

Zambesi, Mr., biology teacher at Pencey Prep who breaks up an informal football game 5

zoo. *See* **Central Park Zoo**

Index to this *Reader's Companion*

Unlike the previous index, which gives the pages in *The Catcher in the Rye* where the people and places can be found, this second index gives page references to my *Reader's Companion* to the novel. In addition to listing people and places mentioned in the novel and discussed in the *Reader's Companion*, this index lists authors, scholars, actors, film directors, literary and historical figures, musical works, novels, plays, poems, songs, and bands.

The Absolutely True Diary of a Part-Time Indian, novel 39

Ackley, Robert, Holden's friend and suite mate at Pencey Prep 3, 21, 59, 61, 91, 105–06, 108–10, 121, 177, 211–12

The Adventures of Huckleberry Finn, novel 15, 68, 110, 140, 175, 179–80, 199, 212

Agerstown, Pennsylvania, town where Pencey Prep is located 59, 80–81, 105–06, 121

Alexander, Paul, scholar 7–8, 17, 26, 32, 46, 64, 98, 115

Alexie, Sherman, author 39

Allen, Henry, author 69

All the Pretty Horses, novel 32–33

Andover (Phillips Academy), private prep school near Boston, Massachusetts 59, 165, 167

Andrews, Dana, actor 15–16, 79

Angela's Ashes, book 61

Aniston, Jennifer, actress 54–55

Annapolis, Maryland, home of the United States Naval Academy 185

Antolini, Mr., Holden's English teacher at Elkton Hills ix, 4, 21, 29, 45, 59, 73, 76, 117, 138, 148, 178, 186, 188, 190–91, 193–95

Antolini, Mrs., wife of English teacher 117, 148, 188, 190–92

Arsenic and Old Lace, film 106

Arteta, Miguel, film director 54

Astaire, Fred, actor and dancer 100

Astor, movie theater on Broadway 152

Aylmer, Felix, actor 155

The Baker's Wife, film 122–23

Balanchine, George, choreographer 99

Ball, Lucille, actress 100–01

Bank, Stanley, scholar 85

Banks, Russell, author 37

Banky, Ed, basketball coach at Pencey Prep 109, 132

Barnes, Bart, scholar 70

Barron, James, scholar 114, 118

Bartholomew, Freddie, actor 30–31

Behrman, S. N., playwright 152–53

Belcher, William F., scholar viii

Bellaman, Henry, scholar 105

Beller, Thomas, scholar 118, 169, 205

Beowulf, epic 87, 147

Bernice, the blonde Seattle woman Holden dances with in the Lavender Room 121

Billy Budd, novella 15

Biltmore Hotel 3, 117, 145–46, 149, 165

Blanchard, Rachel, actress 52–53

The Bloodhound Gang, rock band 56

Bloom, Harold, scholar 64

The Body, novella 39

Bound and Gagged, cartoon 58

Branch, Edgar, scholar 208

Brando, Marlon, actor 12

Brooke, Rupert, poet 73–74

Brossard, Mal, Holden's friend at Pencey Prep (on wrestling team) 3, 105–07, 121

Brown, Rob, actor 47, 49

Bryan, James, scholar 92, 150, 157, 184, 211

Bryfronski, Dedria, scholar 108

Bryn Mawr School, Baltimore prep school where Jane Gallagher may be a student 100, 102, 120

Burden, Carter, buyer of Salinger's letters to Michael Mitchell 67

Burrows, David J., scholar 62–63, 194–95

"A Caddy's Story," short story 94

California, West Coast state where D.B. lives, and where Holden recuperates ix, 21–22, 40, 73, 76, 78–79, 84, 89, 185, 210. *See also* **Hollywood**

California, John David (J. D.) (Fredrik Colting), author x, 43–46

Campbell, Paul, Holden's friend at Pencey Prep 20

Capitol, movie theater on Broadway 152

Captains Courageous, novel and film xi, 30–31, 137–39

Carpenter, Frederic I., scholar 78

Carroll, Madeleine, actress 123–24

carrousel. *See* **Central Park**

Castle, James, student at Elkton Hills who leaps from the window to his death 21, 59 111, 148, 186–87

The Catcher in the Rye, film 46

Cather, Willa, author 16

Caulfield, Allie, Holden's younger brother, now dead 1, 3, 22, 26, 37, 44, 60, 63, 76, 85, 92, 97, 105, 107–09, 133, 142, 148, 173–74, 178, 181, 186, 188, 194, 212

Caulfield, D.B., Holden's older brother 2, 15, 22, 26, 29, 44, 74, 76–77, 79, 81, 97, 103, 122, 134–35, 137, 168, 173, 175–76, 185, 211–12

Caulfield, Mr., Holden's father 2, 186

Caulfield, Phoebe, Holden's younger sister 2, 4, 20–21, 25, 27–28, 44, 60, 63, 92, 117, 121–27, 148–51, 153, 155–57, 177–78, 181–88, 194–96, 200–02, 205, 207, 209–11

Cavendish, Faith, prostitute Holden calls from the Edmont Hotel 113–14, 120

Central Park, large public park in Manhattan ix, xi, 4, 20–21, 34–35, 44, 52–53, 57, 87–90, 92, 113–15, 117–18, 120, 122, 134, 149–50, 157, 181, 189, 197–98, 200, 205–07, 209–10; carrousel 4, 21, 44, 196, 205–11; lagoon 20–21, 88–90, 115, 118–19, 134, 181–82, 210; zoo 4, 117, 196–98, 210

Chabon, Michael, author 64

Channing, Stockard, actress 34–35

Chapman, Mark David, John Lennon's assassin 37, 47, 53–54

Chapter 27, film 54

Charlene, the Caulfields' live-in servant 20

Chasing Holden, film 50, 52, 54, 100

Chaucer, Geoffrey, medieval poet 61, 91

Chbosky, Stephen, author 34, 36

Choate, private school in Wallingford, Connecticut 59, 168

Clarke, Malcolm, film director 50

The Collector, novel 33

"Come All Ye Faithful," song 169

Connery, Sean, actor 47, 49

Conspiracy Theory, film 47–48

Cooper, Gary, actor 129–30

Copperfield, David 5, 58, 74–75, 107, 172

Cornish, New Hampshire, town where J. D. Salinger lived as a recluse 7, 17, 45, 50, 66, 70–71, 199

Costello, Donald P., scholar 75

Costello, Patrick, scholar 194

Creeger, George R., scholar viii

Cutchins, Dennis, scholar 43

D-Day (invasion of Normandy, June 6, 1944) 11, 15, 36, 81, 109, 173, 176. *See also* Normandy, France

Deschanel, Zooey, actress 50–51

DiCaprio, Leonardo, actor 12

Dickens, Charles, author 74–75, 107, 170, 172–73, 191

Dickinson, Emily, poet 173–74

Dinesen, Isak (Karen von Blixen-Finecke), author 93–94

Donat, Robert, actor 123–25

Donner, Richard, film director 47

Douglas, Claire. *See* Salinger, J. D., family

Douglas, Melvyn, actor 30

Edmont Hotel, fictional hotel where Holden dances with three women from Seattle 3, 21, 94, 113–14, 117, 120–22, 132, 136, 145

Edwards, Duane, scholar 195, 203, 211

Edwards, June, scholar 63

Eggers, Dave, author 39–40

Elkton Hills, a school that Holden had attended previously 59, 89, 146, 186

El Morocco, upscale nightclub in Manhattan 129

Ely, Ackley's roommate 109–10

Epstein, Julius J. and Philip G., screenwriters 79

Ernie, African-American pianist and nightclub owner in Greenwich Village 134–35

Ernie's, nightclub in Greenwich Village 21, 29, 117, 120–21, 132, 134–35

Evertson, Matt, scholar 32–33

A Farewell to Arms, novel and film 129–30, 175–76

Fear and Loathing in Las Vegas, novel 32

Feinberg, Barbara, scholar 66

Field of Dreams, film 43

Fiene, Donald M., scholar 32

Finding Forrester, film 47, 49

Fitzgerald, F. Scott, author 57, 76, 177–78

Fontanne, Lynn actress, married to Alfred Lunt 152, 166. *See also* **Lunts**

For Whom the Bell Tolls, novel and film 129

Fowles, John, author 33–34

Frazier, Ian, author 57–58

Freedman, Carl, scholar 64, 147

French, Warren, scholar 5, 62, 79–80, 204

Gale, Herb, Ackley's roommate at Pencey Prep 110

Gallagher, Jane, young woman Holden used to know 3, 21, 26, 60, 99, 102–03, 104–05, 108–09, 113, 132–33, 139, 168, 178

Garland, Judy, actress, singer, and dancer 100

Geismar, Maxwell, scholar 65

"Get It Right," song 56

Gibson, Mel, actor 47–48

Glasser, William, scholar 86, 195

Goldberg, Jay. *See* **Salinger, J. D.,** family

The Good Girl, film 54–55

Gopnik, Adam, author 68

Grand Central Station, New York railway terminal between 42nd and 44th streets on Vanderbilt Avenue 3–4, 21, 114, 117, 145–46, 196

Grant, Cary, actor 105–06

Gray, G. William, scholar 40

The Great Gatsby, novel 57, 68, 76, 177–78

The Great Ziegfeld, film 100

Green Day, rock band 56

Grunwald, Henry Anatole, scholar 4, 15, 187

Guare, John, playwright 33–34

Gyllenhaal, Jake, actor 54–55

Hamilton, Ian, scholar 5, 7–8, 14, 63, 77, 182, 185

Hamlet, Shakespearean play 62, 153–56

Harbach, Otto, lyricist 209

Hardy, Thomas, author 95–96

Harris, Ed, actor 50–51

Harvard, prestigious university in Cambridge, Massachusetts 33, 35, 59, 166

hat, the red hunting cap hat Holden wears ix, 19, 21, 23, 73, 75, 87, 91–93, 188, 196

Hayes, Helen, actress 130

Hayes, Sally, Holden's off-and-on girlfriend 1, 3, 21, 23–25, 28, 145, 152, 165, 181

Hayward, Susan, actress 15–16, 79

A Heartbreaking Work of Staggering Genius, novel 39–40

Heiserman, Arthur, scholar 78

Hemingway, Ernest, author 15, 68, 108, 129–30, 175–76

High Noon, film 129

Hinckley, John, would-be assassin of Ronald Reagan 34, 47

Hitchcock, Alfred, film director 10, 123–24, 128

Hochman Will, scholar x

Holland Tunnel, vehicular tunnel in lower Manhattan 198

Hollywood, famous section of Los Angeles, California, where movies are made 15, 17, 22, 43, 46, 76–77, 79–80, 106, 137, 166, 185

Horne, Lena, actress and singer 100

Horwitz, taxi driver who takes Holden from the Edmont Hotel to Ernie's nightclub 118, 134

I Know My Love, play 3, 149, 152–53, 165–66

Italie, Hillel, scholar 13, 65, 68

Itzkoff, Dave, scholar 12

Jacobs, Robert G., scholar 65, 84–85

Jones, Ernest, scholar 62

Jones, James Earl, actor 43

Julius Caesar, Shakespearean play 147

"Just One of Those Things," song 127–28

Kakutani, Michiko, scholar 68

Kazan, Elia, film director 12

Kelly, Gene, actor and dancer 100, 172

Kern, Jerome, composer 209

Kimmel, Michael, scholar 66

King Dork, novel 41

King, Stephen, author 39

King's Row, novel and film 105

Kinsella, Richard, boy at Pencey Prep in Holden's oral expression class 191

Kinsella, W. P., author 42–43, 191–92

Kipling, Rudyard, author 30, 138–39

Lacayo, Richard, scholar 70

lagoon. *See* **Central Park**

Lardner, Ring, author 94–95, 103–04, 177

Lavender Room, nightclub at the Edmont Hotel 3, 94, 121–22, 129

Laverne, one of the three Seattle women Holden talks with in the Lavender Room 121

LeClerc, Ginette, actress 123

Lee, A. Robert, scholar 78, 194

Lee, James W., scholar viii

Lennon, John, musician 47, 53–54

Leto, Jared, actor 54

Lewis, Jerry, actor 12

Lorre, Peter, actor 106, 128

Luce, Carl, student Holden knew at the Whooton School 3, 21, 23, 25, 168, 177, 179–81

Lundquist, James, scholar 78, 142

Lunt, Alfred, actor, married to Lynn Fontanne 152, 166. *See also* **Lunts**

Lunts, married stage actors 23, 152, 165

Macbeth, Shakespearean play 127

Macklin, Harris, Holden's roommate at Elkton Hills who was a good whistler 61

"Magna Cum Nada," song 56

Marco and Miranda, two dancers Holden mentions in the Lavender Room 128

Marsalla, Edgar, Pencey Prep student who farts in chapel 91

Marsden, Malcolm M., editor 76, 86

Martin, Dexter, scholar 76, 85

Marty, one of three Seattle women Holden talks with in the Lavender Room 1, 121, 129, 131

Mary A. Woodruff, school that Sally Hayes attends 59, 145

Massey, Raymond, actor 106

Maugham, W. Somerset, author 14, 95–96, 99, 108, 192

Maurice, elevator guy at the Edmont Hotel 3, 60, 121, 136, 139, 211–12

Maynard, Joyce, author and Salinger's live-in girlfriend 7, 11–12, 50, 85, 127, 129, 146, 153

McBurney School, New York City school that Pencey Prep competes with in fencing 59, 77, 81–82

McCarthy, Cormac, author 32–33

McCourt, Frank, author 61

McDaniel, Sean, scholar 79

McGrath, Charles, scholar 63, 67, 69

Meacham, Jon, editor 58

Mellard, James M., scholar 78, 92

Melville, Herman, author 15

Menand, Louis, scholar 32, 56–57

Metropolitan Museum of Art, museum on the east edge of Central Park, between 80th and 84th streets ix, x, xi, 4, 21, 117, 196, 200–203

Miller, Edwin Haviland, scholar 75, 92, 212

Miller, James E., Jr., 78

Miller's Tale, Chaucerian tale 91

Miltner, Robert, scholar 1

Mitchell, Michael, artist 67

Moore, Robert P., scholar 91, 128, 176, 211

Morgan Library, midtown Manhattan library that owns letters written by J. D. Salinger to artist Michael Mitchell 67

Morgan, Terence, actor 155

Morrow, Ernest, Holden's classmate at Pencey Prep 61, 112–13

Morrow, Mrs., Ernest's mother whom Holden meets in the train 3, 20–21, 29, 77, 112–13

Mueller, Bruce F., scholar x

Museum of Natural History, museum just west of Central Park, between 77th and 81st streets ix, x, xi, 3, 25, 44, 117, 149, 157–64, 196

My Foolish Heart, film 15–16, 79–80, 84, 185

Nadel, Alan, scholar 92

New Orleans Rhythm Kings, jazz band 165

Newark, New Jersey, city across the Hudson River from New York 112–13

Nicholson, Jack, actor 12

Night and Day, stage musical 106

Normandy, France, site of the Allied Forces' D-Day invasion 11, 15, 36, 81, 109, 173. *See also* D-Day

Norwalk, Connecticut, town that Holden's parents visit 184

NYU, New York University, in Manhattan 59, 188

Oedipus, main character in *Oedipus the King* 98, 186

Oedipus the King, play 98

Of Human Bondage, novel 14, 95–96, 99, 108, 192

The Offspring, rock band 56

Ohmann, Carol and Richard, scholars 63, 111

"Oh Marie," song 208–09

Old School, novel 40–41

Oldsey, Bernard S., scholar 30, 85, 105, 184

Olivier, Sir Laurence, actor 153–56

On Your Toes, stage musical 99

O'Neill, Colleen. *See* Salinger, J. D., family

Out of Africa, novel 93–94

Oxford, famous old university in England 59, 96, 99–100

Pagnol, Marcel, film director 122–23

Paramount, movie theater on Broadway 152

"Paul's Case," short story 16–17

Pencey Prep, private academy for boys, usually just called "Pencey" vii, 3, 11, 20–21, 23, 59, 73–74, 80, 82–83, 87, 94, 102, 109, 112, 121, 135–36, 138, 183, 186–87

Penn Station, New York railway terminal between 31st and 33rd streets and between Seventh and Eighth avenues 3, 113–15, 117–18, 121, 177

The Perks of Being a Wallflower, novel 34, 36

The Personal History of David Copperfield, novel 74–75, 172

Pike, Al, Choate student who dated Jane Gallagher 168

Pinsker, Sanford, scholar 64

Poitier, Sidney, actor 33

Porter, Cole, composer 128

Portman, Frank, author 41

Portnoy's Complaint, novel 36–37

Prep, novel 42

Princeton, exclusive private university in Princeton, New Jersey 7–8, 26, 59, 99, 135

Privitera, Lisa, scholar 78

Qualls, D. J., actor 52–53

Radio City Music Hall, large theater between 50th and 51st streets, just east of Sixth Avenue 3, 21, 23, 25, 80, 117, 121, 128, 131, 165, 167–69, 171–72, 179

Raimu, actor 122–23

Ralston, Nancy C., scholar 62

Rapp, Adam, film director 50

Reagan, Ronald, former U.S. president 47

Remnick, David, editor 68

The Return of the Native, novel 95–97

Roberts, Julia, actress 47–48

Robson, Mark, film director 79

Rockefeller Center, New York City social and entertainment hub, home to NBC studios and Radio City Music Hall 3, 131

Rockettes, dancers 168–69

Rodgers and Hammerstein, composing team 99

Romeo and Juliet, Shakespearean play 145, 147

Rooney, Mickey, actor 139

Ross, Lillian, scholar 69

Roth, Philip, author 36, 63

Rowe, Joyce, scholar 195

Rule of the Bone, novel 37–38

Salerno, Shane, biographer 10

Salinger, Doris. *See* **Salinger, J. D., family**

Salinger, J. D.
autobiographical references in short stories and *The Catcher in the Rye* 8–11, 13–18
bans of *The Catcher in the Rye* 71–72
cover of *TIME* 5–6, 14–15, 19
death 9, 12–13, 65–71
education 11, 14, 80–82
family 7–13, 50, 67, 81, 102–03, 107, 125, 127, 143, 148, 182, 199–202, 210–11; **Claire Douglas**, Salinger's second wife 8–9, 102–03, 111; **Colleen O'Neill**, Salinger's third wife 67; **Doris Salinger**, Salinger's sister 8–9, 143; **Jay Goldberg**, Salinger's cousin 9; **Margaret Salinger**, Salinger's daughter 7–9, 13, 50, 67, 81, 102, 107, 111, 115, 125, 127, 135, 143, 148, 176, 182, 188, 199, 210–11; **Matt Salinger**, Salinger's son 67, 70, 127

legal issues 5, 7, 12, 43, 45–46, 50
reclusiveness in Cornish, New Hampshire 5, 7–8, 10, 17, 40, 43, 45, 50, 54, 66–67, 70–71, 100, 199
relationships, 7–8, 10–11, 50, 85, 127. *See also* **Maynard, Joyce**
religion 8, 11, 111–12, 143, 148, 181–82, 208
short stories: "A Girl I Knew" 9–10; "I'm Crazy" 18–22, 25, 80, 85, 89; "The Last and Best of the Peter Pans" (unpublished) 26–27; "The Last Day of the Last Furlough" 27, 176; "The Laughing Man" 15, 175; "Ocean Full of Bowling Balls" (unpublished) 26; "Slight Rebellion off Madison" 9, 23–25, 85, 145–46, 152; "The Stranger" 27; "This Sandwich Has No Mayonnaise" 9, 27; "Uncle Wiggily in Connecticut" 15–16, 79–80, 84, 137
World War II experience 8, 11, 15, 18, 23, 81, 97, 109, 173, 176

Salinger, Margaret. *See* **Salinger, J. D., family**

Salinger, Matt. *See* **Salinger, J. D., family**

Salzberg, Joel, editor 65, 78, 92, 143, 194

Salzman, Jack, editor 144, 152, 195

The Sands of Iwo Jima, film 83–84

Saxon Hall, Pencey Prep's rival school 3, 20, 59, 74, 81, 132

Schaefer, J. P., film director 54

Schepisi, Fred, film director 34

Schriber, Mary Suzanne, scholar 65–66, 143

Seabrook, John, author 70

Seattle, Washington, Northwest coast city, home to Bernice, Marty, and Laverne 3, 21, 94, 121, 127–31

Sedebego, Lake, fictional lake in Maine where Holden remembers talking to Allie 139

Seelye, John, scholar 144

Seton Hotel, actual hotel on East 40th Street, located on 54th Street in the novel, supposed home to the Wicker Bar 4, 169, 179

Shakespeare, William, English playwright and poet 50, 61, 127, 147, 153–54

Shaw, Peter, scholar 151–52, 195

Shields, David, biographer 10

Shipley School, school that Jane Gallagher may attend 59, 102–03, 120

Shoeless Joe, novel 42–43, 191–92

Silverberg, Mark, scholar 66

Simmons, Jean, actress 153, 155

Simmons, Lillian, old girlfriend of D.B. whom Holden encounters at Ernie's 3, 21, 29, 61, 135

Singer, Buddy, musician whose band plays in the Lavender Room 121–22, 127–28, 131

Sittenfeld, Curtis, author 42

Six Degrees of Separation, play and film 33–35

60 Years Later: Coming Through the Rye, novel 43–46

Skelton, Red, actor 100

Slabey, Robert M., scholar 2, 91, 208

"Slaughter on Tenth Avenue," song 99

Slawenski, Kenneth, scholar x, 9–10, 71, 82

Smith, Will, actor 34–35

"Smoke Gets in Your Eyes," song 209

"Song of India," song 99

Sophocles, Greek playwright 98

Spencer, Mr., history teacher at Pencey Prep 3, 19–21, 25, 74, 80, 83–84, 87–89

Spencer, Mrs., wife of history teacher 19–21, 84, 87

Spielberg, Steven, film director 12

Stanford Arms Hotel, fictional hotel where Faith Cavendish stays 120

Steed, J. P., scholar 1, 17, 33, 43, 66

Steinle, P amela Hunt, scholar 71–72

Stekel, Wilhelm, psychoanalyst 193, 210

Stevens, Dana, scholar 46

Stewart, Patrick, actor 47

Stork Club, upscale nightclub in Manhattan 129

Stradlater, Ward, Holden's roommate at Pencey Prep 3, 21, 28, 42, 44, 53, 60–61, 91–92, 99–100, 102–03, 105, 108–09, 121, 132, 177–78, 211–12

Strand, movie theater on Broadway 152

Strauch, Carl F., scholar 104, 193

Strawberry Fields, John Lennon memorial in Central Park 52–53

Summers, Dana, cartoonist 58

The Sun Also Rises, novel 108

Sunny, prostitute whom Maurice sends to Holden at the Edmont 3, 21, 28–31, 60, 121, 136–39

Sutherland, Donald, actor 34–35

Svogun, Margaret Dumais, scholar 186

Takeuchi, Yasuhiro, scholar 76, 93

"There Are Smiles," short story 95

The 39 Steps, film 123–27

Thompson, Hunter S., author 32

Thurmer, Dr., headmaster at Pencey Prep 89, 117

Thurmer, Selma, daughter of headmaster at Pencey Prep 117

Tichener, Robert, Holden's Pencey Prep friend 20

Timpane, John, scholar 79

"Tin Roof Blues," song 165

Tomm, Nigel, film director 46

Tracy, Spencer, actor 30–31

Trenton, New Jersey, city where Mrs. Morrow boards the train 112–13

Trowbridge, Clinton W., scholar 62, 92, 208

Twain, Mark, author 15, 61, 110, 208

Ursinus College, school in Pennsylvania that J. D. Salinger briefly attended 14

Valley Forge Military Academy, school in Pennsylvania from which J. D. Salinger graduated 11, 80–81, 83, 187

Van Sant, Gus, film director 47

Vickrey, Robert, artist whose painting of Salinger appeared on the cover of *TIME* 5–6

Vye, Eustacia, character in *The Return of the Native* that Holden likes 95–97

Walker, Joseph S., scholar 17, 43

Wayne, John, actor 84

Weinstein, Harvey, film producer 12

Welch, James, author 38

West Side Tennis Club, exclusive club in Forest Hills, Long Island 148, 190

Whitfield, Stephen J., scholar 32

Whooton School, school that Holden had attended previously 59, 87–89, 136

"Who Wrote Holden Caulfield?" song 56

Wicker Bar, fictional bar on 54th Street where Holden meets Carl Luce 4, 21, 25, 28, 117, 168–69, 179

Wilder, Billy, film director 12

Williams, Esther, actress 100

Winter in the Blood, novel 38

Winter Passing, film 50–51

Winter's Tale, Shakespearean play 50

Wolfe, Tom, author 64

Wolff, Tobias, author 40–41

Yale, exclusive private university in New Haven, Connecticut 7, 59, 99, 135

Ziegfeld Follies, film 99–101

zoo. *See* Central Park